THE PARTY HOUSE

THE PARTY HOUSE

THE PARTY HOUSE

TEXAS GULF COAST SCHEMES AND DREAMS

L. WADE POWERS

LUMINARE PRESS

WWW.LUMINAREPRESS.COM

Cover imagery provided by Roslyn McFarland,
Farlands Publishing (www.RoslynMcFarland.com)

Cover Layout and typography by Claire Flint Last

Luminare Press
442 Charnelton St.
Eugene, OR 97401
www.luminarepress.com

LCCN: 2019941766
ISBN: 978-1-64388-139-3

For a small town and the people who lived there

Gone today as it was then

The island in the sun shines forever

Memories, like Gulf breezes, never die

Thank you

ACKNOWLEDGMENTS

Several of the chapters in this book were originally intended as short stories. I am truly grateful to readers and commentators for reviewing and critiquing some of these sections: Eva Lund, Leo Dubray, and Erik Powers. After reorganizing the stories to comprise a more or less coherent novel, the manuscript was subjected to the careful scrutiny of Norman Kings Brady, Jr. and William Cook. Their insights and encouragement kept a light burning and the computer humming.

A very special thanks, as always, to my wife, Alla Vichurina Powers, an English teacher, librarian, and companion extraordinaire. Her sharp wits and even sharper red pen helped me avoid many of the errors that persisted from earlier drafts. No writer is really an island and so once again I extend my appreciation to Luminare Press: Patricia Marshall, and her publishing staff, Claire Flint Last, Melissa Thomas, Kim Harper-Kennedy, and Jamie Passaro. As always, any remaining flaws fall at my feet alone.

Finally, I need to acknowledge the influence and inspiration of John Ernst Steinbeck Jr. (1902–1968), author of numerous outstanding novels and works of nonfiction. If imperfect imitation is a sincere form of flattery, then I shamelessly admit to the literary seduction of his Monterey masterpieces, *Cannery Row* and *Sweet Thursday*.

CONTENTS

"Tain't nothin' to me."

– A frequent barrier island response.
It means what it says, pardner.

The Party House was a real place in a real time, Port Aransas, Texas, in the 1970s. But we'll call it Port Tarpon just to avoid pissing off the Chamber of Commerce and tourist bureaus. Although geographically and legally a part of the Lone Star Republic and the Great State of Texas, it was none of those things. Separated from the mainland by a narrow intracoastal waterway, it sat on the north end of Mustang Island, a land unto itself, bordered by the Gulf of Mexico and surrounded by an alien outside world. The inside world contained approximately 2,000 human residents, around 200 dogs, a few cats thrown in by mistake, countless seagulls and shorebirds, millions of crabs, and a handful of coyotes. There weren't any mustangs, but a few horses idled in fields, along with some chickens, a couple of goats, and a few other critters that no one seemed to be sure about. Some of the latter had names and were frequent denizens of the Party House.

There were memorable characters in the inside world in those days and some of them need to be protected, I suppose. Some of them don't deserve to be, but my lawyer said to go easy and change the names. She also said to be free and loose about the facts and not too heavy on history or memoirs, at least not to the extent that people would recognize themselves and file papers. We don't want any of that, do we? So, if you happen to be reading this, which I strongly doubt, and recognize yourself or someone you think you know, well that's just too damned bad. Oh, I mean, it's probably just a coincidence, and it ain't you at all. Besides, my memory is not what it usta to be (it's been forty years), and I probably got most of it wrong anyway. A lot of it I just made up (it's called fiction). And don't bother looking for the Party House. The bar and its colorful characters went away, or blew away, or just fell down, many years ago.

Port Tarpon in the winter is mostly locals—fishermen, shrimpers, and an assembly of mainstream dropouts, some with college degrees and others that can barely write their names. The town swells to tens of thousands during the spring and summer as college kids, inland pleasure seekers, and family vacationers seek the sun and surf of the Gulf of Mexico. Although there are many watering holes in Port Tarpon, one is home and community center to an eclectic group of residents. At the edge of the city marina, sharing the waterfront with restaurants, bait and tackle stores, and two other bars, sits a wooden bungalow called the Party House. In the early to mid 1970s people gathered there to do what they damn well wanted to do, right or wrong, legal or not. This is the story of that place, that time, and some of the people who passed through it. Their response, when asked about the external affairs of off-islanders, was "Tain't nothin' to me."

CHAPTER ONE

Another Beer Bar Confrontation

LATE SUMMER 1974

The noise has been deafening inside the crude wooden building, reverberating along the adjoining dirt streets outside and across to the docks lining the marina, sounds that were either inviting or threatening, depending on your perspective. But now it is quiet in the Party House, and not a laugh or shout, not a note from the jukebox, is heard. Everyone has shifted, moved, or turned on their seats to get a better view. By this time at night, many of the usually boisterous patrons have slipped down the murky slopes of consciousness. Not even a pool table squabble or a drunken pushing match would distract those who had seen too many barroom brawls or sampled too many longnecks. Friday night carousing is expected to continue for the locals and tourists alike. This time, however, everyone freezes, as if painted onto the late-night tableau of smoke, spilled beer, and half-dressed beach bums.

In the middle of the floor stands a lanky man in jeans and a ragged black T-shirt. On the shirtfront, a lascivious armadillo tears his way out of an outline map of Texas ("From deep in the heart of..."). A coal black handlebar mustache graces his lip. Long hair and sideburns and a very greasy cap with a seafood distributor's logo completes the top end. His face is not without humor—eyes, cheeks, and mouth bare a wrinkled witness to the good times he has shared with the Party House regulars. But not tonight. As usual, he is barefoot, smells bad, and has surpassed his considerable drinking limit. His arms hang limply at his side, his neck is craned forward, and his shoulders are hunched a bit, like an arena bull about to make his run. A heavy glass beer mug, just emptied, sways in his right hand, keeping time to his private internal rhythm.

Many in the crowd have seen it before, his silent and intense stare, the clutched mug, and the open space around him in an otherwise crowded bar. I have also seen it before, and I am not thrilled about what will be coming next. His first words after waking up from a two-hour barstool nap don't surprise any of us.

"Yuh gonna give me 'nother beer, you shit?"

This is directed more or less at me, working behind the bar. It also serves for anyone else that might be inclined to pour him another draft. I look over at K.C., one of the three bar owners standing behind him at the pool table. K.C. gives me a slight smile and shakes his head, barely perceptible, no.

"I can't do it partner. It's for your own…"

"Goddamn you and your mother, I want a beer and I want it now," he roars. He takes one stumbling step forward, almost loses his balance, and recovers with two small steps backward.

A girl snickers from the back of the bar, probably not one of the regular customers. Bart, our featured drunk of the hour, ignores her. This is a bad sign, because if he is only half-drunk, he would curse her or would be embarrassed by his own ineptness. Instead, his displeasure is now focused entirely on me, the reluctant social director of the hour. I'm not even a regular employee of the Party House—I work occasionally for some food and drink and to spell my bartending friends.

Bart starts forward again, but this time his arm comes up and, in one smooth, semiprofessional motion, the glass mug sails through the air and passes cleanly through the space my head occupied less than a second earlier. Anticipating the flying mug, I hit the floor about the time the mug shatters against the back wall. I look up to see Bart coming over the counter, then see him disappear just as quickly. Peering over the barrier, I watch as two of our beefier patrons grab him by the back of the pants and try to take him to the floor.

Bart was a minor league baseball player when he was ten years younger, accounting for his deadly accuracy with beer mugs, and he is also a hell of a lot stronger than his wiry frame seemed to advertise. Grabbing Frank around the shoulders, he pushes the ex-footballer backward and onto the floor. Bart turns on Skip, one of our muscular house musicians. Skip is game to help but he's no match for a dead-drunk Bart.

Skip starts to retreat but makes the fatal error of putting his hands out toward the drunk. Bart grabs the extended wrist, twisting Skip around so Bart stands behind him, one arm wrapped across his chest. Bart picks up Skip, holds him over his head, and runs toward the front screen door. Skip is released about two feet in front of the door and flies through it, taking it cleanly off the hinges. Wood frame, screen, and Skip kiss the dirt, just clearing the front steps of the tavern. He lands at the feet of Henry, one of my friends who was about to come up the steps. He stops next to Skip and the two of them stare through the very open doorway.

K.C. drops his pool stick and joins me as we help Frank up. The three of us advance slowly on Bart, still facing the missing door and seemingly amazed by his dramatic display of strength. The bar remains completely silent as regulars and visitors alike watch the drama play out. Before we can reach and subdue him, Bart turns and faces us, his arms hanging limp at his sides and his hands open.

"Now I really need that beer. Throwing people across the bar gives me a dry mouth, know what I mean?" He is smiling and his shoulders slump, his hands relaxed. K.C. and I stop and look at each other.

Frank steps forward. He is at least four inches taller than Bart and gentle by nature, but he can be imposing, and no one doubts he has the juice to take care of business. Bart looks at Frank as if he has just walked in off the street and none of the preceding has occurred.

"Buy me a beer, Frank. Hell, I'm good for it, you know that. I'll buy you two next week."

K.C. steps forward and puts a hand on Bart's shoulder. He is our voice of dispassionate reason, rarely showing any stress or panicked response to the barroom craziness. He looks in Bart's eyes and addresses him in a slow Texas drawl.

"Man, you almost killed Pete here with that mug. If he had been as drunk as he normally is, he'd a been eatin' glass."

Bart glances at me, almost sheepishly. "Sorry, Pete, I just… you know, I forgot where I was. I was still asleep." He reaches out with his hand, and I shake it.

About this time, Skip stumbles back up the steps and through the open door with Henry. While confronting Bart, we have forgotten about him, and I am glad to see he is more or less alive. He is one of the regular Party House entertainers, and we need him to keep the place rocking, but he seems to be no worse for the experience. Nonetheless, he makes a wide circle around Bart on his way to the men's bathroom, the Buoy's.

"Tell you what," says K.C., his arm still on Bart's shoulder. "If you'll go behind the bar and sweep up the glass and then sit down on a stool like a real human being, I'll pour you another one. Deal?"

"Hey, that'd be gooder than good. Where's the broom and pan?"

"It's in the Gull's room. Darla will get it for you."

Diminutive Darla, unusually sober at the moment, nods and heads for the women's bathroom as I return behind the counter and the rest of the crowd commence to do what they were doing. Darla hands the broom and dustpan to Bart, and he comes around to start sweeping. K.C. looks at me.

"You okay with that, Pete?"

I nod. "Works for me."

As I move along the counter to exchange full bottles and mugs for empties, I finally realize how close the mug has come and where I might be if it had struck me. K.C. was right, many evenings by this time my reflexes wouldn't have been worth a crap. At the Party House and at many of the other bars in Port Tarpon, bartenders drink along with customers and closing time is often a blur.

Bart finishes sweeping and walks back to the customer side, grabbing a stool near the jukebox. The change in Bart is as dramatic as one could hope to witness, one minute throwing Skip through a screen door and a few minutes later sitting at the counter with his elbows on the bar, grinning and patiently waiting for a beer. I pour a Pearl draft and set it in front of him.

"Damn all, I'm really sorry, Petey. You know I wouldn't deliberately hurt you. Here's to you." He drinks about half of the beer down, leaving a layer of white foam on his handlebar. Wiping his face with his bare arm, he sets the beer down gently, making sure none spills.

"You've got the arm, all right, baseball or beer mug, you burn them in." I remember when he played softball earlier in the summer. From third base he could hum a rope across the diamond. The first baseman hardly had to move his glove. Of course, most of the time Bart played sober and serious. It was a tossup over what he loved most, baseball or beer. Connie, his live-in girlfriend agreed. "Whatever, I know I'm third," she told us one night.

"*Hola, Pedro, una cerveza aqui.*"

I turn toward Manuel, who has just entered and sat down at the other end of the bar. He is one of the few Latinos who patronize the Party House. Most of the resident Mexicans and the San Antonio fishermen hang out at El Tejano on the other side of the marina.

"Your usual?" I ask, already knowing the answer.

"*Si, Perla o nada.* Hey, *amigo*, what happen wid your door?"

I grab a bottle of Pearl from the cooler, pop the cap and set it in front of him. "Bart's doing some remodeling for us. Unfortunately, he used Skip as a tool." I say it quietly, not wanting to provoke Bart further. Although they drank the same brand of brew, Bart prefers it from the tap, and Manuel likes it from the bottle. That is as close as the two would ever agree. Bart had gotten into a bad fight, one he lost, at El Tejano. He swore he would never go back or drink with a "spic" again. We had made it clear to Bart that Manuel was one of us, and we wouldn't tolerate any hostility toward him or other Latinos in our place.

Manuel takes a chug and smiles, speaking softly. "And did *el señor* Skip enjoy being a tool?"

"No, but he must have landed well." I nod toward the pool tables where Skip is chatting with Darla and K.C. as if nothing has happened. Manuel glances once at Bart, but the mustached one is looking at the jukebox. I know it will only be a few minutes before he offers to play something if I will get a quarter or two from the register. I'm also concerned about getting him another beer when he drains the one he has. Despite his current deportment, I know too well that Bart can still go off again. The problem is we don't know when or what will trigger it. K.C. walks behind the counter and stands next to me.

"Pete, you want me to take over. You've more than earned a break."

"Yes sir, boss, thanks." I grab a mug, pour some Shiner, and walk out the back door and onto the deck overlooking the marina.

Melanie is sitting next to Willie, one of the other owners. She is new in town, has long curly brown hair, an alluring smile, and a well-endowed bosom. She lives by herself in a one-room house about four blocks from the bar. Unattached, she fits readily into the Party House scene, partitioning her life as an art teacher for the island school system by day and a gamer by night, one willing to do the crazy things we take for granted. She isn't as wild as some, but she is friendly, and a lot of the guys are trying to make a play. So far, she hasn't accommodated anyone that we know about. She prefers to hang around with Willie and me, partly because we don't harass her and partly because we can entertain her with our arguments about almost anything, from the most trivial and esoteric to the big questions of the universe. Willie and I are into the one-up game, trying to impress each other with our vast storehouses of knowledge and nonsense. Melanie once summarized it nicely.

"Peter, you hardly say anything to anyone, unless Willie is around. When he is, you can't shut up."

Melanie moves closer to Willie so I have a spot next to her on the bench. We don't say anything for a while. The breeze off of the marina is gentle and warm, a typical summer Texas evening. The gentle lapping of waves at the piers contrast with the constant buzz, laughter, and noise from inside the bar.

Willie also drinks Shiner. It is a kind of hippie-come-redneck thing in South Texas. He has a college degree in philosophy, just the perfect credentials to be an island bar owner. He was one of my first acquaintances when I arrived on the island the previous year.

"Bart's pretty good with a hammer and stapler, so I'll see if he'll fix the door tomorrow. After he sobers up and before he starts in again." Willie has some of the same temperament as K.C.—quiet, reflective, and concise. The other owner, Arnie, had dropped from a different tree. He is excitable, passionate, and more inclined to take action against some of the town drunks like Bart. He is out of town this evening, a good thing. Although he could get as wasted as anyone and has his mellow moments, I'm sure he would have called the cops on Bart, just to prevent further damages.

"Close one, huh, Pete?" Melanie puts her hand on my arm. It is warm and her large blue cow-like eyes look into mine. I have to admit, she can quicken a pulse and raise blood pressure, but in a nicer way than oncoming beer mugs.

"Uh-huh. Got my attention, to be sure."

"Got ours, too," said Willie. "Figured we step out here for a spell."

A loud crash inside the bar is followed by yelling from several in the crowd. K.C.'s voice pierces the noise. "Damn it, Bart, put it down. Right now."

Willie starts to react, thinks better of it, and sits back, cigarette in one hand, longneck in the other. "I'm getting too old for this. If not too old, too tired of it. He can take care of it."

Another crash, more yelling, and a high-pitched scream from one of the girls, probably a tourist. The floor boards are shaking, evidence of bodies thumping, slamming, rolling across the floor, accompanied by chairs sliding and bumping. A couple of girls exit the rear door and hastily retreat down the steps, looking back over their shoulders. My attention is on Melanie's hand, which has tightened on my wrist. Her right thigh is pressed against my left leg and I am responding accordingly.

"I'm calling the cops, Bart. Head out now while you can," hollers K.C. It must have worked because the crashing and thumping stops. For about ten seconds. Then there is another round, and I stand up to peer inside the back door.

Bart is engaged with about four guys, some bigger and some smaller. He is lunging at the counter trying to get to K.C., standing calmly with the phone in his hand. One young guy, shirtless and shoeless, is lying face down on the floor and a girl is kneeling beside him, crying and trying to get him up. K.C. speaks quietly into the phone and hangs up. He comes around the counter to help the others subdue Bart. They finally manage to force him to the floor, pinning him there while he curses and pants, occasionally kicking. As I watch, Bart stops struggling and silently waits for the police.

"K.C. called the cop shop, and they have Bart on the floor," I tell my bench companions. Melanie seems nervous but doesn't get up. Willie just smiles, takes another drag, and stares out at the marina.

Calling the law is the last resort for the Party House. We would rather handle it ourselves, taking care of friends, and dealing with foes. Bart could be either, but we don't want to see him in jail. I haven't seen what started the latest row, but sometimes it doesn't take much, especially from an out-of-towner, like the guy on the floor. K.C. is bending over him and talking to the girl. I can make out blood oozing from his scalp. He has short hair, a frat type that probably should have been drinking somewhere else. In addition to Latinos, Bart isn't fond of clean-cut college boys. He makes an exception for Willie and me because we aren't particularly clean cut.

I sit down and move close to Melanie. There is nothing like a hot thigh at a moment of stress. That and the cold beer restore my mental equilibrium.

"You okay, Pete?" she asks.

I look at our legs pressed together and sip my suds again. "It works, Mel, it works."

The cops pull up behind the bar five minutes later. One car, two cops. We all know them, and Willie lifts his longneck in salute as they climb the stairs and enter the bar. A few more people exit, including a couple of kids that might have been underage. Age isn't a problem in the Party House—families with kids often eat here—they just can't be caught drinking anything with alcohol. A couple of the ones on the back deck probably have, despite our intent not to serve them. Willie rises, tosses the cigarette butt into the street, and makes his way inside. Melanie and I follow, joining the crowd to watch the cops, Charlie and Stuart, cuff Bart and get him to his feet. While Charlie escorts Bart out to the patrol car, Stuart talks to the guy with the bleeding head. He is now sitting up, embraced by the girl, but not looking too happy. The nearest hospital is across the waterway from the island, about a fifteen-minute ferryboat ride. Willie returns to Melanie and me and informs us of what has happened.

Seems that mister crew cut had not only bumped Bart while getting a drink but had spilled some of it on him. When Bart protested, the frat boy cursed and laughed at him. He also mentioned he had a few friends with him. Bart grabbed him and yelled for them to jump in and they did, three of them. Bart took the crew cut out with his mug and the brawl was on.

The wounded one is up and talking, and Stuart asks him to wait until they return and get him to the hospital. K.C. puts some money in the jukebox and encourages a few of the regulars to dance and get the mood "readjusted," as he puts it.

"I'm not sure they, the four of them, would've been enough to put Bad Bart away," adds Willie. "K.C. knows how to use a sleeper hold and that's what finally got him down."

Melanie looks at both of us. "Speaking of sleeper, I think it's about time. Could you guys walk me home?"

She usually has both of us play escort. It is a not-so-subtle way of making sure that neither of us has a clear shot at her. She could flirt with the best of them and be sizzling warm, but she isn't ready to entertain anyone in particular. "Biding my time and waitin' to see" is the way she puts it. What she's waiting to see we aren't sure about, but you have to respect her wishes and we do. Although she lives close by, the streets are dark and a weekend night brings strangers to Port Tarpon. We won't let anything bad happen to our schoolteacher, so Willie and I stroll with her, one on each side.

"Will Bart be pissed because K.C. called the cops?" she asks.

"Nah," Willie answers. "We've had to do that a few times. They'll take care of him, wake him in the morning, give him a better breakfast than he would have gotten otherwise, and let him go without charges."

"Unless the frat boy really had some damage, then there may be some medical expenses to face," I note.

"For Bart, it will probably be money well spent," says Willie.

"How's that?" she asks.

"It's been almost four months since Bart has been in a notable fight. Taking on four and beating one of them to the floor won't ruin his reputation any. And for Bart, that's about all he's got going for him anymore. A fast ball and a reputation."

I answer Willie. "I sure as hell hope I'll have more than that going for me when I reach his age."

Melanie smiles up at me in the half-moon light. "Did you play baseball, Pete?"

"Not so as you'd notice it. And I never beat anybody in a bar room fight either."

Willie takes a last drag on his cig and tosses the butt away. "That's okay, Petey, we can't all be heroes."

I bid good night to Melanie and then to Willie. Walking back to my small cabin at the Marine Science Institute, I think about the night, the near miss with the glass mug, and how strange the past year has been. *Is this what I thought it would be like? When I was still among friends and safe in Austin, did I imagine a life like this? Where am I going?*

CHAPTER TWO

Island in the Sun

MARCH 1973

Seventeen months earlier, being a part-time volunteer bartender wouldn't have occurred to me. Port Tarpon and the island craziness was still in the future, a world that I barely knew existed. My world centered on the university, The University, the hallowed halls of academia where enterprising graduate students vied for research opportunities with esteemed faculty sponsors. This was to be followed by post-docs and prestigious positions somewhere pursuing esoteric scientific investigations. The future was yet to be revealed, but the pathway was clear. I had proposed a project in behavioral ecology, describing the social interactions within a newly discovered species of fiddler crabs. My graduate advisor approved the project, and I was on my way to the university's Marine Science Institute on a Texas barrier island to begin two to three years of fieldwork.

My first impressions of my new home were not compelling. It wasn't awe and wonder I felt, more like terms of enduring than endearing. It didn't resemble a Caribbean paradise, not by a long shot. There weren't any nearshore coral reefs—turquoise blue waters rarely appeared. Silt and mud runoff from land provided the characteristic lack of clarity in the northern Gulf of Mexico. A few palm trees hinted that the sandy barrier island had pretenses of being tropical, but it required only a few minutes exploration to quickly dispel any geographical misconceptions.

Situated about a hundred miles north of the Mexican border, the island clings to the Texas coast like a Western movie sidekick, but it seems to belong elsewhere, as do most of its inhabitants. They started gathering more than a hundred years earlier, lonely fisherman and itinerant beachcombers, wrecked ship scavengers, outlaws and goat farmers. They came, settled, lived, and died. Recognition of the island as a gateway to the large inner bay and its commercial potential led to attempts to dredge a connecting channel from the Gulf. The Civil War resulted in several skirmishes for control of the waterway. Railroads, lighthouses, and hurricanes had their impact on the island's future. Not until the turn of the century and completion of protective jetties for the waterway did the resemblance of a real town appear on the northern tip of the island. There weren't any tourists in those days, or college kids, or automobiles, or much of anything. To get there, you crossed the lagoons and waterways by boat. If you had to transport something big, it required a barge and the use of makeshift piers, one on the island and the other on the inland shore.

During the 1930s and 40s, sports fishermen discovered the Gulf and the inland waterway, a place to catch red snapper, cod, sea bass, and the biggest prize, tarpon. The town acquired a name and a reputation and people followed, building streets, stores, motels, and bars—lots of bars. The Texas Highway Department connected the southern end of the island by bridge to Corpus Christi and served the northern end with two twelve-car ferryboats running between the town and the mainland several times a day. Summer tourists and spring break kids soon followed. There wasn't any surf to speak of—the nearshore Gulf was too shallow, and the sand bars prevented all but a few ripples. Occasional storms created some four-foot waves, but surfboards were available anyway, along with banana oil, increasingly provocative swimsuits, loud music, and an unmistakable party atmosphere. The sixties and seventies created a mixed island culture of rural Texans, Hispanics, hippies, entrepreneurs, and dogs. The island boasted a population of over 50,000 during the summer and about 2,000 during the winter, including a transient population of Midwestern snowbirds and regular employees of the Coast Guard station and the university's Marine Science Institute. The latter produced a rotating population of professors, students, and staff to add to the island melting pot. From propertied high rollers in their condominiums to homeless lowlifes scrounging for beer and beans, the island life was a tapestry of individuals of all ages and educational backgrounds.

I didn't know any of this when I arrived at Port Tarpon in late winter, March of 1973. It was a bitter wet afternoon as I drove my beat-up station wagon onto the ferry and set the brake. There were four other cars besides mine, and most of the passengers got out and stood along the front of the boat as it crossed the narrow waterway. I joined them, protected by a thick flannel coat against a stiff sea breeze. The constant cry of sea gulls and the briny smell of the ocean reminded me of how different the coast was from the heart of Texas. Two large oil tankers were docked along the mainland shore. Ahead, on the island, I could make out a few low buildings and an occasional palm tree. It looked dreary and colorless, hardly inviting, but there I was, committed to the island for two years or more, "come hell or high water," as my dad used to say.

My friends in Austin warned me the island wasn't worth visiting in the winter. Wait until it gets warmer and crowds enliven the beaches and bars, they said. Only then would there be sufficient food, beer, music, and women, enough to satisfy any appetite. Except for music, I didn't have a notable appetite. By Austin standards, Mustang Island would be semi-deserted, inhabited by pathetic parochial people of little value or interest. Most of the stores and restaurants would be shuttered until spring break brought the first wave of party-seeking students. Only the Institute and its activity promised a relief from winter boredom.

The ferry docked with a noticeable bump, and the gate lifted. I started the station wagon's engine and slowly, carefully, eased the car off the boat and onto the wooden dock, followed by a two-lane paved street. Maybe "paved" was being generous. It was full of potholes, had no sidewalks, and the surrounding view appeared to confirm the forecast rendered in Austin. I saw few people but there were several dogs strolling nonchalantly down the middle of the street. The wind blew a slight mist onto the windshield after each pass of the wiper. Welcome to paradise. Was this it, what I really wanted? I could have finished a degree in Austin, in a comfortable lab with a protected field site, surrounded by friends and all of the technical support I could want. I only knew one person in Port Tarpon, a fellow graduate student at the Marine Science Institute or MSI. Carl had encouraged me to join him—to be partners in exile, separated from the great university and its bustling students, faculty, and impressive facilities.

■　■　■

I ARRIVE AT THE MAIN JUNCTION IN TOWN, WHERE FERRY Street crosses Island Road. The latter runs the island's length, connecting twenty miles south with another barrier island and with the mainland. Across the street lies the Coast Guard station and on my left is a marina with several buildings and a number of moored boats. The Institute is farther ahead, past the CG station, but I turn right to get a preliminary glimpse of the town. A number of small motels, a couple of restaurants, a church, and a baseball field line the road, along with houses, three real estate offices, and bars. As foretold, most of the restaurants are closed. All of the motels have vacancy signs, except those shuttered for the season. More dogs, a few people, only a few cars.

At the southern edge of town, I make a U-turn, returning to the junction and turning right to continue to the MSI. It sits at the end of the ferry dock road, next to a jetty, and in back of dunes bordering the Gulf Coast beach. The MSI is by far the most impressive building in town—concrete and glass, modern and efficient looking. Two stories high but spread over a considerable footprint, it conveys some of the strength of the university with which it is affiliated. I hope the people inside are more like those in Austin than what I expect of the people in Port Tarpon. Parking in front of the building, I get out and walk into a reception area on the first floor.

The receptionist, a young tall blonde about my age, mid-twenties or so, smiles and asks if she can help me.

"I hope so. I'm Peter Gilbert, Professor Stevens' graduate student."

"Oh good, we're expecting you. How was the trip down?"

"Long, but not a bad drive. It didn't rain until I hit the coast."

She looks at me in sympathy. "Yes, it's winter here. I'm afraid our island in the sun is a bit wet at the moment. The Chamber of Commerce doesn't brag about the winters." The outer door behind me opens and a blast of cold air underscores her comment. "We have a temporary place for you to put your things. In a few days we can offer you a cottage to live in. Unless you want to take your chances in town? There may be some places to stay, and I can get you started, if you'd like." She gives me an encouraging smile.

I return her smile, already feeling more at ease. "No, I'll stay here. It'll be fine." I am underwhelmed by what I had seen in town. Maybe later, I think. When I know my way around, I'll venture out, but the Institute seems like sanctuary, the best choice for the present.

She rises and walks around the desk, a set of keys in her right hand. "Follow me, and I'll show you what we have." She is almost as tall as me, just less than six feet by my estimate. Wearing a tight skirt and sporting a feminine sway, decisive but not overdone, she leads the way down a long hallway toward the jetty end of the building. She stops, opens the outer door, and points to a small group of adjacent wooden buildings. "The one on the left is yours." She hands me the keys. "I won't go out with you, but the large key opens the outer door. Inside there are four rooms. The small key opens room C. You can pull your car around to the building. After you unload, come back to me, and I'll get you registered, give you a parking permit, and get you a key to the library and to this building."

"Thanks. Efficient, really efficient." I take the keys and give her an appreciative glance as she turns and walks back to her office. *No ring? Available? Maybe this won't be so gruesome after all. And, no trace of an accent. Probably not local, could be from somewhere else, like me.*

Passing through the door into the increasing wind and rain, I turn the corner, enter my car, and drive it to a parking area next to the temporary housing. I travel light, a duffle bag with clothes and personal items and two boxes of books and field equipment. Towels and bedding are to be provided as part of my room, paid for by a predoctoral training grant. I also receive a small stipend for expenses, including food. It isn't much but I knew that when I agreed to leave Austin.

The room is small and simple, but adequate for the present. A single bed, a desk, a chair, and a set of drawers comprise the accommodations. A small bathroom with a shower at the end of the short hall serves the four rooms. I quickly stow my clothes and return to the office.

Again, the warm relaxed smile. "Ready to see your lab, Peter?" she says.

I nod. "Call me Pete, if you will."

"Call you, or call you Pete?" Her voice is flirty, but not with the exaggerated sweetness that some southern women exude.

I smile but lower my head. Once again she rounds her desk with a set of keys. "I believe your colleague is down there and he can fill you in." She looks back at me coyly and sings in a cheerful lilt, "Follow me, follow me."

Yes, I will.

We descend into the basement of the building (three stories, even bigger than it looks) and walk past several open doors. The rooms, offices and laboratories, are lit and mostly occupied. The deserted exterior and quiet office upstairs belie the bustle and intensity in the basement. Students, staff, and faculty populate the area, busily working on critical research projects, no doubt. The open doors beckon, reminding me of the main campus and the buzz of intellectual curiosity that pervades those corridors and meeting rooms. It's what I came for, to join the ranks of investigators, the scientists I hope to become. It is a prize I am willing to sacrifice a comfortable life in Austin for. But there is more. It is also the ocean, the marine world to which

I have always been drawn. Surrounding Port Tarpon is a vast wonderland of marshes and intertidal beaches inhabited by equally marvelous creatures—crabs. I hope my project will be sufficient for a dissertation and a doctoral degree in marine biology.

She pauses outside of an open door near the end of the corridor and hands me the keys. "Good luck," she says softly and turns to leave.

"Wait, I don't know your name."

She turns back with a teasing smile. "For an up and coming scientist, you're not very observant," she states matter-of-factly. "There is a sign on my desk and on the sign is my name. You still have some paperwork to complete and at that time you can perhaps learn and memorize my name. See you in about twenty minutes?"

I gulp, not sure what to say. All I can manage is, "Sure, I'll be there."

My student colleague is standing in the door, looking at me and watching the receptionist walk away. Carl is about my height and age. He's from Canada and studies neurobiology in squids. We walk into his, now our, lab and sit down. Most of the room is occupied by two large round tanks of circulating seawater. Two desks and bookshelves line one wall of the two-person office.

"Made it at last, did ya?" He retains a bit of his northern accent.

"Um-hm. Stevens sends his regards. He'll be down in about two weeks to check on us, to see if there is anything we need."

Carl sits back and glances at the shelf above his desk. "I'll need some papers from the library. I can send him a list by electronic mail."

"We have a computer here?"

"On the second floor. We have a terminal in the corner." He points at the stand and keyboard next to my desk, the empty one. His is littered with notebooks and papers.

"Convenient," I say.

"Checked into your room? Which one?"

"3C."

"My first room. Same one, before Cindi got here."

"Where do you live now?"

"About two blocks from here. We have a small house, just about right for Cindi and Samantha." Their daughter is only three months old. I knew them in Austin during the past year. Carl is Professor Stevens' first grad student, and I am his second. Stevens is only a year older than Carl and me.

"I'll bring my books over tomorrow. This lab is obviously yours." I look toward the tanks and the bench of electronic equipment beside them.

"They have an outside shed with some similar tanks set aside for you. I gathered most of your research would be in the field." This was a half statement-half question.

The truth was, I wasn't sure. I had been told my research subjects were on the island, but I didn't know where or how accessible. I hoped to do most of my work in the field, a combined ecological and ethological study of the crabs and how they behaved around their burrows. Supplemental studies involved bringing them into the lab for detailed observations and photography. My main use of Carl's room would be as an office. A phone and a computer would keep me linked to the outside world, especially the main campus.

"Where's a good place to eat?"

"Tonight, a good place is our house. Cindi is expecting you and we never get enough company here. We've been looking forward to it."

"Really? What about the other students? I thought that

there were quite a few people working here."

"There are, about two dozen, plus some faculty and a few post-docs. A few exceptions, but many of them run with a different crowd, the locals." He says this with a slight grimace, as if he found the subject somewhat distasteful.

"Oh? What does that mean?" I sense another side to this coin, one that I had only been indirectly and incompletely warned about.

"Port Tarpon is a different world. You're either gonna love it or hate it. You'll find out soon enough." He looks at his watch and I read mine: four thirty.

"I need to get upstairs and complete some paperwork for what's-her-name."

He doesn't take the bait. He smiles and says, "How's about five thirty or so?"

"Can I bring anything?" I was thinking about stopping for beer or wine.

"Not this time, mate." Carl hands me a notebook page with a penciled map to his house, along with his address and phone number. "You won't always find street signs and house numbers here, so maps are the best directions."

I stand up, give him a nod, and walk back to the office of the mystery receptionist. The smell of seawater, seaweed, sea fish and all things marine pervade the building. I take a deep breath before climbing the stairs. I like it. I always have.

Her name is Penelope Stokesberry. It says so, on a sign plainly visible on her desk. As I enter the office, she points at it, just to make sure my previous lack of attention is remembered. I thank her, sit down, and we fill out registration papers for graduate research credits, a parking permit, housing form, and a general information sheet. She gives me a map of the town, showing the names and locations of restaurants, motels, three churches, and the grade school. The marina, Coast Guard station, and Institute are prominently featured, along with some basic facts on the population and a brief historical introduction. It is five o'clock when we finish. She stands, puts on her coat, and smiles at me as we prepare to leave.

"We close at five, but if you need anything, there is a security guard on duty around the clock. His number is on your copy of the info sheet. Again, welcome to MSI, Peter… um, Pete. I hope to talk to you again, soon."

"I'm sure we will, Penelope."

"It's Penny. The sign is just to make me look more important than I am."

We walk out together—she turns out the lights and locks the office door. Penny leaves by the front entrance, and I stroll down the corridor toward my building, my new temporary home.

Thirty minutes later I'm at Carl and Cindi's, having a Molson and digging into a great stew. It has been a full day—leaving Austin, driving two hundred miles, and the arrival formalities. I am weary and the beer relaxes me further. By ten I thank them and say good night. I pull into the MSI parking lot reflecting on Austin and the island, noting how different the environments and the expectations are, but also anticipating the opportunities. It is like an iceberg on the surface, the biggest part to be discovered later, lurking in the depths of the future. I am still blissfully naïve about the iceberg and even more so about my future navigating the unknown seas.

CHAPTER THREE

Port Tarpon

MARCH 1973

My room has one window facing east, and the rising sun strikes my pillow. I awake, glance at my watch, and jump from the bed. Almost nine! Although I don't have any appointments or pressing tasks, I had hoped to get an earlier start. The first business, after a shower and dressing, is breakfast. It has always been my favorite meal of the day, but I had forgotten to ask Penny or Carl about a good place to eat. *Just as well. I should be able to figure out a few things for myself.*

Walking to the car, I pass two other guys coming into the main building. Thinking they might be students who know their way around, I ask one of them, a fellow of medium height with long blond hair and a beard, if he can recommend a place to eat.

"What'cha got in mind, laddie?" he says with a grin. "Not looking for an I-Hop, I hope?" He pronounces hop and hope almost identically, like a chant.

"No, just some place to get some eggs or pancakes."

"New here, huh? I'm Willie. This is Kenny." He nods toward the taller guy behind him, decked out with red hair and a beard, wearing glasses.

"I'm Peter, just arrived yesterday. I'll be sharing an office with Carl. Doctor Stevens is our graduate advisor in Austin."

Kenny just nods and picks his nose, but Willie smiles and shakes my hand. "Welcome aboard, Pete. Can I call you that? Peter sounds out of place here. But you probably don't know that yet, right?"

Kenny mumbles something about staying on schedule and Willie says, "Right. There's a restaurant on Island Road, on your right about three blocks from the junction. Only place to go. It's called, strange as it seems, The Island Restaurant. There's another one on the way to the ferry, but I recommend the first. Better class of client." Kenny laughs and shuffles toward the building. I thank them and get in the car.

I won't be able to eat meals out forever, in fact, not for longer than a week. Penny mentioned the small cabin next to the jetty with a kitchen. I would share it with another student, a Chinese biochemistry grad. The building has two double bunk beds, but they only plan to rent it to two single, long-term students. That's me. Single and long-term. It will be ready for us next Monday, in four days.

I had passed The Island Restaurant the day before. There are several cars in the lot—always a good sign—and it looks right. I had also noticed there were no obvious franchise fast food places, at least on the two streets I had driven so far. That was also a plus, but I hoped the prices in the locally owned eateries weren't going to be prohibitive. I later learned I didn't need to worry. During the off-season, many places struggled just to break even—high prices on an island of limited winter income weren't justifiable. Conversely, I would learn the high tourist season resulted in considerable competition for visitors with mostly modest pocketbooks. Except for a few high-end restaurants, most places were affordable and the food, surprisingly, was better than average.

The restaurant is bigger inside than it looks from the street. There are a few booths along the front wall, a counter near the kitchen, and some tables and chairs in the middle. It isn't quite half full and I have a choice of seats. I pick one at the counter and sit. A middle-aged woman brings me a cup and saucer before I can say a word.

"Coffee, sugar?" She's chewing gum and holds a pot of coffee poised over the upturned cup.

"Coffee, no sugar," I reply.

She laughs loose and loud. "You must be a new sugar, sugar. Unless you're not sweet."

She pours and walks away before I realize what she means. *Okay, Peter, time to go to school. This ain't Austin.* I scan the menu on the wall in front of me and decide on scrambled eggs and sausage patties with a glass of orange juice. Prices are quite reasonable, even for my student budget. *Hard to go wrong here.* She returns, takes my order, and brings the juice.

I look around the restaurant. Most of the patrons are men, middle-aged working types in jeans, overalls, flannel shirts, and baseball caps. A couple of young women occupy one table in a far corner. One older woman sits alone at the counter and between us two men are talking in an animated fashion about local politics. A number of the men are reading newspapers, and there are several scattered around the room, apparently available for the taking. The door opens and another young woman, about my age, enters, nods at a couple of the men, and joins the women at their table. I can't be sure, but they don't look or act like students. Must be locals. It's good to know the island isn't just occupied by fishermen.

"Here ya go, sugar. More coffee?"

The plate in front of me is not short on food. At least three eggs, two large patties, two pieces of thick Texas toast, jelly and butter. I nod a yes and she refills my cup. The men at the counter pay their tab and leave, still talking politics. The women are whooping it up, commenting on last night's social events, from what I can gather. The waitress makes her rounds, chatting and filling coffee cups. Endless refills for one price guarantee to attract and retain those with nothing more critical to do. The place has character and warmth, and I am beginning to recognize and appreciate the relaxed down-home atmosphere. I understand why Willie recommended it, but I am also curious about the other restaurant and vow to give it a try as well.

Three cups of black coffee get my engine started, and I am ready for my first full day at MSI. I pay the bill, leaving the waitress a decent tip—"Thank ya much, sugar, come back." I glance at the three women as I make my exit, but they ignore me. A little cooler reception than I was used to in Austin, where it seemed even strangers were quick with a smile.

A few minutes later, I'm in my room, gathering up books and the box of equipment. I drop them off at the lab and thank Carl for the previous evening. He is already at work on a squid.

"Where did you have breakfast?" He sits at a dissecting microscope, teasing out a large axon for recording nerve impulses. He doesn't look up.

"Island Restaurant. Lots of food and not bad."

"There'll be more and better choices during the summer, including a meal plan here. We have our own kitchen to serve the summer classes and all of the students that come, starting in May."

"Great, I'll look forward to that." By then I knew I would be tired of my own limited repertoire of cooking. "See ya later. I'm off to do a preliminary field survey, especially while the weather is decent."

I already knew that the coastal weather could change dramatically during winter and spring. Blue northers (a.k.a., Texas northers) pushing down from the Midwest could drop temperatures by 40 degrees Fahrenheit or more in just an hour. It could be sweating hot and humid at noon and freezing cold by two. Snow and ice were unusual, but bitter chills were not. I had to be prepared for both.

Fiddler crabs are semi-social intertidal animals. The literature typically describes them as tropical and semi-tropical (there are a few temperate species here and there), occupying the sand and mud flats between the high and low tide marks. They aggregate in these areas to feed, dig burrows, and mate. The burrows are inundated at high tide and they retreat inside after plugging the opening. Most of their social interactions occur on the surface during low tide. These consist of territorial fighting between the males and sporadic bouts of males courting females, enticing them to enter a burrow for the purpose of conjugal bliss and promulgation of the species. *Big words, Peter. Is anyone impressed? I hope my committee will be.*

My task is to describe this in a species recently named and described, but with little information available on ecology or specific behavior patterns. But first I have to find them and in suitable locations where I could set up long-term studies with minimal interference. This meant away from the thousands of visitors that would overwhelm the island during the summer, the season when the crabs would be most active. Fortunately, most visitors either went to the beach to sunbathe and swim or to the piers or boats to fish. Vegetated sand or mud flats, preferably on the backside or inland waterway side of the island, would be ideal. If the crabs were present, I could set up cameras, recording equipment and do surveys, some requiring observations at the same site for several days at a time. It was essential that the sites be remote and free from random visits by the curious and careless.

The weather is great, shirtsleeve comfortable, temperature in the mid-sixties, with only a slight breeze. I drive south down the island road, clearing the last buildings, and observe a large expanse of dry salt flats to my right hand on the inland side of the island. Here and there are channels and ponds. They aren't intertidal, but I speculate that the margins along the water's edge might be suitable habitats. Parking the car off road, I walk across the flats with a pair of binoculars and a notebook. It isn't the kind of environment that is characteristic for most fiddler crab species, but this is South Texas. I have been told there were fiddler crabs here and I mean to find them. I walk along the ponds and channels, not knowing exactly what to expect.

I had read about them, large groups of crabs gathering to feed at the water's edge, the dramatic claw-to-claw combats of the males, and the frantic courtship dances as females passed by the male burrows. Although the details for each species varied, the activity patterns were similar. All were cued to one sequence: the rise and fall of the tides. But tides along the Texas Gulf Coast are minimal and this presented an enigma. How would periods of combat and courtship, if they existed here, be determined? More important, where would these activities take place? I knew I couldn't expect to find them along exposed ocean beaches—they needed a rich organic substrate to feed from and the sandy beaches were sterile by comparison. In addition, larger predatory ghost crabs occupied the ocean beaches, not to mention automobiles, beach blankets, and thousands of tourist feet.

I keep looking, hoping to find open burrows near the waterline, pellets deposited from their feeding, or some claws or other shell remnants. But there is nothing! As I drive back to MSI I start regretting my decision to leave Austin. Four hours of walking the flats turn up zilch. I need to consult with someone from the Institute, with someone familiar with the habitats where I thought the crabs might live. I was positive some of the local fishermen used them as bait. I was also positive I wanted a cold beer, the next item on my agenda.

I return to my room, take a shower, change clothes, and give some thought about dinner. A soft drink and a bag of chips comprised my field lunch. The warm sun and the disappointment of my first day of searching have stimulated a sharp craving for food. Pizza sounds great, but where? As far as I can tell, there are no pizza parlors on the island. Consulting the map Penny gave me, I see there are at least two restaurants around the marina near the Coast Guard station.

I walk to the marina, only three blocks from MSI. Next to the station is a nice-looking sit-down restaurant. A menu with prices is posted on a front window. It is mainly steaks and seafood rendered Cajun style. Nice, but expensive—one meal kills my budget for a month. Across the street are three bars sitting next to each other and adjacent to the marina. On my left is a weathered wood frame building. A small sign over the door identifies it as "The Party House." Next to it is a small white stucco building with a red tile roof, the "Gun 'n Reel." A rifle and fishing rod are crossed on its sign and it appears to be a traditional small-town tavern, but it probably doesn't offer much in the way of food. The bar to my right is a white wood frame building resembling a small cottage. The sign over its front porch identifies it simply as "Mary's Place." Acting in the blind, I opt for the Party House. Up three front wood steps and entry through a screen door.

It's obviously a bar, with pool tables in the back, some tables and chairs, and a bar counter. The menu overhead draws my immediate attention—sandwiches, pizza, and a few other snacks. A few customers sit at the bar and two guys shoot stick in the back. A very tanned barmaid, looking to be in her early-to-mid-thirties, is pouring beer and talking to one of the guys. An old-fashioned jukebox is close to the front door. I sit down and notice no booze is evident. It's a beer bar. Or so I thought.

She steps in front of me and, in neither a friendly nor a hostile tone, says, "What can I getcha?" She has a slight but not extreme Texas drawl, lots of freckles, and short dark hair that seems to require minimal upkeep. She's wearing a plaid work shirt and cutoff jean shorts. She is slim and looks like an active outdoor type.

"A beer and a pizza." I'm looking at the menu and it appears they have three choices: cheese, pepperoni, and "the house." "What's on the house?" I ask, anticipating it may have peppers, onions, meat, or something else to fill an empty stomach.

"Ain't nothing on the house here honey, ya gotta pay for everything." She laughs and the guys at the bar laugh with her, enjoying what must be a traditional joke at the expense of newcomers. I also laugh, realizing I really want a pizza and may have to settle for pepperoni.

She suddenly gets serious and leans forward to whisper, as if protecting some great secret known only to the inside locals. "It has ground sausage, onions, and olives. Will that do?"

"Oh yeah," I say. "How big is it?" She holds her hands out, indicating about six inches. I nod.

"What beer talks to ya?"

I look at the taps and see they have Shiner. I liked it

when living in Austin, a good local beer but not to every-one's taste. I also like Lone Star, and they had both. "Shiner from the tap," I answer.

She looks at me with a different expression. "Hey, good call." She walks to the tap, grabs a large frosted mug from a box under the counter, and pours it exactly right, leaving just enough foam at the top so you know what you're drink-ing. She puts it down in front of me and walks around the back counter into a small kitchen. The pizzas are frozen so it takes only a few minutes to heat one in a small counter oven and get it next to my mug. I also notice there is about one-half of a pie sitting on the back counter, although it isn't listed on the overhead menu. I finish the pizza, order a second beer, and point to the pie.

"That for sale?"

"Sure thang," she drawls, "Just 'bout everythang here is. You want a piece?" That produces a reaction from one of the counter guys, nearly choking and spraying beer on the bar in front of him.

She looks at him in mock disgust, but it seems to be a familiar routine, possibly played for my benefit.

"Yeah, I'll have some." I don't care what kind of pie it is. A piece is a piece. The beer is only twenty-five cents a glass, the pizza two dollars. I'm getting off cheap, even though it might not be the most nutritious or balanced meal I have ever had. It's also not the worst. She brings me a generous slice of peach pie, and I down it with my second beer. I look around the bar.

Over the tables near the front door is a bookshelf. A sign reads: "Community Library. Take one, bring one back." I walk back to the restrooms. One is marked "Buoys" and the other "Gulls." A sign above the two doors states: "If you can't figure out which one to use, get the fuck out of here."

A second sentence advises: "If you do use it and you work here, wash your damned hands." I use the john, actually a much cleaner facility than I expected, wash my hands, and step into the poolroom. A dartboard hangs on one wall, and there are two coin-operated tables. A full water dish sits beneath one of the tables. The back porch area is screened on two sides, one facing the marina. There is an additional porch outside of the bar with benches and two picnic tables. A lanky bearded man in blue jeans and a disintegrating T-shirt is lying across one of the benches, snoring loudly.

Inside, I pay the tab plus a small tip. The barmaid gives me a quick smile and a see-ya-later. Promising myself to return, I step out and take a deep breath of salty evening air. The walk back to MSI is a pleasant one, helped by a full stomach and a mellow glow, courtesy of Shiner. Tomorrow will be another day, and this time I'll ask questions and find someone who knows what I'm looking for. Maybe Penny knows where I should go. Maybe she'll tell me where to go. Nothing would surprise me.

Penny tells me where to go. She's a tease and nothing is going to be easy for me with her. My approach is honest and straightforward. I ask her if she knows what a fiddler crab is. Her eyes get big, and she sits back in her chair. No, she answers, she knows what a crab is, but could I please explain what I mean by a fiddler crab. I'm surprised; while she is a receptionist, she works at a marine science facility. Surely she must have seen or heard about them. They are neither exotic nor rare. I apologize and begin describing them—what they look like and how they behave. When I mention the males, with their one large claw and one small claw, perform a waving dance to attract females, she looks puzzled and asks me to explain. Yes, stupid me, I have to show her. I rock back and forth on my feet while waving one arm over my head, moving across the office in an unabashed spectacle of exuberant dancing. This coincides with the entrance of Willie and another guy into the office behind me. Penny can't take it any longer. She rolls forward onto her desk, head down, laughing uncontrollably. I sense Willie behind me silently breaking up.

The other guy looks at me with a smile, but asks, "Fiddler crab, right?" Willie is no longer silent—he and Penny are laughing loud enough to bring others out of their nearby offices to observe the object of their entertainment. It is I, the new student who looks ridiculous, but at least the other guy knows what I am inquiring about. I turn to him, trying my best to ignore Willie and Penny.

"The crabs will be my dissertation project if I can find them. Do you know where I should go?"

This brings another spasm of laughter from the easily amused. "Go west, young man, go west," gasps Willie, trying to catch his breath.

Penelope sits up straight, suddenly somber. She looks at the guy next to me. "Mitch, should I tell him where to go?"

By this time I realize I have two options: I can retreat and try to preserve what little is left of my dignity or I can join in the fun and continue playing the clown. I quickly decide on the latter.

"I'll go wherever you say, and I won't pass go and I won't collect two hundred dollars."

Penny, still serious, gives me another wide-eyed look, and says, "Peter, will you dance for me just one more time? That was adorable." She holds her hands in front of her and turns to one side, like Olive Oyl flirting with Popeye.

Now it is my turn to laugh, and I know my decision was the right one. Mitch holds out his hand and introduces himself. He is a research tech working on fish populations.

Willie is also not a student but a staff member who helps out on geological and oceanographic projects conducted by two of the MSI faculty. Red-bearded Kenny, the fellow I met yesterday, is a recent post-doc and one of the faculty. Mitch indicates he can direct me to several areas where my crabs should abound. I turn to Penny.

"And you? Did you know what I was talking about?"

She sits up straight and tells me in a very prim and proper voice, "You are looking for *Uca panacea*, the Gulf Coast sand fiddler crab. They won't be in the intertidal, as I am sure you will soon find out. And by the way, we have three other species of *Uca* here, in case you are interested."

Mitch nods in agreement, and Willie walks out of the office, his purpose in coming apparently forgotten or postponed. I thank Penny for all her help, and she tells me I can dance for her anytime. I will keep her offer in mind. Mitch and I walk down the corridor together and descend to the lower level. He tells me Penny assists the education director with his public presentations, and they had recently done one on fiddler crabs.

"Oh," I say, learning once again about assumptions. I won't make the mistake of presuming the ignorance of others again, especially receptionists with a sense of humor.

We stop at his lab, and he unrolls a detailed topographic map of the island. Along the backside, lining the Intracoastal Waterway, this is where you'll find the crabs, he says. He points to a dirt access road near the ferry landing. The road is about a mile in length, originally terminating at a landfill, but the dump has been relocated. The road passes a fisheries laboratory operated by Texas Fish and Wildlife, but after that there is nothing but salt flats and fiddler crabs. He informs me the MSI library can provide copies of the map. I thank him, and as I leave, he does a brief rendition of my crab dance. I walk away, shaking my head but grateful for his help. After yesterday, I thought nothing would surprise me. Wrong again!

The morning is still only half gone when I obtain map copies from the library, located next to the administrative offices. I decide to stroll around the Institute and orient myself. I might have avoided the first day's frustration if I had explored first, but a day in the field is never a total loss. Fresh air, exercise, and just observing a new environment bring its own rewards, or so they say.

I don't enter any of the labs, but merely note names on doors and peek in to see what and who is housed within. About half of them seem to be reserved for fish or fisheries research. There are also a few smaller labs and research offices on the main floor, along the corridor leading to my building. I walk back to the office area and turn down a different corridor, one that crosses over a walkway to a second building. This newer structure also contains laboratories on two floors. Behind this building is another parking lot backed by sand dunes and the Gulf beach. To the left I can see the stone jetty marking the northern boundary of the island and the Institute. It also lines the entranceway from the Gulf into the Inland Coastal Waterway, providing access to mainland towns and industrial docks. All ships arriving and leaving Corpus Christi transit this narrow passage.

Leaving the main building complex, I walk about the grounds. In addition to the small octagonal building where I sleep, there are two similar ones. There is also a rectangular building with a broad porch that serves as a kitchen and mess hall during the summer. Next to the jetty are three other structures Carl had told me about at dinner. The first is the small white cottage located a few steps from the jetty, my future shared residence. The second structure consists of a complex of covered sheds lacking vertical walls and divided by interior partitions. A number of large and small round plastic tanks occupy most of this area. This is where I can maintain some of my animals for experiments and controlled observations. The third structure is mounted on a pier jutting several feet into the waterway. Within the small locked building is a tide trap, a trawling net lowered with a winch when the tide is moving water in or out of the pass. It is a convenient way to collect fish, shrimp, crabs, and other marine creatures for study or for dinner. The latter use isn't official, since it's not licensed for such, but many of the Institute staff employ it discreetly to supplement their menus.

Local fishermen use the jetty for fishing, and there are always several of them busy on the concrete walkway. They are often accompanied by feral jetty cats that scavenge for fish heads, unused bait, and anything else smelly and oily. A couple of great blue herons also patrol the walkway and are known to steal bait from the buckets of the unwary or distracted.

Missing breakfast, I decide to grab some lunch before my next trip to the field. It is Friday, and a fish sandwich sounds good. I stop and ask Mitch if there is a suitable place for such on the island. Mitch is slim and a few inches shorter than me. He has dark curly hair and a full beard. He greets me with a smile and motions for me to take a chair.

"You haven't driven down the beach, yet?"

"No, are there restaurants there as well?"

"A few close to town that aren't open yet, but one is right on the beach about three miles from here. You can take any of the beach access roads before you go that far. It's a motel called Charlie's—you can't miss it. They don't have a lot of roomers at this time, but there's a restaurant that caters to wharf fishermen and beach strollers. They've got burgers, other sandwiches, chowder, fries, and shakes. You going there?"

"Yeah, I'll give it a try."

"Want some company?"

"Great, your car or mine?"

"I ride an old bike, not really built for two."

"Let's go." I lead the way out the door to my car.

"I hear you'll be staying in the jetty dorm," he says, getting into the passenger side.

"News gets around, huh?"

"Yeah, you'll be shacking with Chun, the student from Taiwan."

"Chun?"

"He's got a longer name, which none of us can pronounce, but he tells us to call him Chun." Mitch speaks slowly and softly, but he talks with less reservation when he's one-on-one.

I start the car, and we drive the Island Road out of town. "What's he like?"

Mitch looks straight ahead and reels off a description, as if reading from a biography abstract. "Quiet, hardly says anything unless you ask him a question. His English isn't great, but he gets by. He's older than he looks. Appears to be seventeen, but he's over thirty. Been up in Austin until about a month ago. He started working on some jellyfish enzymes and was staying in one of the smaller dorms. I guess they decided to pair the two of you. He works all day and well into the night, so you might not even notice him as a roommate." He glances at me as we near the first beach turnoff. "You can take this road."

We pass a couple of houses tucked among the dunes and emerge onto the beach. There are a couple of other cars and pickup trucks, either parked or driving along the water's edge where the sand is firmer. Mitch directs me to turn right, toward the south, and I can see a weathered building in the distance, partly on the beach and partly among the dunes.

"It's been here awhile," he says. "You can't build on the beach side of the dunes anymore. They need the dunes to protect the rest of the island during storms. Charlie's has been here for about forty years, survived several storms, kind of a landmark for the locals. We like to come out here from time to time."

"Good food?" I ask.

"That and more." He is silent for a moment and then asks, "Do you play poker?"

"I used to play when I was in the military, mostly on payday nights. I'm not big-time or anything, but I like the game. What kind of stakes?"

"It's a friendly game, usually. He smiles. Some of the locals, including a few of the MSI guys, sit in. Change and a few dollars, mostly for laughs and beer. Interested?"

"Could be, could be. When do you play?" By now we are pulling up to Charlie's. Only three cars are parked in a sandy area on one side, in front of a row of attached cabins.

"It's irregular, whenever the mood strikes. Or when we smell new bait in the water." Mitch looks at me when he says that, but it's not threatening.

We get out and walk up a stairway to a large porch overlooking the Gulf and the nearby wharf. Inside, there are several guys and two gals sitting around a large table. Only two of the guys are eating, but they all have longnecks in hand. A number of empties are stacked in the center of the table. Mitch greets them, and they answer as we walk to the counter. The smell of frying fish, frying fries, and frying burgers permeates everything, good smells when you're hungry. There is nothing like the sea, sand, and sun to make an appetite soar. And to my delight, they have fish sandwiches at the top of the menu.

"These are actually made from local, fresh catches, not frozen. The tartar sauce is also home made." Mitch relates this with more than a trace of pride.

"Can't wait," I reply, and we give a twenties-something woman our order. "Buy ya a beer?" I ask Mitch, but he is looking over at the table we passed.

"Can't now, honey, I'm working," answers the gal behind the counter.

"Umm, actually I was offering…"

Mitch smiles and says to the woman, "Sure, two long-necks." To me, "If you don't specify, just about anyone will let ya buy them a brew."

It seems like every waitress in town is a comedian. I would have to get used to that. We take our beer to a corner table looking over the beach. A cop car passes, moving slowly toward town. Groups of seagulls attack open trash-cans, and several plovers are walking along the waterline. The surf is minimal, mostly just water sliding smoothly onto shore. Most of the small waves are located over sandbars paralleling the beach. A slight breeze is not enough to disturb a limp flag hanging over the porch. Laid back it is, as foretold less than a week ago in Austin.

I tell Mitch more about my crab research, and he confirms the presence of fiddlers in several sites around the island, including along the jetty at the Institute. A small runoff stream from the holding tanks provides a limited habitat for them, but he warns me that the area is popular with fishermen. I am interested because that would only be a short walk from where I'll be staying. Anything I can save on gas costs and time will be an advantage. When I mention the lack of crab activity where I expected to find it, Mitch shakes his head and smiles.

"Northers, man, it gets cold here. Why would you come out if you had a comfy burrow to stay in?" He says this matter-of-factly, as if I should have known this before I arrived on the island.

"I guess it is too early, and my research subjects probably won't make an appearance for a while. Have any idea how long?"

"At least another month. That'll give you some time to meet folks and find your way around town."

I sip on the beer. "Shouldn't take long. There doesn't seem to be much to it. What do you do for entertainment here? Besides, poker?"

"Are you married or have a girlfriend?"

I consider this a moment before answering. "I was living with someone in Austin, but it was pretty casual. She decided to stay there and work, but we'll probably see each other now and then." I pause and Mitch gives me a nod to encourage additional information. "We've been together for about a year. We arrived from California last summer and rented the house Carl and Cindi had in Austin. She likes the neighbors and the town, so I'm pretty much on my own."

Mitch shifted in his chair to face me straight on. "Will you be getting a masters or a doctorate?"

"Doctorate. I already have a master of biology from Cal State Humboldt." Then I remember Carl's comment about some of the Institute staff and the locals. It had also come up briefly at dinner when Cindi made a comment about the Party House crowd and things to avoid. "I ate at the Party House yesterday evening. Seemed friendly and quiet and the pizza wasn't that bad. Do you go there?"

"Yeah, Willie and I, and most of our poker gang hang out there. During the winter, there isn't a lot of excitement, so we make our own. Play some pool, listen to music provided by some of the locals, dance a bit, and there are always a few of the ladies looking for a partner."

"To dance with?"

Mitch gives me one of those are-you-for-real looks. "That and anything else that comes to mind. Winter is a good time to do things indoors."

"Yeah, that's what my crabs supposedly do—have sex indoors, in their burrows." As soon as I say it I wish I hadn't. My reputation at MSI is already hanging by a thread and claiming to be an expert on crustacean sex isn't going to help matters.

The counter girl brings the sandwiches to the table. Mitch smiles and holds his empty bottle out, and she takes it in a smooth motion, as if it is something they rehearsed often. I'm only half-finished with mine, but the girl walks back to the cooler and brings two opened bottles to the table. Trying to drain the remainder of the first longneck, I nearly choke on it. Mitch smiles but does so with subtle control. He seems to be studying me, as if trying to classify me, to decide who and what I am. I'm starting to wonder the same thing. Am I in the right place?

"How about you, Mitch? You tied down?" The sandwich is hot, and the tartar is tasty, with a pronounced Cajun zest. The fries are large, Texas style, and the table has a couple of different hot sauces in addition to mustard and catsup.

Mitch swallows a bite, wipes his mouth with a napkin, and takes a slow sip of beer. Everything steady and reserved. He answers carefully, as if making sure there is no misunderstanding. "I have a gal who stays at my place some of the time, but no, no ties. You'll probably see her sooner or later. She goes by Moonshine."

"Pardon?"

"Moonshine. Her real name is Pamela, but everyone calls her Moonshine. A bit crazy, but in our group, it's hard to tell."

"Your group? Besides Willie, who else from the Institute belongs?"

"Henry is another one of the research techs. Frank is a graduate student working on fish populations in the same lab where I work. His wife also drinks with us. You'll probably run into them in the next few days. Most of the regular Party House people are not Institute people. Randy and his wife, especially his wife, spend a lot of time in the bar, and there are the three owners, K.C. and Arnie, along with Willie."

"Willie is one of the owners?"

"Yep. There are a bunch of people from around town and on any given night you can find many of them social-izing at the bar."

"What about Carl? Does he ever drink with you?"

"Not once. He seems to be a nice guy and gets along with everyone, but his wife is a bit strange. She doesn't care for the rest of us and has made it clear on a couple of occasions. I think if he was here by himself, he'd probably join in."

Mitch looks at his watch and indicates it's time for him to return. He has finished his second beer, and I am barely started on mine. Mitch tells me to bring it with us—just keep it out of sight while driving, he says. "They're not big on pulling you over as long as you're not weaving or run-ning over sunbathers," he tells me. Fortunately, there are very few beach loungers today.

I drop him at the Institute and drive back to the ferry landing. I turn west onto the dirt road, arriving at a deserted sand-mud flat along the Inland Waterway. Mitch is right—evidence of the crabs is everywhere on the flats: burrows, feeding pellets, and even a few claws and carapaces. There are no crabs on the surface, but it's early afternoon in late March and the air is cold. As I kneel, I feel some heat rising from the sandy surface. I'll return in the morning.

Driving back to the Institute and feeling relief at finding the crabs, I'm in the mood to celebrate. After dropping my field gear in the room, I walk over to my office. Carl is in the middle of recording a squid, so I don't disturb him. I pick up the phone and call my advisor in Austin and tell him the good news about the field site. Leaving Carl to his task, I wander upstairs and poke my head into Mitch's lab. Willie and Mitch are laughing about something, looking very relaxed. After sharing my afternoon news and once again thanking Mitch, Willie proposes we adjourn to "the local oasis of refreshment" and grab a few cold ones.

"Seems like a plan," I tell them.

"Ah, the laddie catches on quickly, doesn't he?" remarks Willie in a faux-Scottish accent.

The three of us walk to the marina and into the Party House. It is quiet, and Mitch indicates it probably won't get a crowd until after seven. Mitch, as usual in a group of several people, doesn't say much, but Willie is in the mood to talk. Sara, his girlfriend and trailer mate, joins us. Over a couple of pitchers of beer, I learn a lot more about Willie, his girlfriend, Sara, and his arrival in Port Tarpon two years before.

Willie and Sara

SUMMER 1971 AND SPRING 1973

Sara and Willie take turns telling their story, and Arnie joins us at the table, passing smokes around to those who want or need them. Willie always wants one. Sara doesn't like tobacco but will gladly toke a joint now and then. She is thin, tall, and has long blond hair done in a ponytail. Sara is a second-generation islander, and she has a casual familiarity with and is completely adapted to the island and its lifestyle. She could have been here since the first pioneers built a shanty or cast a net into the surf. She looks and talks the part, a pronounced South Texas twang combined with an open smile and a generous heart.

The daughter of a cigar-chomping realtor, she took up the trade as her dad got older, but in a casual manner that would never do for Century-21 or Re/Max. It kept her respectable but not well financed in the days before the land rush for beach property, before people thought of the island as a place to live instead of merely visit. She was unattached, carefree, and everyone's friend.

Willie arrived in Texas from the upper Midwest in the summer of 1971 looking for a job. Eager to give up the urban lifestyle in which he was raised and educated by overly restrictive parents, he fled south to the Gulf Coast and Port Tarpon. He had a philosophy degree and a minor in biology. He also knew his way around a boat. After a brief and successful interview, the Marine Science Institute hired him as a research assistant. He needed a place to stay and walked into Sara's real estate office just as Sara's dad was on his way to lunch.

"My daughter 'll take care of ya," he said in passing, exhaling a thick gray cloud as he stepped through the door.

Indeed, she did. Willie had short blond hair, was slim like Sara, and possessed a purposeful look about him that is frequently absent in many of the PT residents. He had opinions on a lot of things, much of which he readily shared with Sara as she asked him about his living preferences.

After an hour of smiles and some quick thinking, she told him about a trailer she had for rent in the center of town that was walking distance from the Institute. Willie paused and frowned. Finally, he confessed his lack of money for a deposit and that he couldn't pay a month's rent in advance. He had fled home in a hurry and didn't bring a lot of resources.

"Not yet," he told her. "But, I have a job and …" he continued with a broad grin, "I have my best asset, a quick mind."

Sara sat there a moment, a smile slowly forming at Willie's blatant display of immodesty. Her eyes never left Willie as she leaned forward, put her hand on his, and revealed her proposal. He could have the trailer free of charge, since she and her dad owned it. Only one catch. Willie would have to share it with her. She wanted to move out of the house she and her dad shared, and this seemed like a golden opportunity.

Willie, for once, was at a loss for words. For the past hour, he had been thoroughly beguiled by Sara's comely looks and charming smile. He had only been in town two days, staying at a small family motel. He had yet to visit a bar, meet any of the local gals, or discern the priorities of anyone, much less those of his prospective landlady. They were about the same age, but her invitation seemed precipitous to someone who has just recently left the land of prohibitions and proper decorum.

"You don't know me," he said, "I might be a serial killer or something worse."

"Well, if it's worse, then I guess I'll be in real trouble," she answered, still smiling and staring.

Willie couldn't seem to come back with anything snappy. She had caught him off guard, something that he rarely experienced. She withdrew her hand and sat back in her chair.

"I already have a pot patch started behind the trailer," she told him, hoping her prospective housemate would appreciate the bonus.

Willie had just started smoking cigarettes—for him, pot was in another universe.

"Isn't marijuana illegal in Texas? In fact, isn't it a felony?" Although lacking personal experience with the magic weed, he had read about the penalties, which included significant time in the state pen at Huntsville.

"Yeah, I guess in Texas it can be a problem, but this isn't really Texas, or at least not so as y'all would notice. No one here seems to care, Willie."

She said this with all of the assurance of a legal authority, but Willie was far from convinced. The proposal required some careful consideration. He asked to see the trailer and for some time to think it over. It was more than a place to live. Although Sara had proposed that they share living arrangements, she hadn't specified what that entailed. Same bedroom and bed? Did this domestic arrangement come with an intimate relationship or something less? Sara showed him the two-bedroom trailer, nicely furnished, and gave him twenty-four hours.

"I don't make this offer to just anyone," she informed him, eyes as intense as before.

Willie nodded his head and thanked her as they walked out of the trailer. He got in his car and she waved at him as he drove away. He made his way to a nearby tavern to grab a beer and sandwich and do some heavy contemplation. The proposal was appealing, and it fit his budget. The second bedroom remained a mystery. Would that be his, or would they share the queen-sized bed in the back bedroom?

When asked again about rent, Sara told him he could pay the utilities, keep up the maintenance, and "make himself useful." She didn't define what she meant by "useful," but her eyes seemed to flash with some inner light, as if she was enjoying a drama that only she was privy to.

The island and the town appealed to his newly realized sense of freedom. It wasn't sophisticated, more of a Wild West scene in an island setting, Cannery Row gone Texan-Caribbean. Before leaving home, he had threatened to major in everything until his father declared a financial moratorium. Philosophy and politics were particularly dear to his heart and debating—a.k.a. bullshitting—was a skill that came naturally. Willie reached the realization he could do a lot worse. The price was right and, who knows, she seemed intelligent and it might work. If it didn't, he assured himself there would be other options available down the road. Two hours later he was back in her office, sealing the deal with a handshake. No lease, nothing written, just a smile and a promise to give it a go.

Later that day, Willie moved a suitcase and two boxes of books out of his motel and into the trailer. Sara told him to drop his stuff in the second bedroom and make himself at home. He started to put his clothes in a small closet in the smaller bedroom, but she told him that there was room enough in the back bedroom closet.

"Hope you don't mind sharing a bed," she said, as if they were discussing the weather. Actually, she was. "It gets pretty damned cold here during the winter and sometimes a space heater just doesn't get it."

"Oh," Willie said. He guessed, correctly, that she may have had bedmates in this trailer before. *Not her first rodeo, but then why would it be?*

She handed him a key at the front door, gave him a brief, almost sisterly, kiss on the cheek, and told him she had to get back to the office. He watched her leave, wondering how it had all happened at what seemed like light speed, and what the future expectations would be.

Within six months, Willie and Sara were permanent housemates and considered married by Texas common law. It didn't stop either of them from occasionally looking hard at someone else. Willie's hair grew out, accompanied by a golden-brown beard, and he assumed the role as the town's foremost pot cultivator. It grew high enough behind their trailer that the local electricity meter reader asked Willie to cut it back a bit so he could see the dials. Sara took over the realtor business from her dad so he could spend more time in the local cafes and bars talking politics and complaining about the economy. In addition to Willie's day job at the Institute, a couple of the locals talked him into becoming a part owner of the beer bar where he made his decision to move in with Sara. The three owners named it the Party House, and it was the perfect forum for Willie to share his knowledge and opinions. Everyone was happy.

■　■　■

We order a third pitcher as Willie and Sara finish their tale of togetherness. The two ashtrays on the table are full of butts. Arnie is back behind the bar as thirsty customers arrive and order.

Mitch is quiet until the tale is completed. "So that's how it all happened? One look and instant romance?"

He is looking at Sara. I have also been silent, taking it all in—new place, new friends.

Willie decides it is past time to take a leak and leaves the table for Sara to speak her mind.

"Yep, that was Willie, always the sweet talker. Guess I couldn't resist him."

"Seems to me that you were the one that made the moves," replied Mitch, pouring beer into everyone's glasses. "But we're glad you did. You two grow better grass than anyone else around."

"Well, I needed someone to weed the garden," she laughs. "Actually, the real estate business wasn't doing all that great, so I married him for his money. Heaven knows, it wasn't his looks."

Willie yells from the bathroom, "I heard that." He shuffles out the door of the Buoy's room, zipping his pants. "I never claimed to be a looker, just the one with the brilliant mind."

"And ego," adds Sara, taking a long sip of brew. "And what about you, Pete? Shall we find you a playmate?"

"He's got a cute Chinese roommate, already," says Willie, rejoining us at the table.

"And crabs," adds Mitch. "Sexy crabs."

"Works for me," I reply, "at least for now." I'm sure that once summer arrives and the beaches fill with bikinis, I'll find a playmate.

By this time, the bar is filling with the usual mix of tourists and locals, and the jukebox is pounding out some loud reggae. Sara grabs Willie and begins dancing. Mitch and I look at each other, tilt our glasses slightly, and drink to the good life.

CHAPTER FIVE

Research and All That Jazz

SPRING AND SUMMER 1973

Mitch was right on—Chun was quiet and unobtrusive. We moved into the small jetty cabin five days after I arrived. The first thing I noticed was what we had in common. Practically nothing, except that he had about as much money as I did. We decided to pool our resources for a few groceries. For him, that meant rice, lots of rice. He wasn't fond of American rice, especially the brands he could buy locally. White paste, he called it, but it was cheap. I started buying packs of ramen noodles. The original idea was to use them for soup, and I had several other types of canned soup as well: chicken noodle, bean with bacon, and golden mushroom. One day, I opened a can of the mushroom soup when I discovered I still had a packet of ramen noodles opened but not moistened. Instead of making soup from the noodles, I boiled them like I would pasta, and I poured the heated but condensed mushroom soup over them, creating a poor man's casserole.

Chun watched me with interest and had a taste of the result. He approved of our new concoction and also used the ramen noodles from time to time, taking a break from white paste. Vegetarian spaghetti was another budget selection in our culinary repertoire, and I showed him how to fix that. He had chopsticks, so I also bought a pair at a store in Corpus Christi. The two of us must have been a sight, leaning over our bowls of rice or pasta, shoveling it in to our mouths Asian style. Didn't work as well on soup.

I started visiting the crab fields every morning, and I quickly discovered that activity was present but minimal, at least by the expectations I had read about them and seen in photos. But they were there, males and females, feeding around their burrows. What was missing was water. No cycles of activity relating to tides, but they did come out onto the surface during the morning and late evening. I watched them through binoculars and took a few telephoto shots with my Nikon.

The next task was to dig up a few burrows, measure the depth, and see how far down the water level was below the surface. Crabs needed to keep their gills wet in order to respire, and the mudflats were mostly dry on top. Sure enough, the substrate became damper at about four inches depth, and standing water was present at about nine inches. I began keeping an elaborate notebook on my findings, measuring population density by counting the number of burrows per square meter of substrate and mapping the surface, noting positions of plants and any minor topographical features. I constructed a wooden frame to drop onto the surface for my counts and also dug up all of the burrows in selected areas and recorded any crabs I caught: their size, sex (males had the one large claw), and whether left-handed or right. Although it was only April, by ten or eleven on most mornings it became unbearably hot on the flats. I measured surface temperatures of 105 to 110 degrees Fahrenheit in the direct sun. By noon, I was hungry and thirsty, but I could only afford to eat out once a week. It was soup, sandwiches, and pasta most of the time. Thank the island deities for cheap beer.

Cindi took pity on me, and she and Carl had me over for a dinner about once every two weeks. I would bring the beer or wine. Fortunately, neither of them were heavy drinkers. At these times, Cindi would tease me about getting a local girlfriend. Someone who can cook, she emphasized. Know anyone suitable, I'd ask. She would smile and tell me she was working on it and to be patient. Sara and Cindi both wanted to fix me up. I had little doubt that their choices in local ladies would be quite different.

When June of that first summer approached, I was offered the chance to supervise an undergraduate student of my advisor. She attended college at the main campus, but her parents had a condo on the beach, and she could stay there during the summer. Prof. Stevens brought Fran down with him while he was visiting Carl and me one day in late May. He had informed Fran about my crab behavior project, and she wanted to do something like it for her senior essay in biology. I agreed to help her and supervise the study.

Fran was a bright-eyed brunette with an aggressive but generally pleasant personality. She was also good looking, medium height, slim, and possessed a variety of clinging one-piece and skimpy two-piece swimsuits. It only took two days in the field to convince her she would need long-sleeved protection under the brutal South Texas sun, but our morning sessions were usually followed by a beachside dip in the surf, and that's when she paraded her wardrobe for the easily stimulated. She wasn't openly flirtatious, but she did like to sway and shimmy and attract the admiring looks of others at the beach. I knew better than to attempt a play because I would be largely responsible for helping Stevens assign a grade for her study. I decided the best solution was to put her on a project she could do independently from me, at her own schedule and pace.

I had been assigned two large plastic containers, each measuring about three meters across. They were located in the large open shed by the jetty, not far from our cabin. They served as convenient arenas for controlled behavioral observations. The main advantage was they were covered, and a cool breeze often blew through the shed, providing much more comfortable working conditions. I needed to get some data on interactions between crabs, so I set up Fran for ethological observations, recording any contacts, aggression, or other behaviors of our captive population. I had transported a considerable amount of sand from the field into the tubs with the help of Fran and Carl. It was deep enough to provide for burrow depth and a wet bottom. She would do her observations in the shed, while I continued working in the field, and we would meet once a week to compare notes.

During the third week of her studies, the breezes died, the shed became very hot, and Fran decided she needed to take a shower rather than going to the beach, which was only about four blocks from the Institute. Although there was a shower room in both of the regular dormitory buildings, summer students were arriving, and Fran decided my shower would do. I had told her where we kept a spare key in case she wanted a cold drink from the fridge or wanted to use the toilet.

I returned from the field at about noon, parked beside the cabin, and walked in. I could hear the shower running and assumed it was Chun. I should have looked in the bedroom because I would have seen Fran's clothes lying on my bed. I didn't. An ice-cold coke was the only thing on my mind, and I was enjoying every drop of it when Chun walked in the door, gave me a slight bow with his head as he always did, then looked toward the bathroom.

"Who in there?"

I stared at the bathroom door just as the shower stopped. Out stepped Fran, barely covered by my towel. She froze, looked at Chun, looked at me, and jumped back into the bathroom, pulling the door shut.

"My clothes. They're on the bed. Get them, please." Her voice had a trace of panic, but whether it was because of me or Chun or both of us, I couldn't tell.

Chun started to exit the cabin, not sure what he had interrupted and not anxious to find out.

"Stay, Chun," I said, waving him back into the kitchen with my hand, as if he was the household dog. "I'll get her out of here. This is just a big mistake."

He grinned, lighting up his face like a marquee announcing a new musical. "Big mistake, huh? You bet, mister Pete. Big mistake."

"My clothes, Peter, please," came the desperate voice from the bathroom.

I grabbed her shorts, blouse, and swimsuit from the bed, returned to the kitchen, and knocked on the bathroom door. It opened slightly as an arm and hand emerged. I put her clothes across her wrist, and it withdrew. The door closed.

He was still grinning. "You tell me, I go. Leave you here with big mistake."

"Don't you dare. Stay here." Already thoughts were flashing through my head about reports to Austin and the seduction of an undergrad in my cabin. Stevens would probably see it as a comedy of errors, but the Institute administration didn't seem to have a sense of humor.

Fran came out, mostly dressed, wet hair dripping, a pink blush evident even in the subdued light of our kitchen. I introduced my cabin mate. He bowed, and she laughed nervously, grabbed her notebook, and was out the door.

"Very pretty. She your woman, Pete?"

"No, she is not. She is a student I supervise. I didn't know she was going to use the shower. I thought it was you." I looked at him, hoping he fully understood me.

"No, not me. I was in lab." And that was that. He never mentioned Fran again, and Fran never mentioned the encounter, but she also never used my shower or the cabin for anything else that summer.

Penelope had been my first female contact when I arrived. Her manner had both amused and intrigued me. From a few discreet—and some not so discreet—questions, I was able to discover that she was indeed single, lived in a modern condo, and had been working at MSI for four years. She occasionally dated, usually off-island older men with money. She didn't make the bar scene and didn't spend her off hours socializing with Institute staff. One thing became clear immediately. Neither Penny nor any other staff member was allowed to date students. Dating other staff members was not forbidden, but it wasn't encouraged. The Institute comprised a small world within the world that was Port Tarpon. Although some of the staff were townies, like Mitch and Willie, others maintained a rigid isolation, keeping their distance from the unwashed, the unenlightened.

Carl and Cindi provided me with some of the perspective. They were clearly in the academic camp, and they assumed I would be with them all the way. When I mentioned some of my encounters with the locals and particularly my patronage of the marina watering holes, I was met with a combination of shock and disapproval.

"Peter," said Cindi, taking my hand as if she was having an attack of maternal concern for my health, "Those places can be dangerous. Most of us know better than to go down there during the daytime. I can't imagine what goes on there at night."

Carl hung his head, as if confirming his wife's opinion. I quickly decided that this was not an issue I wanted to draw lines for, either with my Canadian friends or with anyone else at MSI. At that time I had only eaten a few lunches and enjoyed a few beers at the Party House and at Charlie's on the beach, but that appeared to be threatening to Carl and Cindi. I found out later that many of the institute personnel were in agreement.

Because of Fran's studies at the shed, I decided to set up a small field study along the jetty. The fiddler crabs were active there, even though fishermen and visitors strolled along the walkway about twenty feet away. A small stream of water from the fish tanks created a sand flat habitat that was quite different from the algal mud flats on the island's back roads. The species of crab was the same, however, providing testimony to the adaptability of these animals to a variety of environmental conditions.

I had several boxes of wood applicator sticks to use with paper flags, marking individual burrows for later reference. I carefully marked off several meters, recorded the x- and y-coordinates of each burrow, measured the opening diameter, then sat to one side with binoculars and a camera to observe the burrow occupants as they returned to the surface and commenced their social interactions. I started early in the morning so my observation period fell between ten o'clock and noon, before it became uncomfortably hot. The site also kept me near Fran in case she had questions or needed help, but she knew better than to interrupt me while I was making observations. Unfortunately, others were not trained in this regard.

On the third day of my jetty site study, I heard a digging sound behind me. The crabs had suddenly disappeared, but this wasn't unusual—a close overhead flight by a seagull or heron often produced the same reaction. The crabs usually resumed their surface activity within a minute or so. I looked behind me and about six feet away a woman was digging in the sand with a large shovel. She stooped down and retrieved crabs and threw them into a plastic pail. She had to be in her seventies or older, was wearing a bandana over her straggly gray hair, and she had more wrinkles than I had ever seen in a human face. She had obviously spent a lot of time in the sun, and she had a determined grin on her face. She was also standing squarely in one of my measured and flagged study quadrats.

Still holding my binoculars, I looked up at her in shock, just beginning to comprehend that she was destroying in a few seconds what had taken me painstaking hours to prepare. She looked at me, stood up and leaned on her shovel.

"Yep, them little critters makes sum o' the best bait there is. Been using' em since I was a little sand flea." She said this with distinct pride and gave me a big grin before lowering her head and digging into more of the flagged burrows. It never occurred to her why I would be sitting there on the sand with binoculars and camera amidst a crab colony with sticks and flags.

I stood up, looked once at the devastation she had made of my research site, wished her a good day and good luck fishing, and took my permanent leave of an area I now knew was not only vulnerable to disturbance, but was subject to complete destruction. Back in the shed, I waited until Fran took a break from her observations and told her what happened. She laughed and offered me one of the Cokes she kept in a cooler by the crab tank. I looked over her notes, complimented her good technique, and decided it was time for lunch, a liquid lunch.

■ ■ ■

ONE OF MY STUDY OBJECTIVES WAS TO COMPLETE A twenty-four-hour cycle of temperature measurements and behavior observations. After my disaster near the jetty—later known as "the Great Fiddler Massacre"—I knew that future studies needed to be conducted well away from people, especially fishermen. I had a Yellow Springs multi-probe thermometer to record temperatures simultaneously from ten different locations. I also had a sleeping bag, but I needed a tent to provide relief from the overhead sun and from swarms of mosquitos and biting flies both during the day and at night. I asked Penny if there was a tent at the Institute I could borrow, and I explained why I wanted it.

"No problem, Pete. We have one we sometimes use for our own field trips. It will be big enough to hold all your gear and two sleeping bags." She said this in such a nonchalant tone, I wasn't sure I had heard it right.

"Two bags? It's only me. I'll be there by myself."

"The loan comes with a catch, Peter. You know, there is always a catch." She looked at me with an evil gleam in her eye, something I hadn't seen before. "The second bag is for me. I want to see what you are doing and maybe take a few pictures of you in the field. It will be used for our education presentations, something we like to have for all of our student and faculty research projects."

Indeed, I had seen posters of other projects in the hallways of the Institute, and their periodic newsletter often featured short reports of ongoing studies. I was flattered that my study might be displayed as well. However, Penny was proposing that she spend the night with me in a tent. Actually, proposal wasn't quite correct. It had been decided and finalized. She would join me shortly after four, bring some dinner for both of us, and leave about ten the following morning, when my twenty-four-hour observation period ended. It was a weekend, but she considered it an extension of her duties as an education assistant. She made it very clear that this wasn't a "date," and I wasn't to consider it as such.

Friday evening, I picked up the tent from the Institute warehouse and gathered my equipment for Saturday's marathon study. The temperature equipment was not automated, so I had to make each reading manually and record it, but I could do this from the tent. Penny asked me to provide the drinks.

"Alcoholic?" I asked her.

"Peter, oh Peter, you know better than that. What would you have me do? Get drunk with a student in a tent out away from everybody, defenseless, at your mercy?" There was no smile, only a bright glint in her eyes, challenging me to provide a suitable answer.

I gulped and said okay, not sure of what she had actually said or what I answered. On Saturday morning, I picked up a cooler and two six packs of soft drinks. I drove to the site, set up the tent, placed my sleeping bag near the entrance, and rigged the temperature probes. Five of them I buried in the sand-mud substrate, at zero, and at ten-centimeter intervals, down to forty cm depth. The other five I used for aerial measurements, at ten, twenty and fifty cm above the surface. Two of them were used for shade and direct sunlight comparisons. All of the probes had long lead wires that came back to the instrument in the tent. I had also marked a number of burrows with flagged sticks for photos and observation reference. I had grabbed a quick breakfast at the Institute (the food service was open on weekdays and Saturdays) and had made some sandwiches and bought chips and cookies. I began the study at ten o'clock sharp, recording observations. In between readings, I read Steinbeck's *Tortilla Flat.*

The day was hot, and there was little breeze. The crabs were mostly inactive during the midday, but the study was progressing. Just after my four o'clock reading, Penny drove up in her station wagon. She waited for me to signal her approach, and she brought a sleeping bag and backpack to the tent. The crabs disappeared momentarily as she arranged her things in the tent, placing her bag next to mine so that both of the bag openings faced the tent opening. She was wearing short shorts and a tie-off plaid top, exposing her midriff, a nice sight indeed.

She looked into the cooler and appraised my choice of drinks. "Well, Pete, I don't know whether to be thankful or disappointed." It was her old flirty self speaking, but I was still unsure about her and her expectations. She was the official MSI receptionist and the gateway to the administration—I couldn't afford a misinterpretation or misstep. Better to be cautious and conservative. We talked for a while, and she looked at the novel I was reading and told me it was also one of her favorites, along with *Cannery Row* and *Sweet Thursday.* I told her Port Tarpon reminded me at times of Steinbeck's description of Cannery Row.

She took a photo of me doing the five o'clock and six o'clock readings. We ate dinner at six thirty: fried chicken and hot biscuits with sweet butter. There was also a side of green beans and sweet potatoes.

"Where'd you buy this?" I asked between chomps on the chicken.

She slapped me on the arm. "I *can* cook. I'm not just a beautiful receptionist and expert on fiddler crabs, you know." Her eyes were on fire, but her slightly upturned mouth gave her mood away. Playful, teasing, but always at arm's distance.

"Yes, well, you are a great cook, you are," I continued, proving it by digging into the potatoes.

"I bought these at the Island Cafe," she said.

As dark approached, many of the crabs entered their burrows. I had a small Coleman lantern plus two flashlights. I had a screen for the lantern so that disturbance to the observation area was minimized. Penny asked me what happens at night. I was surprised she didn't know that in addition to everything else she knew, but I told her that this was my first night observation. I assumed she was referring to what happens to the crabs at night. I needed to make temperature measurements every hour, and I had an alarm clock to make sure I was awake for each one, but other than that I was prepared for a long boring night. Penny's presence would make it considerably less boring, but I remained committed to observations only.

About nine o'clock, just as I was finishing my temperature recordings, we heard the first taps. Penny and I had been sitting in the tent on our bags, talking quietly about her time at the Institute. She wanted to shift the conversation to me, what I was doing, who I was doing it with, and where I was going after my graduate days. Except for the first part, I didn't have any answers. I kept thinking about her earlier question, what happens at night?

The tapping was distinct, a single small sound within the observation area, not more than a few feet from the tent. The lantern cast just enough glow to make out the movements of some of the crabs near us, but the telephoto lens and binoculars didn't capture enough light to see what was making the sound. Within a minute, other taps were heard until the entire area seemed to be filled with the rapping sounds, like a chorus of crickets or frogs at night, but lacking the melody. Then it occurred to me. I had read that some fiddler species did produce auditory signals during nocturnal low tides. The males used their large claws to drum on the ground near their burrow openings. The burrow acted as a resonating chamber, and the taps served as a courtship display to attract females when the visual waving displays were not effective.

Penny and I sat side by side at the tent entrance listening to the ongoing mating game. I didn't have a tape recorder, and I told her I would need to return one night and get a record of the drumming sounds so I could determine frequency. We could see one male, only about four feet away, tapping at his burrow entrance. Every minute of so, he would stop and pick up some sand with his small claw and a few seconds later deposit it as a small spherical pellet beside his burrow. Females wandered about the area, feeding and occasionally stopping beside a drumming male.

"Whether waving during the day or drumming at night, the males seem to have only infrequent success attracting a mate," I observed.

"Yes, I know how that goes," Penny answered softly, as if to herself.

After several minutes of observation, we settled back into the tent, I noted the phenomenon in my field book, and we talked about the amazing world of mating and courtship. I had taken a couple of courses on animal behavior, and I described some of the bizarre outcomes: female black widows eating their mates, female praying mantids biting the head off of the male to complete the physical act, and other examples of fatal rewards for the unsuspecting males. Penny remarked that some males deserve all that and more. I couldn't tell if she was speaking from experience or was just projecting her dissatisfaction with the human pairing ceremony in general.

I didn't go to sleep until after the midnight reading, but Penny fell asleep about ten fifteen. We were head to head, about two feet apart in the sleeping bags, both of us still dressed except for sandals. I didn't set the clock until after midnight, but Penny awoke each time I did, without complaint. She seemed to fall asleep within a few minutes after each session, but it took me longer. Sometimes, it seemed the clock went off just as I was finally drifting back to dreamland.

Dawn came just after six and we stretched after the reading. The crabs were showing little surface activity. It was cold (about 55 degrees Fahrenheit on the surface), and I didn't expect them to start feeding and courting until about eight or nine. Penny had brought some hard-boiled eggs and toast with blackberry jam. There was also a bottle of orange juice and two paper cups. We ate outside the tent, enjoying the freedom after several hours cramped under the canvas.

"What, no coffee?" I asked.

She just looked at me, saying nothing, as if I was the naïve, young student that I was. Suddenly, I felt like a young kid entertaining a fantasy about an older woman I knew I would never have, never had a reasonable expectation of having.

"You need to find yourself a girlfriend, Peter. Someone who can cook."

"Have you been talking to Cindi? She said the same thing."

"No, I haven't, but you are a healthy young man with healthy desires, and I am sure that your Taiwanese roommate doesn't provide all of the amusement you need." She said this as if she was a guidance counselor advising me on my next career move. The advice wasn't off base, and I told her so.

The ten o'clock reading signaled the end of our observation session. The crabs were now fully active, and the males were doing their dances, waving their claws, going into frenzies as females neared their burrows. Penny sang a few bars of Rosemary Clooney's "Come On-a My House" as we packed up our gear and folded the tent. I looked at her and mentioned that candy and other food was probably not in the crab's offering.

She smiled and said, "Thanks, Pete, for an unforgettable night. I mean it, it was great, interesting, and thank you for being a gentleman."

"It works for me," I mumbled to myself as I watched her drive away. I took a few reference photos and followed her back into town. I was exhausted and decided a nap was in order, so I returned to my room and crashed until four that afternoon.

INTERLUDE

FALL 1973 AND WINTER 1974

When I decided to pursue research on Mustang Island, it had always been my intention to return to Austin and the main campus during the dark and cold days of winter. My first few weeks on the island confirmed that decision. There would be little chance to conduct meaningful field studies with my subjects underground. The winter months would allow me to continue searching the literature, quantitate and analyze my initial observations, and consult with my advisor and others on my doctoral committee. If necessary, I could also collect a few crabs and keep them in tanks in lab space I had in the complex assigned to Stevens.

There were other good reasons to head north. My former housemate, Sonya, was still maintaining the modest two-bedroom frame house we had rented in central Austin. I had called her a couple of times during the summer and she seemed to be doing well. She rode down to the coast with Stevens twice. The first time was a weekend trip for Stevens to see how Carl and I were getting on. I was able to show him my field sites, and Sonya inspected the jetty cabin I shared with Chun. We rented a cheap motel room in Tarpon Pass for Friday and Saturday nights. She paid for it, and we renewed our casual affair.

Sonya and I met in California while I was completing an MS in marine ecology. She was on the rebound from a brief unpleasant marriage, and I had broken up with a young woman that I might have married. Sonya had a modest income and I had considerably less, surviving on a small stipend and a graduate teaching assistantship. We met at a dance club, spent the night, and somehow decided that pooling our meager resources was better than going it alone. I moved into her house, and shortly after I was accepted for graduate work at the University of Texas. We were getting along well but we made no promises of permanent commitment. She accepted the chance to accompany me to Texas, and we packed up her car, a U-Haul truck, and arrived in July 1972.

I spent a few months studying for, and passing, written predoctoral exams. My graduate student status with Stevens was confirmed. A few months after that, I decided to continue my studies in behavioral ecology, selecting crabs over spiders, scorpions, and some other terrestrial invertebrate options. This meant extended time at the coast, an environment I had always loved, but it also meant separation from Sonya.

Her second visit to Port Tarpon came during midsummer. By this time, I had become an integral part of the Party House crowd, working hard in the field during the day and playing equally hard with my new friends in the evenings and during the night. The candle was burning at both ends, I had lost weight, and my hair was halfway to my shoulders. I also had started a beard and adopted some of the mannerisms of my Port Tarpon associates. Again, Sonya and I shared a room in Snapper Pass, and she paid the tab. We ate out, sunned on the beach, and looked forward to our reunion later in the year.

She asked me if I was seeing anyone special on the island. Aware of the student crowds, the party atmosphere, and the almost unlimited opportunities for pairing off, she was curious about what I was doing when not playing with crabs. It was not a jealous woman asking—we had never displayed a sense of possession about each other. We enjoyed a mutual attraction for each other and respected the other's privacy and right to make decisions. I confirmed the social craziness that existed during the summer, but I told her that I had no "special interests" and the fieldwork would be ending by late September. I confirmed that a shared bed in Austin with her would be welcome.

She mentioned that she had met a guy from San Antonio during a party at our neighbors' house. He had taken an interest in her, and they had eaten out once and gone to a movie, but nothing more serious than mild flirtation. We took pride in our honest relationship, and we were well aware we had lived together and shared finances for more than six months. In Texas, we were common-law husband and wife, not an unusual relationship in either Austin or Port Tarpon.

Late September arrived. A few storms quieted the beaches, the barroom crowds had thinned, and I informed the MSI administration I would be leaving, hopefully to return the following spring. They graciously agreed to hold a space for me, either in the jetty cabin or in another location. The Institute owned several houses in town for visiting researchers and other personnel. I said goodbye to Chun, to Carl and Cindi, and to many of the Party House gang. Mitch and Willie hosted me at an aloha party—not a permanent farewell, they said—where drinks and pizza were provided in exchange for my promise to return the following year.

The station wagon made it back to Austin with my belongings, but just barely. That was another reason to return to the city: I needed to put some money into car repairs if I wanted it to last another year on dirt roads and salty sand beaches. I drove to our house, and Sonya greeted me warmly. After a modest dinner out, we returned to the house and settled in again as a hippie neighborhood couple.

Sonya was five feet eight, slender, with black hair that hung down her back. She resembled Cher and when she dressed up, she could turn heads and draw admiring comments from men and women alike. I was not beyond feeling like the top tomcat when she was on my arm. We were not desperately passionate lovers, but we were comfortable and happy.

One of my drinking buddies from the first months in Austin was also waiting to renew good times. Gordon was a research tech for Stevens, operating an electron microscope for his studies on neuromuscular ultrastructure. He was several years older, in his late thirties or early forties, and had a full beard, resembling Jerry Garcia of the Grateful Dead. His personality belied the somber responsibility and technical expertise his job demanded. Gordon would have fit right into the Party House crowd, which I didn't realize until after I returned from the island. Gordon and I occasionally met for a few beers after a day's work in the UT zoology department labs. A street corner restaurant provided a pleasant outdoor observation post to watch people passing by. Although Gordon was a lifelong bachelor, he had an appreciative eye and was known to entertain the fair sex from time to time in his rural log cabin north of the city.

Gordon and I talked about the island and its hippie-redneck hybrid culture. We were comfortable with both, enjoying the progressive music scene sweeping the country as well as the hard and soft rock sounds that could be sampled in various clubs and venues around Austin. The laid-back people were in sharp contrast to the rah-rah football atmosphere that dominated Austin during its championship years. Fraternities, sororities, and Longhorn burnt orange were not part of our universe. Sonya, our neighbors, Gordon, and a few of the other zoology department students and staff remained mellow and socially out of touch with the university.

Gordon's first question, after I described life in Port Tarpon, was "What the hell are you doing back here?" He asked this while refilling my glass from a pitcher of Shiner draft. I told him he should come down and visit next year, that he would be a natural for the beach, the bars, and the babes. He agreed but never made the trip.

The fall and winter passed, and my studies were productive. I took an advanced course in nonparametric statistics, co-wrote a simple analytical program for nearest neighbor distance measurements, and began preparations for the 1974 summer field season. I was able to secure an additional small grant of my own for some equipment and travel expenses, and I had an outline of my dissertation in draft form. On the academic front, everything looked bright and rosy. Not so on the domestic horizon, where storm clouds were gathering.

Despite the tolerance Sonya and I had for each other's personal decisions, there was a limit, a boundary that we had not previously recognized. In retrospect, I probably overreacted, not giving her enough benefit of the doubt, not considering the sacrifices she was making to maintain a house in Austin while I was immersed in research and gallivanting about the island.

The storm broke in February when I told Sonya I would return to Port Tarpon in a few weeks and would probably remain there the following winter. In other words, I would not be returning to Austin. We were sitting on the floor in our living room, sharing a bottle of wine, passing it back and forth without using glasses. She held onto the bottle as I informed her of my plans.

"What about us?" she asked, in a voice that was even quieter than her usual mild manner of speaking. "Is this it? Did I follow you from California just to have you leave me here, by myself?"

I could see the wetness gathering at the corner of her eyes. The only time I had ever seen her cry was a few times when she had experienced severe migraines. Twice I had to take her to an emergency room for them to sedate her. She took a swig and handed the bottle back to me, almost empty.

"This might require another bottle," I said, emptying and setting it aside. "You could come down to Port Tarpon. You might be able to get a job in one of the shops, or in a restaurant, or something…"

"I have a job here. It pays our rent and most of our other expenses. Have you forgotten?"

Unsaid, but not forgotten, was the fact she had paid for our motel room and dinner out both times she had visited me. I had barely survived on my predoctoral stipend that summer. Most of the available work in Port Tarpon was minimum wage, temporary, and in high demand. I had to agree that job prospects were not promising. She got up and retrieved another bottle of Merlot from the kitchen. I opened it and passed it to her for the first hit.

"Sonya, I am so sorry. I want to stay with you, but I can finish my degree in two years if I push on through. I can have it wrapped up by the end of summer 1975."

"If your beer parties don't get in the way." She was angry now, the tears gone, the meek voice replaced by an accusatory challenge. She lowered her head, as if giving careful thought to what she was going to say next.

I took the bottle, tilted it up, and slowly sipped, as if I had all of the time in the world to enjoy a fine vintage. The vintage wasn't bad, but the time was up.

She looked up and focused on my eyes, fixing them with hers, as if there was a solid bar that kept them locked together. "Mario wants me to come to Reno with him."

I waited for her to explain, to provide additional commentary to a statement that had seemed to come from out of nowhere. It was the lightning that accompanies the violent front of the storm, and it broke as I sat with her, our knees nearly touching.

"Who is Mario?" I finally managed, passing the bottle back to her, hoping that the additional wine would swing the mood back to hippie mellow.

"He's the guy I met at the party next door, the one from San Antonio I told you about. He wants to go to Nevada. He says I could get a job in a casino and make good money and that we could find a reasonable place to live." She took another hit but didn't extend the bottle.

"Is this something you want, Sonya? Do you want to go to Reno?" I said this quietly, but inside my heart was pounding.

"If you're leaving for the coast, why not? Why should I stay here? I can't come with you, and I don't see a future path for us. For *us*, Peter, do you understand that? I know we didn't make any promises or long-term commitments, but you can't expect me to accept this. I won't. Damn it, I won't."

I reached for the bottle, but she held onto it, as if it represented a treasure we had shared but I had lost. Now it was hers alone. I nodded, slid backward onto my elbows, and slowly resigned to the termination of our relationship. "When would you go?"

"Mario mentioned April. The weather is better for travel, and he will finish his business in San Antonio."

"What business would that be?" I asked, not really interested.

"He repossesses automobiles, ones that bill collectors want back."

"You're going to run away with a repo man?" I was incredulous. I was suddenly pissed. I was being traded for a guy that snuck around and stole cars, albeit legally, from deadbeats that couldn't pay their bills. "Are you out of your ever-lovin' fuckin' mind?" I lost all traces of calm, cool, and collected. Her look told me not to pursue it, that she probably considered my bar-crawling lifestyle to be less than a model of exemplary conduct.

Sonya and I spent the next month sorting out our financial affairs, dividing up our common possessions, and arranging for my departure. We said our farewells, with hugs, tears, and more than a few regrets in mid-March. I returned to Port Tarpon and my jetty cabin, leaving Austin and a significant chapter in my life behind. Sonya left for Reno with Mario a month after that. We never communicated again, and I have no clue what happened to her. I hope life went well, she found the happiness she so much deserved, and that she eventually forgave me for not being the supportive partner she wanted.

The spring heralded a year of significant surprises and meaningful discoveries. From the time I arrived on the island, it seemed that every day was different and represented a story, a chapter in an unwinding saga that would alter my life forever.

CHAPTER SIX

The Good Ship George Dewey

SPRING 1974

t ain't much to look at, abandoned high on the beach, exposed to onshore winds and blistering sun on a back-bay island of the Intracoastal Waterway. Casual beachcombers and serious scavengers have either ignored the nineteen-foot metal lifeboat, or it has been covered by the drifting sand and only recently exposed by a late winter storm. The overturned hull lies like a stranded whale. Its bolts are rusting, and wooden seats are weathering—it provides no evidence of life or ownership. A few old timers believe the boat has been there for years, possibly decades. Others think it washed up recently, a drifter from some place along the waterway or the Gulf. "Perhaps it abandoned its owners, leaving them stranded somewhere or drowned," they say. There are always a cheerful few in the crowd. Others just shrug and say, "Anything is possible."

A faded inscription on one side of the bow reads "George Dewey." The name belongs to a liberty ship, hastily built to transport troops and supplies during World War II. It has been thirty years since the lifeboat served its role with the SS *George Dewey* during frequent passages across the Atlantic. Where has it been since? Like many of the inhabitants along the central Texas Gulf Coast, the boat is a derelict, arriving without notice or purpose and staying without reason. It turns out some of the old timers were wrong. The *Dewey* had been deliberately sunk recently off the Texas coast to form, with eleven other liberty ships, artificial reefs for marine wildlife. The local papers had duly reported it, but for many on the island, there are always other priorities.

Willie and Mitch discover it on a Sunday afternoon in late April 1974 while scrounging for rope and other debris deposited by a recent storm. The boat is upside down and the stern half buried, the port side obscured by dense marsh grass. Mud plasters the hull so that from a distance the structure is barely recognizable. When they examine it closer, the fittings seem tight and the hull intact. A number of dents and scrapes along the bottom and sides testify to use and abuse, but nothing that primer and paint can't disguise. Best of all, it's their discovery and by any measure, legal or otherwise, theirs. Willie, always the opportunist, sees the potential immediately. Mitch, more thoughtful and less flamboyant, agrees after a moment's consideration. They flip it over, drag it into the water, and tie it to their motorboat. Twenty minutes later, it is tied to a pier in the Port Tarpon marina, directly across from the Party House.

Willie tugs at his beard as Mitch finishes tying the motorboat to the wharf. The long blond hair across his forehead only partly disguises the thinning that will lead to early baldness. He pulls out a cigarette and lights it—he is rarely without one in hand or mouth. He and Mitch are about the same age, in their late twenties, and they work well together, whether at the Party House, the Institute, or at any number of island schemes and ventures.

Mitch and Willie walk into the Party House, ready for a couple of cold ones after spending much of the day in the pre-summer sun. They join an unusually large crowd for a spring weekend. All are welcome at the tavern—local fisher-men, laborers, drifters, hippies, rednecks, tourists, children, dogs, and anyone else that can walk up the short steps in front and get through the screen door. For a few of Port Tarpon's denizens, that can be a formidable challenge. The rear of the tavern, facing the marina, has a longer flight of steps straddling the piers that support the back deck—even more challenging for those leaving at closing time.

The lifeboat lies along the dock, floating high but still covered with mud, future uncertain. Mitch and Willie suck on a couple of longnecks and think on the matter. No use rushing into it, they agree—boats don't turn up every day. From the wrap-around deck, early evening celebrants offer comments of praise, derision, bemusement, envy, and encouragement. For three days the vessel waits while ideas are announced, debated, and abandoned. Some sug-gestions are serious, others insane, but all have one thing in common—they lack corresponding offers of labor or funding.

For the price of a pitcher or two, Willie and Mitch are finally able to recruit help lifting the boat from the water. They drag it across the road and onto sawhorses at the side of the bar. From the Party House deck the patrons look down on the gleaming hull as Mitch hoses it down. Henry, his short, curly-haired Jewish sidekick, is always cheerful and willing to help with the dirty jobs. He attacks stubborn patches of mud, barnacles, and algae with a putty scraper and chisel while Willie, cigarette dangling, super-vises. Willie is good at that, using his education and logic to insert himself as the leader at every opportunity. Most of the group knows he is more often right than wrong, so they listen as he directs Mitch and Henry in the technical details of scrubbing. Moonshine, Mitch's on-again, off-again girlfriend and an all-around crazy, joins the gathering crowd on the deck as the sun sinks over the marina. She is thin and short, a brunette with a pixie hair cut, sporting a flirtatious smile and ultra short cutoffs. As a labor addition, she is about useless, but sometimes it's the visuals that count. Finally, it is time for Willie to address the assembled multitude, waving a Lone Star longneck with one hand and a cigarette with the other.

"I'm happy to announce…" He pauses, looking at Mitch and Henry. They stop cleaning to stare at Willie. "… to announce the arrival of the fleet."

One or two cheers erupt from the tavern deck. The others stare in stony silence, not sure they received the correct announcement. Moonshine does a shimmy along the rail, thrusting her hips back and forth, lost in a song that only she can hear. Bad Bart, the designated drunk for the day and for most days, stumbles out the back door of the bar, falling into several people seated at the nearest table. He is blissfully inebriated.

Willie continues, oblivious to the ever-present distractions and disturbances of the Party House regulars. "This is the first, only the first, vessel to be commissioned in the Party House Yacht Club and Exploration Society." He pauses again, scanning the group for approval. Only he could come up with such a pretentious title, but it seems to fit. Meeting numerous amused grins but no disagreement, he takes a leisurely pull on the longneck. A trickle of beer runs down one side of his mouth, wetting his beard and dampening his T-shirt.

Moonshine climbs onto a table, moving in quick small steps, raising and lowering her arms, her dance but not her legs largely ignored by most of those gathered. They have seen her routine before, but it's all good. Bart stumbles to his feet and manages to land in a chair, still clutching a bottle of Pearl. Miraculously, little of the beer has spilled. Henry knocks the last daubs of debris from the hull as Mitch works the hose up inside the overturned boat. The runoff finally drips clear as the last sand and mud come loose. Willie joins the group on the porch to admire their latest material possession.

"What'll we call her?" asks K.C. Tall and blond with a sharp jaw line and prominent cheekbones, the second owner and the most frequent manager of the bar is good looking, according to those who know about such things. He is well spoken and has a graduate degree in literature. This is not an unusual qualification among the Port Tarpon residents, although it doesn't seem to provide a great deal of help in running the bar. Everyone on the deck understands that the lifeboat has now become common property, and its fate is therefore a communal decision.

"I think we should keep the name *George Dewey*," says Mitch, turning off the water and walking up the gangplank to the deck. "And let's make it the Good Ship, the *Good Ship George Dewey*, an honorable and proud title to commemorate good fortune when it comes unbidden." Mitch looks like an old-time seadog, speaks softly, and has an undergraduate degree in fisheries biology. Like most of the others, he is mostly but not entirely a dropout from conventional jobs and lifestyles.

"That's my man," shouts Moonshine to no one in particular. "He sure can say the fancy things."

"What the hell kinda name is that? *George Dewey*? George? Sounds like some kinda fag," laughs Bart. "Not sure I wanna sail in some fag boat."

This gets a few laughs and a slap on the back, but Mitch folds his arms and looks to Willie for support. Willie and

Mitch are colleagues and try to represent the voice of reason in an unreasonable environment. Despite having ties to the academic community and claiming to be almost respectable, they take every opportunity to remind the others they can be just as degenerate as anyone in Port Tarpon.

Willie makes an executive decision. "Let's have a contest. We'll put a box on the counter, and anyone can put in a name on a slip of paper. We'll draw them out in a week and judge the best one. And don't put *your* name on it. That way we won't be influenced by how much money you have or how much we dislike you personally."

A few murmurs of approval are interrupted by a question from Darla. She is married to Randy, the owner of Tarpon Marina Labs, a commercial specimen-collecting lab. "Who's gonna be the judges?" Eyes turn to Willie.

"I'll be a judge," says Bart.

"You can't even read when you're sober and that isn't very often," replies Willie.

"That's the truth," adds Connie, Bart's live-in girlfriend, joining the party from the street and sitting next to her man. They put their arms around each other while she takes a hit from his bottle. Connie's blouse is thin and wet, easily revealing her shapely braless breasts.

Moonshine hasn't stopped gyrating. Willie smiles up at her. "We'll have Moonshine do it. Her and K.C. can be the judges. I'll set up a box." Moonshine pauses, looks at Willie, then around at the crowd, aware her name has been mentioned but unsure of the context or whether to be pleased or not. Someone yells "All right" and the issue is settled.

"What do you think, Pete? Will this work?" Willie turns to Pete, whom he now also regards as a colleague and a solid member of the Party House community.

Pete nods and takes a sip. "Works for me."

A week later, a small gathering inside the bar watches as Moonshine pulls several dozen slips of paper out of a shoebox decorated with Christmas paper and hands them to K.C. As he reads them aloud, Willie writes the nominations on the blackboard above the kitchen counter. Suggestions include: *H.M.S. Party House, Drunken Tug, Floating Turd, Dildo Dreadnaught*, and, amazingly, five votes to retain the name *George Dewey*. Although Mitch isn't present, it doesn't escape the attention of several people that Moonshine is Mitch's live-in. Willie dismisses it, saying he favored the original name all along and it received the most votes. So decided, the *George Dewey* is reborn to serve a new noble cause. From scrubbing and sanding to paint and epoxy, for six weeks the lifeboat lies alongside the Party House as onlookers gawk, offer advice, and occasionally help with the restoration. More than one drunk staggers onto the outer porch late at night to use the boat's metal surface as a urinal. The *Dewey* represents the flagship of the Party House flotilla, to be joined by a rubber raft badly in need of repair and a small Boston Whaler that has seen better days. A crew slowly assembles, and eleven sign on as the Port Tarpon Renegade Armada Navy, formalizing the occasion with a bottle of truly God-awful mescal. Willie swallows the *gusano rojo*, the coveted red worm, and earns the title of Rear-end Admiral. Mitch is named first mate, and Moonshine is designated Cruise Director and Morale Superintendent.

The launch party and shakedown cruise are planned with meticulous care. Suggestions come forth for crew costumes, food, drink, and entertainment to appease the anticipated horde of celebrants. And what would a flagship be without a flag? Designs and colors are alternately proposed and dismissed.

"Black on black, " suggests Bart. "That'll make the design real easy, even for you assholes."

"How about a bright pink background and a blue beer bottle?" This comes from Sara, sitting in Willie's lap. Several people stare at her, knowing pink isn't her style. She shrugs and chugs, dismissing her own suggestion. Mitch proposes a small white bow flag adorned with a bright green marijuana branch—no, not the emblem—an actual branch from the local harvest. Mitch and Willie are persistent proponents of the magic weed. The white flag could also be used to surrender, if the occasion should so warrant.

Other discussions focus on worthy mission objectives, as Willie has phrased it. Some favor the cruise scenario—leisurely drifting along the Intracoastal Waterway, stocked with munchies and beverages, the Port Tarpon version of Carnival Cruise Lines. The vision expands as the drunk and delirious contribute—the cruise ship *George Dewey* should provide casino gambling (afternoon poker games) and cabaret entertainment (a portable radio accompanied by Moonshine's morale-lifting dancing and Connie's wet thin blouses).

Other advocates promote a more active itinerary. The boat should be equipped with a small outboard motor and a stern flag featuring a porpoise or a shark, signifying speed, grace, and derring-do. The *G.S. George Dewey* could become the envy of the waterway, weaving with agility among the incoming tankers, competing fashionably with the posh sloops of the local aristocrats' Boat and Gun Club. There is yet a third proposal. Small in numbers but aggressive by nature, the would-be pirates, always a colorful and bawdy bunch, envision a *Dewey* with skull and crossbones (Moonshine requested pelvis and crossbones), propelled by a monstrous outboard, a drug-runner special. Stores would consist of one or more cases of Jack Daniels and José Cuervo. Dressed in black leathers and red headbands, the crew could launch lightning raids in broad daylight on unsuspecting tourists. As the night wears on and partial sobriety gives way to full-fledged fantasy, the proposed raids manifest greater consequences: attacks on the auto ferries crossing the Intracoastal between the island and mainland and raids at neighboring marinas to secure additional "stores." Sideboard shields, horned helmets, and blazing torches are proposed as essential accessories. The women see plundering as a form of freelance shopping, while the men are attracted to the image of a miniature longboat, complete with dragon prow and square sails, bearing down on cabin cruisers and yachts, invoking a surrealistic mixture of comedy and terror on the waterway and adjacent bays. Later, the tapestry of great deeds to be done comes unraveled, as it often does, sliding from ambitious but ridiculous dreaming into morning hangover. In addition, the increasing heat of approaching summer dictates a minimum of clothing, ruling out heavy armor.

When the day finally arrives, a tattered red shirt is hoisted over the bow and a small outboard, liberated from an unnamed garage, powers the *Dewey*. On a mid-May Wednesday evening, the Party House's finest vessel is declared seaworthy, unbeknownst to the U.S. Coast Guard, and launch day is set for Saturday morning.

Mitch and Pete propose a party site on a small, uninhabited island in the waterway, about three miles from town. They have been there before to collect animals, and it offers some seclusion from the traffic on the Intracoastal. Nick and Toni, an older, long-time common-law couple, have a small houseboat, slow but with a shallow draft. They arrive at the remote sand spit locally but not officially known as

St. Melancholy on Friday, transporting cooking gear, ice chests, food, musical instruments, four kegs of beer, three large tents, and two portable toilets. Willie determines, by a method known only to himself, that by avoiding the wakes of tankers and larger motorboats, a crew of two could ferry about fifteen people, their overnight baggage, and three or four dogs per trip in the *Dewey* with only minimal risk of swamping and sinking. Just in case, a life vest is thrown in for good measure. Friday night sees Nick and Toni labor on St. Melancholy while the Party House Crew, now expanded by about fifty eager celebrants, supports the launch effort in the bar with numerous toasts and ad hoc chants for the success and fortune of the *Good Ship George Dewey*. Outside the bar, the lifeboat gleams in the moonlight with new silver paint.

Saturday morning arrives in Port Tarpon with cloudless skies and a mild, warm breeze, perfect sailing conditions for an overloaded boat and semi-loaded passengers. The participants gather around the marina and other onlookers roar their approval from the Party House deck as six members of the designated crew wrestle the boat across the street and onto the wooden dock. Willie calls signals as the men flip the boat upright and place it in the water. It floats, much to the amazement of more than a few of the dubious bystanders. Her name is emblazoned in dark blue lettering. Texas registration letters, chosen at random by K.C., add to the illusion of legitimacy. A wooden pole at the bow sports the red shirt flag, donated by Arnie on behalf of his dog Chuck.

"It was Chuck's favorite bed," he had confided to the group the night before. "He woulda wanted it this way, flying in fronta us on our way to a party." Arnie mumbles a lot, but as far as anyone knew, he didn't have a speech impediment. Except for maybe the bottle in his mouth.

Chuck, before the semi had rolled over him a month ago, had been a notorious guest at island parties. The Irish setter had enjoyed a reputation for guzzling beer, eating burritos, and emitting some of the foulest farts in town. No gathering was considered complete without the straggly, often filthy, neighborhood vagabond and scrounger. Although he seemed to belong to Arnie, he wandered from door to door, bar to bar, begging for handouts and passing gas with enthusiasm. His unique scent still emanated like an enveloping cloud from the red rag flag.

The crowd pushes forward, longnecks in hand, appraising the capabilities of the boat and the crew.

"Ain't worried about the *Dewey*, just the crewey," says Bart, already several beers on his way. As he staggers onto the wooden wharf, he slips and is rescued from a dunk in the marina only by a desperate grab at his pants from Connie.

"Put him on board first," calls Willie. "I don't want him landing on top of us when we're full."

Helping hands guide Bart toward the boat, assisting him to the middle bench. Bart grins and pulls Connie down beside him.

K.C. holds up a mostly empty bottle of tequila. "We gotta christen her. It's bad luck to sail without an official blessing."

"Isn't there supposed to be some liquor left in the bottle?" Arnie asks.

"Hell if I'm gonna waste it. This is good enough," answers K.C. He reaches for the bow and swings the bottle onto the metal cleat. It cracks with a decisive blast, sending glass all over the dock and into the water.

"I thought a woman was supposed to break the bottle," remarks Henry.

"K.C. is good enough," retorts Willie.

A small cut is dripping red from K.C.'s right hand. Willie hands him a handkerchief.

"Umm, great start, man," says Mitch, standing by the stern with a rope in his hand. "Anyone else on this run?"

A few people murmur but no one steps forward. Several of them watch Connie and Bart grapple with each other while his beer liberally sprinkles the boat.

"Sure it'll get there?"

"Will it get back?"

"If Kelly goes, can we use her for flotation?"

"Mitch, are you sober enough to find Melancholy?"

"Shit, here comes the Coast Guard!"

Willie and Mitch respond as one, "Where?"

The crowd laughs as Randy approaches, decked out in an old Navy uniform, complete with bell-bottoms and swabby cap, grinning and swaggering, thumbs tucked in his belt. Randy is clean-shaven and industrious. A Boy Scout type with a legal wife and children, Randy seems to be an exception to much of the Party House contingent, but everyone likes him and his wife, Darla.

"Our military escort has arrived. Let's go," announces Willie, grabbing at the bowline. "There will be only one maiden voyage."

"Connie, are you sure you qualify for a maiden voyage?" asks Whisky Joe, her former lover and Bart's carousing buddy.

Bart lifts his bottle, smiling as broad as his mustache, and downs another mouthful of Pearl. Scrambling for seats, an assortment of Party House regulars board, bringing the tops of the gunwales closer and closer to the water's surface. Pete is one of the last to step aboard, not wanting to miss the opening bell on St. Melancholy.

With six inches of waterline to spare, Mitch calls out, "That's it, we're full," and he climbs aboard, sinking the boat another inch.

Everyone looks at Kelly, big blonde buxomly Kelly sitting near the stern, who weighs every bit of two hundred and fifty pounds. She ignores them, turning her head toward the open waters beyond the marina. Mitch casts off, promising those on the dock he will return soon.

"That's what they said about the *Titanic*," shouts Arnie. "Just be sure to save Chuck's flag."

"Poor Arnie, he's never been the same since his dog got squished," observes Darla, standing on the dock. She puts her head on Arnie's shoulder as Randy looks on. He is used to his wife playing the community social worker.

With a practiced start of the outboard, the maiden voyage commences at nine o'clock in the morning, a remarkable feat considering the bar room regulars rarely stir before noon on weekends. Only an event as historic and potentially disastrous could draw a large crowd this early. Even then, other Friday night celebrants will not appear on the dock until late morning or early afternoon.

The first trip is almost uneventful. Gunning the motor and turning sharply to port or starboard to lift a cooling wall of spray, the *Dewey* circles tankers and shrimpers, races past fishermen and sailboats. The bow rides high when moving at full speed but threatens to dive when slowing, so the passengers shift aft and Mitch revs the motor. Fortunately, the Intracoastal surface is almost as smooth as glass. Approaching St. Melancholy at full speed, the bow bites the shore sooner than expected, throwing several of the passengers to the right and almost capsizing the boat. A small amount of water slops over the starboard side.

"Avast, damn it, avast," shouts Willie as he gingerly

launches himself over the side and wades the last few feet to the beach.

The overloaded boat has a deeper draft than expected so disembarking means wet knees. Connie gathers her full thin summer skirt around her waist and stumbles ashore with an appreciated display of immodesty. The *Dewey* rises five inches when Bart and Henry help Kelly over the side.

"Hey pilgrims, let the party begin," calls Nick as he emerges from one of the tents, zipper in one hand and a beer in the other. Toni buttons her blouse as she exits behind him, smiling like the hostess of a debutante coming out.

"Disturb sumpin?" remarks Bart, "I shore wouldn't want y'all to stop a cuz a us. We jus here to do the same thang."

Toni looks at Bart, then at Connie. "Connie, can he do the same thing?"

"Wha' thing?" replies Connie, still somewhat dazed by being out of bed and in the fresh air before noon. Her brief attention span disappears completely as she follows Bart to the open grill where Nick prepares coals for the fish bake.

Most of the crowd gathers around an open keg as Mitch and Willie push off to retrieve another boatload from the marina. In front of the largest tent a tape recorder blasts the Allman Brothers' instrumental "Jessica." Maggie and Jet, two unattached ladies, spread a blanket on the sand at the water's edge, removing their tops to gather rays. Jet is new to the crowd. A tall willowy blonde with very fair skin, she earns a passing glance of interest from several of the guys. Crazy Maggie has been a familiar fixture in Port Tarpon for many years. She is naked almost as often as she is clothed and is barely noticed by the regular Party House men. Her bisexuality turns off some guys, and she tends to swing toward the ladies as she gets drunker, further discouraging some male egos and urges. Pete takes a moment to look admiringly at both of them, always willing to appreciate a bit of feminine pulchritude.

"Appreciating some feminine pulchritude?" asks Willie, handing him a longneck.

With his eyes still feasting on Jet, he replies, "Uh-huh, but only from a biological perspective. You know, birds, bees, and raunchy sex."

Willie smiles and they clink their bottles in professional concordance.

Music, hot sun, cold beer, and another hour pass before the second boatload arrives, bringing Sherry, Fast Eddie, Leonard, Frank, Debbie, Jill, three of the island mutts, and a large cooking pot. The aluminum vessel is placed in the center of a clearing by the three tents and next to a pile of driftwood. Willie drops a burlap sack next to the pot.

"Three weeks' worth," he notes with obvious satisfaction, answered by several murmurs of approval and anticipation. Sherry, one of the Party House bartenders, and Toni fill the pot with water from the houseboat while Frank and Nick start a fire. Frank is about twice the size of his wife Debbie, a comparison that occasionally leads to drunken speculation among the group about whether she is of legal size and should he "throw her back." Leonard, one of the Party House musicians, opens the sack and dumps about a hundred small brown buttons into the steamy water. Peyote stew requires several hours to brew, rendering it fit, sort of, for consumption around sunset. Jill, who also works the Party House occasionally, immediately removes her blouse and joins Maggie and Jet

A third and fourth trip by the *Dewey* brings more people, more dogs, and a few kids. Everyone is welcome at the Party House and on the island. By mid-afternoon St. Melancholy has become a carnival of noise and movement, dancing, spinning Frisbees, water tag, sunbathing, kite flying, and card playing—in other words, something for everyone. Food appears from baskets, bags, and boxes in the houseboat: baked beans, potato salad, coleslaw, hushpuppies, hot dogs, hamburgers, grilled kingfish and snapper, burritos, and tacos. Lemonade, tea, cokes, beer, wine, tequila, and bourbon pass freely among the crowd. Everyone has contributed something—everyone is served. Live music replaces the radio and tape recorder as Skip, Leonard, and Little Joe pound out their well-known repertoire, including "Enchilada from Ensenada" and "Hesitation Blues." Maggie, Jill, and Jet bake on their towels, bodies bounce to guitars and drums, dogs chase each other from dirty plate to dirty plate, a few lovers mingle here and there, and everywhere there is the smell of food and suntan oil. Willie and Mitch, their roles as ferrymen completed, join the throng as the sun descends to the horizon.

Bart, having achieved a considerable head start on the festivities, is out cold in the blue tent. He lies in peace, hands folded across his chest, breathing the steady rhythm of deep dreams, an angelic smile on an untroubled face. Connie kneels beside him, alcohol-induced adoration the order of the moment. Clasping Bart's hand, she casually remarks to Sherry that if Bart could remain like this, she would marry him. Sherry is never the one to let a stray remark go unnoticed. She nods and leaves the tent, returning a few minutes later with Fast Eddie. Others crowd into the tent behind them.

"Connie, now's your chance," Sherry explains. She hands Connie a piece of white lace. "Tie this around your head."

Someone calls out of the tent for flowers and soon the tent is filled with late spring blooms, all of them weeds, but colorful ones. A larger crowd gathers outside the open tent flaps. Fast Eddie stands up and begins his best imitation of a solemn ceremony. Eddie, in fact, works for an island tourist agency, and he is regarded as one of the normal ones, meaning he isn't given to the crazy binges and all-night celebrations of others. Eddie plays poker with the bar group, but he is clean cut and looks more professional than most of them. He tolerates their excesses with good humor, and he is perfect for the performance. He recalls what a mean drunk Bart can be but how he seems to have reformed for this special occasion. He also reminds the crowd of how crazy Bart has been, like the time he drove a hijacked police car into the Gulf surf, leaving it on the second sand bar with the red and blue lights flashing. Arnie reminds Eddie of the time Bart drove his pickup truck off the ferry dock without a ferryboat present. Everyone agrees Bart is a step beyond the usual Port Tarpon insane, but Bart sleeps on, oblivious to all but his reverie. The best of the flowers are placed on his chest, and he takes on the appearance of the newly deceased awaiting final interment. The resemblance is not lost on the witnesses as the ceremony proceeds.

"Is Eddie doing this for real?" asks Melanie, the newly hired school art teacher. At the time, she is one of the more naïve members of the group.

"Yes, definitely," answers K.C. "He once attended Bible school, and he learned all about weddings and burials."

"Which one are we doing?" grunts Henry, followed by a soft ripple of laughter. Eddie turns and frowns in Henry's direction and the crowd resumes a respectful silence.

"Do you, Connie Ronstadt, take this man to be yours, despite his present condition, regardless of what he may say if… I mean, when… he wakes up?" Eddie's level gaze and steady voice leave no doubt as to his sincerity and authority.

Connie's eyes try to focus for a minute and the slightest

hint of a frown creases her brow. "I guess so."

"Good enough," says Eddie. He turns to the crowd. "And who speaks for Bart… what the hell is his last name anyway?"

Dead silence. People shrug and shake their heads. The question has never arisen before.

Eddie turns back to Connie. "You live with him, what *is* his last name?"

No answer. She looks down at her hands and a tear appears at the corner of each eye. "I didn't know it would be this complicated. I just thought we could… well, you know… get married."

"You're right, we'll do it." Eddie glances at the crowd and resumes. "Does anyone speak for Bart?"

"Sure, I'll speak for Bart," answers Jimmy, and he steps forward to kneel beside Connie. Jimmy is a third-generation islander, descended from a large family of Gulf and Bay fishermen. He is one of the unsurpassed party animals, thus considered a respectable citizen. "Looks like I'll have to fill in for Bart during the honeymoon, too."

Connie shrugs and smiles, but she doesn't let go of Bart's hand.

"Do you, Bart a la Jimmy, take Connie Ronstadt to be your woman, even though it may be the biggest mistake of your short, miserable life, without you even knowing you did it?" Eddie nods at Jimmy.

"You betcha," laughs Jimmy, "any day of the week, as she well knows."

"Well, then, by the power invested in me as the Most Reverend Person on St. Melancholy, I now pronounce you man and wife." Fast Eddie bows his head and spreads his arms wide.

Jimmy grabs Connie and plants a wet kiss on her lips.

Wild cheers and applause drown Connie's somewhat hesitant thank you. Someone hands a twined grass ring to Jimmy. He slips it onto Connie's ring finger and gives her another more passionate and lingering kiss. More cheers rise from the crowd as they exit the tent with a jubilant Jimmy, leaving Connie and Bart alone to consummate, more or less, the union.

Shadows lengthen and a cooler breeze caresses St. Melancholy, welcoming a few late arrivals and bidding farewell to some early departures. The *Dewey* has been beached since mid-afternoon and its crew is appropriately incapacitated, but a few outboards and a large canoe have provided additional transport.

As dusk settles on the party, Nick and Willie announce that the stew is ready. Sun, drink, and the ever-present weed have taken a toll, and at least half of the forty or more remaining people are asleep or seriously sedated. But others party on —food and beer still abundant and the music and laughter several decibels higher. Nick lifts the pot lid as a dozen of the hard-core gather around. The greenish brown liquid bubbles and belches, filling the campsite with a pungent aroma. Only a few of the assemblage have actually experienced the full impact of the strange concoction. As the thick goo is stirred, revealing lumpy residues of the peyote buttons, many of the uninitiated express reservations.

"Ackkk, are you for real?"

"We're really supposed to drink this… this shit?"

"You first, I'll take notes."

Nervous laughter is heard as Willie ladles the hot stew into paper cups and passes them around.

"You might want to keep a brew handy for it," advises Mitch, one of the few with prior tasting experience.

"Yeah, and we know you never suffered any ill effects, huh?" observes Darla. Everyone stares at Mitch, trying to determine his relative normality. Not easy, under the circumstances.

Sara, experienced in the ways of magic buttons and herbs, sips first, trying unsuccessfully to suppress a shudder. She chases it quickly with a gulp of beer and smiles. The crowd watches in silence, as if expecting her to collapse momentarily in the throes of a painful death. Willie takes another chug on his Lone Star, hoping he won't need to find another lover.

"Not bad," she says, "but it could use more salt... and more Tabasco... and more..."

A visible wave of relief arises from the group and consumption commences in earnest, though not without grimaces and remarks about the taste from hell. Tequila is the chaser of choice for several as they settle down around a large fire, telling stories, toasting the Good Ship and its magnificent crew, and experiencing the mellowness and camaraderie that accompanies a South Texas spring evening on the coast. As the last fires die and the remaining celebrants curl up to pass the night, Bart wakes up and wonders why he smells like a perfume factory.

Sunday morning arrives bright but late on St. Melancholy. The campsite is strewn with paper cups, paper plates, some clothes, a few sleeping bags and blankets, beer cans and bottles, and a number of bodies in strange positions and seemingly random locations. Already the oppressive Gulf Coast heat is upon the sleepers as they stir and grapple with the realization that peyote stew leaves a morning aftertaste even worse than the first horrible sip of the night before. Throbbing temples, pained eyes shut against light reflected from sand and water, stomachs ready to rebel (many do)—

serious hangovers seize the survivors. Dogs wait patiently in the shade of tents; some sprawl across the houseboat deck, bored with the community recovery they have witnessed so many times before. Clean-up ensues, using garbage bags that were thoughtfully brought along. Remnants of the stew, unpalatable even to the hardiest, are thrown into the bushes. Remaining ice and a few beers bring relief to some. The tents are struck, and the supplies are brought to the beach to load onto the houseboat. The *Dewey* stands ready for the first load of passengers to the marina and the Party House.

"Great party, " mumbles Bart as Connie helps him into the lifeboat.

"You have no idea," she says. Sherry and Fast Eddie look at her and smile.

Willie stands next to Pete, his ever-present longneck in one hand and a cigarette in the other. "Have a good time, Pete?"

Pete sucks on an ice cube, still trying to clear the peyote aftertaste. "Works for me," he says. They join Mitch and the others as the lifeboat pushes off.

■   ■   ■

THE *GOOD SHIP GEORGE DEWEY* SAILED MANY MORE times along the Intracoastal Waterway to adventures big and small, realized and fantasized. Over the next two years she would rescue stranded boaters, play host to fishing parties, conduct an occasional raid, and narrowly escape from close encounters with the Coast Guard. On two occasions she was hijacked, first by a whiskey-toting band of shrimpers from across the bay, and later she was commandeered by some of the Party House ladies to kidnap Willie on his wedding night. But that, as the saying goes, is another story.

The end of the *George Dewey* came almost three years after her maiden Party House cruise. It didn't come in the middle of the channel while overloaded with the dazed and delirious nor did she blunder through the ship lanes into a tanker or shrimp boat. A middle-aged fisherman, experienced and one of the minority around Port Tarpon regarded as careful and sober, rented the lifeboat for the day. Returning from fishing in the Gulf, he and the *Dewey* were caught by a summer squall that materialized without warning. Motor flooded by following eight-foot waves, she capsized and sank while crossing the bar at the ship channel entrance. A witness on the jetty reported the accident to the Coast Guard, and the fisherman's body was recovered in the bay the next day. The lifeboat was never found. That might have been just as well since it had been a refugee from Coast Guard inspection and approval for three years. Perhaps it lies half buried on some other coastal beach, awaiting another discovery and restoration.

At the Party House, life continues to the rhythmic, tidal-based pace of Port Tarpon. Schemes and dreams keep time with the click of pool balls and clinking glasses. Over it all, Chuck's red flag, the last reminder of the greatest ship in Party House history, hangs over the mirror at the back of the bar, still emitting an unmistakable odor.

The Great Barroom Bicycle Race

MAY 1974

There comes a time when great athletes gather and challenge each other in great contests, championships that will live in people's memories as testaments to human will and effort, attempts to reach for victory and glory and to be recognized as the best who gave their best. The Great Barroom Race wasn't one of those times.

The race actually came together from two very different ideas and sources. The first was the recognition that many of the dogs of Port Tarpon were not only mangy and flea-ridden, but they were breeding like … well, like dogs. Port Tarpon lacked an animal control service and dog pound. There was a veterinarian in town, but most of his business was tending to the pampered pets of the more affluent residents. He had neither the time nor the resources to deal with the hordes of roaming dogs that many people fed but couldn't medically care for. It was Mickie that talked up the idea one early spring night at the Party House. We need to raise some money to get the dogs treated and spayed, she said. She had a friend in Corpus Christi who had connections with a similar program in the city, and they offered to come out to the island for a week if their expenses and money for the supplies could be raised.

Like many of the discussions that ensued over a few pitchers of beer, this one seemed like a great idea. Most of the bar regulars liked dogs, mangy or otherwise. They all saw the need to intervene and do something, but how? By coincidence, happy fate, or the will of the Gulf Coast gods, a different discussion was taking place at the next table.

Frank and his wife, Debbie, were talking about bicycles and bicycle racing. Frank was an athlete through and through. In addition to being a graduate student at the Institute, he had played varsity football as an undergrad and had been drafted as a punter for the Houston Oilers. He had made it into two preseason games before injuring his knee and finishing his pro career. He looked like a footballer and he kept in shape, partly by riding his ten-speeder up and down the island road and on the beach. The latter wasn't easy, and it had to be done along the waterline, where the sand was wet and hard enough to provide a suitable surface. His short but wiry wife was also a rider and could keep pace with him most of the time. Frank was recalling a bicycle race they had entered in Austin the year before. It had attracted a number of racers from around the Midwest, coming from as far away as Kansas and Louisiana. He took fifth out of a field of over one hundred, and Debbie had beaten all but two of the women. Her time had also bested most of the men. Neither of them had the professional bikes and gear that most of the others sported. As the beer took hold and Frank speculated on how well those same racers would do on a rutted island road and a sandy beach, Debbie sat up and in a suddenly sober voice exclaimed, "That's it."

"What's it?" asked K.C., sitting alongside Frank. The other table quieted as Mickie, Willie, Pete, Bart, and Connie turned toward Debbie.

"Why don't we have a bicycle race here on the island?

Instead of a groomed track or a state highway, we can run it half on the beach and half on the island road, which in some places is more like the beach than a road."

"Well you'd have an advantage over some of the bikers that have never raced on a beach, I suppose," said K.C., stroking his chin and tilting back in his chair.

Willie picked up his mug and sat down on the other side of K.C., facing Debbie and Frank. "I know another thing you can do that most of them probably can't."

Debbie put her arm around Frank and gave Willie a faux shy smile. "No they can't, I'm with him, aren't I darling?"

"Yeah, you are. What would that be Willie?"

"Besides writing boring papers about fish and bike riding, what else do you do well?" Willie looked at Frank as Frank looked down at Debbie, her head against his chest. "Not including that."

Frank thought a minute. "I can kick a ball a long way. Maybe not as far as I used to, but still better than most." Willie just stared at him, obviously not getting the correct answer.

"Well I can chug a beer better than most of the guys around here."

"Bingo, laddie, bingo. You can drink beer, and not only a beer, but several in succession and still bang a bike down the beach." Willie looked around at the others for some sign of comprehension, but it had been a long night and it wasn't coming. "A bicycle race combined with chugging beer. A barroom bicycle race." He had their attention now, along with several of the other bar patrons. They gathered around the table as Willie explained.

"We adopt your idea of combining the beach and the hard road portions, but the contestants have to stop at several bars in town and at each bar chug down a can or bottle of beer. We can lay out a route that'll challenge the best of them."

"Why a can or bottle, why not a mug?" asked Arnie.

"Because it's harder to gulp it down from a bottle and especially from a can. Try it."

Several of them had, too many times, but everyone knew that Frank was a master of the art. He had learned it during his fraternity days—he could pour it down his throat and swallow with hardly a pause for air. One loud burp and twelve ounces of the amber brew was done and gone. Debbie was almost but not quite as good at inhaling the suds, but, combined with their beach biking, the proposed race seemed like a natural.

Mickie was not to be forgotten. "Suppose we had an entry fee? That would pay for the beer they consume, a few prizes for the top bikers, and the rest we could put toward doggie care?"

"We could do better than that," Darla added, joining the discussion. "We should be able to get some publicity, talk the bars into making a donation for the cause, and sell extra beer to the onlookers, donating the profits for the day."

K.C. looked at Arnie and Willie. "I think we're good for that and I bet we can talk most of the other bar owners into it."

"What about publicity and PR?" asked Mitch.

"Sara can do something through our town newspaper and maybe something over in Snapper Pass," said Willie. "What we really need is to get Corpus Christi and Austin on board."

Skip, one of the PT musicians, spoke up. "I can handle Austin. I know someone at the *American-Statesman,* and I have a few friends at a radio station."

"Great, what about Corpus?"

Pete raised his hand. "I know one of the reporters at KRIS-TV. I can ask her."

By now there were about twenty people gathered around the table, offering suggestions for the race route, the number of beers required, and how much to charge.

Since Frank and Debbie were sure to be entrants, they excused themselves from the planning discussion. Mickie acted as recording secretary and designated several people for specific tasks. The decision was made to hold the race at the end of May. There would be crowds and the weather should still be pleasant. It would give them just enough time to make arrangements and get the word out.

The race was scheduled to begin at Charlie's on the beach. The sandy part would be the hardest cycling and would tire out some of the better racers who weren't used to soft terrain. It would start with the consumption of a beer at the start, followed by a two- mile run along the water and a mile on the road to town and the second stop at the Party House to consume the second can. Next, a one-mile race to Bud's near the Ferry for the third can. Then a mile-ride back to Mary's near the Party House for the fourth can. The fifth drink waited out at Ahab's, three miles along Island Road. The sixth and final can was back at Charlie's on the beach, about one mile from Ahab's. About nine miles by the odometer and six brews by the bar-o-meter.

■　■　■

Saturday morning at ten saw over 200 contestants lined up at the beach motel. Each had paid twenty dollars to enter and they had brought an assortment of bikes, from rusty one-speed junkers to professional lightweight racing cycles. Part of their money was used to offset the beer provided by the five sponsoring bars, but each of the bars had donated money toward the Save Our Dogs Day Fund as well. KRIS-TV had cameras at the start and finish lines and a couple of portable cams roaming around town to catch the action. The onlookers at each location also formed a consuming multitude that made the effort profitable for both the bars and the doggie fund. The size of the crowds and number of contestants exceeded all expectations by the organizers. Frank and Debbie, once confident that they were in charge of "their" race, were now less so. Still, they had practiced with riding and chugging and knew they had a good chance to place in the top five of the men's group and women's group, respectively.

People filled the top balcony of Charlie's and lined the beach ten to fifteen deep for the first quarter mile of the race. A lane from the start line to the waterline had been cleared and a green ribbon provided to keep the spectators from getting in the way. Flags and a volunteer stood at each turn along the route. A map was also provided to each rider. Another problem was serving so many drinks to the large number of contestants, a good reason to use cans instead of mugs. There would be no differences in how much beer was poured. At each consumption point, the rider had to turn the can upside down to indicate he or she had finished the drink. One other rule had been added as an afterthought. If at any point a rider/drinker couldn't hold the beer down, they would be eliminated from the race. They were also told that they couldn't deliberately puke along the route, that if seen, they would be eliminated. Each rider was identified by an armband with a large number.

At ten after the hour, all of the 212 riders, including thirty-seven women, sat on their bikes with a full beer in hand. The bartenders and helpers in town were ready, the route volunteers posted. Newspaper photographers and television cameramen were recording the scene. Of the Party House regulars, only Frank, Debbie, and Nick were entered. Nick was riding one on the rustier three speeds, but he was strong and had a determined look. Bart had planned to enter, but during the early hours "planning sessions" of race day, the mustached one passed out and had to be scratched. Several island volunteers circulated among the riders to affirm their initial beer consumption before pushing off. Willie served as Master of Ceremonies, raising a longneck above his head from his position on the balcony. All eyes turned to him as he shouted down to them, "For the Doggies, lads and lassies, down it and be off for the doggies."

Down it they did, although it was obvious that most of them didn't have the head back and open throat technique Frank had perfected. He was one of the first ones off the line and Debbie wasn't far behind him. Several of the riders were struggling with the drinking phase, and it took them a couple of minutes to get the first one down. This was a good thing because there was no way a herd of 200-plus bicycles would be able to ride together along the water. The desirable zone was less than five feet wide and shifted up and down the beach as the waves slid ashore. Navigating the zone required a compromise of aiming for where the sweet spot would be when you got there but without too much lateral movement up and down the beach. It was a wavy course, if you did it right. Most of the others, bunched together, needed to either ride through the shallow surf or higher in the dry sand, either way a slow and gruesome task.

Pete stood next to Nancy, one of the roving reporters from KRIS-TV, while her cameraman shot scenes of the crowd and the race start. She had short dark hair and braces on her teeth, making her look younger than her mid-twenties. She had been working in Corpus for less than a year. The island was part of her beat, and she had covered a few events at the Institute, including a brief interview with Pete about his fieldwork on crab behavior. He had a crush on her, but they moved in different worlds. After most of the riders had left the line, the cameraman turned toward Nancy, and she gave her spiel about the race and the dogs that would benefit. One of Randy's ragged Airedales served as the poster dog for the canine spot.

Finished, she turned to Pete and gave him a metallic smile. "I'm good until they return. Buy me a beer?"

"Works for me." He walked inside to get her a longneck as she wrapped up her mike and found a place to sit in the sun. It was a beautiful coastal spring day, a slight breeze accompanied by lazy ripples of waves sliding onto the sand. Most of the send-off crowd stayed at Charlie's, waiting for the racers' return, expected before noon. Jimmy Buffet was blasting from the speakers, and a number of impromptu dances were underway.

Down the beach, the riders were digging in, trying to maintain their place in the wet sand zone and pushing as hard as they could on a surface not ideally suited for biking. After the first mile, they were already strung out, with the last drinkers just leaving the start line. The professional racers with their fancy multiple speed gears had no advantage on this stretch. In addition, the entire course was essentially flat, no rises requiring lower gears.

An unexpected route feature occurred just before the second mile mark.

Maggie and Jet decided to sunbathe just high enough on the beach to avoid the racers but close enough for the riders to get an eyeful. The brunette and blonde spread out on their brightly colored towels without tops and only the smallest bikini bottoms they could wear and still avoid arrest. Technically, nudity wasn't against the law and most of those who wanted full exposure used areas of the beach farther from town and the heavier traffic. There were no signs warning the unwary, but all of the locals knew where to swim and sun with minimal cloth. Because families and younger visitors clustered closer to town, topless ladies were less common, and they usually huddled closer to the dunes, away from beach runners and car traffic.

Maggie and Jet weren't trying to be subtle. As the first riders approached, they sat up to watch them pass, waving and giving the men and women big smiles and pushing their chests out proudly. Frank and Debbie, among the top twenty, had seen their show before and easily ignored it, but several of the other riders couldn't help themselves. Even a glance away from the waterline worked against their wave timing. Two of them ended up in deeper water than they wanted, and three others cut through semidry sand, which slowed their bikes noticeably.

After the topless ladies, the riders turned left onto a short, paved access road that took them into town and to the second beer point, the Party House. Jumping off their bikes and running up the stairs, they rushed inside to the counter where one can of beer, of twenty lined up, waited for each contestant. There were other beers waiting on tables in case more than twenty racers were drinking simultaneously, but that turned out to be unnecessary. The field was now well strung out, and only seven riders, Frank included, hit the door and started drinking together. He was in fifth place. It was no contest—Frank poured it down and was out the door before the sixth rider was half-finished. Frank was on his bike and starting for Bud's as the next rider burst out the door.

Inside, one of the leaders, in seventh, was puffing and had a bright red face. He got about a third of his second can down and up came the first one. Arnie pointed at him and said, "Sorry, mate, you're gone." Four others took a bit more time finishing theirs as Sherry grabbed a mop to clean up the mess. Others rushed in, and the Party House was deep into the hoopla.

Frank was the fastest, and by the time he arrived at Bud's he was in fourth. Debbie was leading the women and was ninth overall by then. Only a few spectators were gathered around the bar by the ferry and some of those were arrivals that were clueless about the ongoing race. The police were monitoring the crowds, and volunteer police from Snapper Pass and Corpus helped with the increased traffic. Motorists were told to look out for and avoid the bikers—they were encouraged to park and watch for the rest of the morning.

In the meantime, Frank downed his third can, albeit a bit slower than the first two. Again, one of the closer competitors wasn't able to finish his. In fact, all along the route, many of the riders were finding out that the beach ride wasn't the toughest part of the race. It wasn't that most of them were unfamiliar with the suds—many of them prided themselves on being able to swill with the best of them. It was the combination of tough terrain and instant chugging they weren't prepared for. Debbie had a decisive lead over the second woman behind her, but she hardly cared. It was the men she wanted to beat and if she could pass her husband that would be even better. But she was less than half his size and when consuming alcohol, size counted. It should be mentioned here that no one had ever suggested that beer volume should be adjusted for the size of the contestant or that the women should have to drink smaller portions than the men. Not with this crowd, no way.

Out of Bud's and back up the Ferry Road to Mary's. It was a smaller place, but cans were lined up and ready. The length of the race stretched out longer, giving the later bars time to replace cans and mop up messes. And, there were fewer riders as the race wore on. Several of the Party House regulars were helping Mary serve the beer and watch for the completed chug. At Mary's, Frank hit the street first, and Debbie was fourth overall. They knew the long three-mile pull to Ahab's would give some of the pure racers an advantage, and they would need all of the head start they could muster to stay in competition.

The rough road also took its toll, blowing out more than one tire, especially those not suitable for rougher pavement. There were no SAG (support and gear) cars or teams to help the riders—they were on their own. Despite the climbing temperatures and free-flowing perspiration, more than one biker desperately needed to pee. Small bladder, you lose. Debbie had a small bladder, but she did what a lot of long-distance racers did and simply peed while she peddled. Her dark shorts didn't show it, and she didn't care if they did.

It wasn't quite eleven when the small group of leaders, Frank and Debbie still among them, pulled up in front of Ahab's. A number of spectators had gathered there, and they were in a party mood, dancing in the parking lot and inside, but well away from the bar. This time, after the three-mile ride from town, the beer was welcome and refreshing. It was going down slower but Frank still finished his before the others. He ran out the door and jumped on his bike to complete the final lap back to Charlie's. He rode to the three-mile access road, a particularly bumpy strip, and onto the beach and within sight of the waiting crowd. Willie was prepared and saw him coming from about 200 yards away, from the opposite side of the motel where riders had left.

He grabbed his microphone and alerted the crowd. Nancy tapped the shoulder of the cameraman, and he zoomed in on Frank, peddling hard and peddling alone. The nearest rider was about fifty yards behind him. The cheering reached a tumultuous climax as Frank crossed the finish line and jumped off his bike. He was grinning from ear to ear as he raced up to the steps of the motel and was handed his last task, downing the sixth and last can. It should be noted that the beer consumed was Lone Star. Some of the planners had suggested other brands, including Shiner, but they finally decided to give some of the less local and less hip riders a break.

The crowd quieted as Frank lifted the red and white can high in the air, tilted his head back, and poured it into his mouth without spilling a single drop. Many of the spectators hadn't seen him do it at the start and they murmured in amazement as he finished the race like the undisputed champion he was. The second rider, a tall thin male who was one of the professional entries, stumbled up to the table and reached for his can. He was clearly a bit bewildered, and he managed to down the beer but without the spectacular performance by Frank.

The winner, in the meantime, had climbed up to the balcony amidst handshakes and a flurry of congratulations. He was scanning the beach for Debbie, and here she came, fourth overall and by far the first female. She finished her beer in a more leisurely fashion and showed some noticeable effects from the alcohol. She also emanated a distinctly sour odor.

Willie announced the number, name, and place of finish as each rider consumed the last can. Only one of the 123 riders who finished at Charlie's puked at the finish line. The last rider came in at two thirty, but only a few witnesses were there to greet her. By that time, most had adjourned to parties on the beach or at one of the several bars in town, all doing a better than average business for a spring Saturday afternoon.

Frank and Debbie received their first-place trophies, and Mickie happily announced that several thousand dollars had been raised to provide flea and mange treatments and spaying for the island dogs. As soon as she had been interviewed by Nancy, she left to join Maggie and Jet, making it a delightful triple play for the topless. Pete thanked Nancy and said goodbye to her before joining Willie for a ride back to the Party House.

The event had been exciting, a fund-raising success, and it was time to celebrate well into the night. It was also the start of the real summer season, when things got crazy, and peace and quiet could be forgotten for the next three and a half months.

Frank and Debbie joined the party late and ordered a pitcher of beer between them. "Time to sip, then sleep," he said, and Debbie nodded agreement. Each of them had a medal attached to a green and gold ribbon around their neck.

At seven in the evening, Bart stumbled into the bar, sleepy-eyed but thirsty. "Did I miss anythang?"

"Nary a thing," replied Willie. "I'll buy you the first beer." And he did.

CHAPTER EIGHT

All That Glitters

SUMMER 1974

Despite the party at St. Melancholy, the celebrations after the barroom race, and my return to the Party House scene, I hadn't found a woman to replace the vacancy left by Sonya. There had been a few encounters at the beach, some flirty moments at the bars, and a couple of one-nighters with visitors. None of these provided the comfort and familiarity of a steady lady, and most of them were either occupied with someone else or were never to be seen again. Fortunately, the arrival of warmer weather stimulated the surface activity of the fiddler crabs, and my days were fully occupied. Unfortunately, lonely nights in the cabin had to be accounted for. I had vowed to spend fewer late nights at the bar so I could get earlier starts on fieldwork and complete the research during the next two years. It was too late to save the relationship with Sonya, but obtaining my degree in a timely fashion might serve me well in the future.

Enter Angela, stage right. In early May, two weeks after the festivities on St. Melancholy, I found myself at the main campus, consulting with Stevens and picking up some additional equipment from the zoology department. A student from UCLA had enrolled in the MSI summer session and was temporarily staying with relatives in Austin. Stevens asked me if I would be willing to give her a ride to Port Tarpon. A special course involving a cruise on the R/V *Longhorn* in the Gulf of Mexico would kick off the summer teaching schedule. The steel-hulled trawler was equipped for sampling geological cores, dredging, plankton towing, and a variety of other oceanographic tasks. The cruise was scheduled for the third week of May and I was asked to help out with some of the sampling procedures.

Angela had a dark-complexion, was about five-two high, and had long black hair. She wasn't slim, but she was athletic. On the way to the island, she told me she was a member of the UCLA women's fencing team. Her practice foils (non-electric), two masks, and two chest protectors were in bags along with the rest of her luggage.

"I hope I can find someone to practice with at the Institute," she remarked. She was in the front seat beside me, looking out her right-side window.

"I'm sure someone will be interested."

She looked over at me and asked, "How about you? Ever fenced before?"

"Never had the chance. You're the first person I've met that knew anything about it. You must be pretty good if you're on a major university varsity team."

"It's actually considered a club sport, but we compete in a local conference that includes USC and other California schools. So, are you game? I can teach you to move, hold the foil, and parry, enough to give me some practice time."

"I'll think about it. Usually, I'm pretty busy in the field."

For the next few hours we talked about her undergraduate degree in biology, and I told her what I was doing in the field. She was attentive and seemed genuinely interested. I also realized she was lonely and didn't know anyone else at the Institute. Unlike Fran from last year, she was not under my supervision and therefore I was free to go out with her, if she was willing.

Her willingness became apparent that evening after dinner. The MSI mess hall was open and serving. Angela had just turned twenty, and she was of legal age in Texas. I suggested we visit the Party House for a brew or two and she readily accepted. We should have walked over because it was a pleasant night, and at the time I had no other intentions toward her. But the car was parked next to the mess hall and we climbed in.

At the tavern, I introduced her to Mitch, and we shared a pitcher of draft. Angela made friends easily and seemed very much at home. Skip and Leonard were playing guitars and singing country rock. We had a second pitcher, and I asked her if she had ever seen the Gulf of Mexico at night. She had barely caught a glimpse of it when we arrived on the island.

"Should we go back so I can get a swimsuit?"

I almost said yes, since I would have liked to see what she really looked like, but I said, "No, we'll just walk on the beach. Swimming at night is probably not the best of ideas." Her puzzled look prompted me to add, "Sharks sometimes wander in closer to feed."

"Oh." She paused and stared at me. " Has anyone been attacked?"

"Not that I know of, but I'm not interested in being the first."

We left the Party House and drove down the beach, past the pier, to an area that appeared to be deserted. We left off our sandals in the car. A half moon provided just enough light to see the surf line, so we walked along the water, moving up and down to avoid the waves. The night was warm with no breeze, and we both noticed the sparkle in the shallow water and on the beach at the same time.

"What is that?" she asked, stooping to pick up a handful of sand. The waves lapped around her ankles, and we could see the glow appear and disappear as the water wet the sand and withdrew.

"Bioluminescent algae," I answered. "They're dinoflagellates and every so often we have a big bloom of them. When the water hits the sandbars or the beach, it causes them to glow. Haven't you seen them in California?"

"No, never. They are beautiful. It's like magic." She was laughing, running in the shallow waves like a small child, completely delighted.

Moving quickly over to where a wave had just wet the sand, I wrote my name in it, creating a temporary glowing signature. She did the same and we both laughed.

"I want to swim in it, to be surrounded by the shining water."

"We didn't bring our suits, remember?"

"Do we need them?" She looked around at the darkness in both directions. "We seem to be the only ones here."

"Sharks?"

"We'll only go out a little ways. Just for a few minutes. Please." Her bubbling enthusiasm dispelled any remaining reluctance on my part.

"All right, but let's put our clothes in the car. Uh, I don't have towels, so we'll have to air dry."

We returned to the car and undressed, leaving the interior light off. I could make out her body in the moonlight, her long hair hanging down in front, over her breasts. We ran back to the water and waded to our waists. It was cool and we laughed as we jumped up and down, but I warned her to avoid excess splashing. She dripped water across her face and shoulders, watching it sparkle as it ran down her arms and across her chest. Her hair was wet and pressed to her back. I could see her clearly when she turned toward the Gulf and faced the moon. She knelt in the shallow water, letting the waves wash around her, and I sat beside her. One wave nearly toppled her, and I reached out to grab her shoulder. Still unsteady, she leaned forward and fell into my lap. She put her arms around me and gave me a quick, wet kiss on the mouth.

"Thanks, Pete, this is fantastic. I've been on the Texas coast for less than a day, and I've already experienced my first night swim in the sea and written my name in sparkling letters. I wonder, what is next?"

"My pleasure, ma'am, welcome to Texas," I drawled slowly, doing a poor John Wayne imitation. *Yes, what is next?*

We stood up and waded through the splash zone for a few more minutes. I was also caught up in the bioluminescent display. I had seen it a few times before, but had never waded in it, and never viewed it with such charming company. Without saying anything, we both felt the need to return to the car and dry off. She reached for my hand as we crossed the sand, as if we had been good friends or lovers for some time. The rapid rush to familiarity was more than I expected or had ever experienced. *Must be the moonlight and the algae*, I thought, but I wasn't going to second-guess nature or fate.

We climbed into the car and I turned on the engine and heater to dispel the chill that we both felt. There was something else I felt, sitting next to the naked Latina. We smiled at each other, almost with shyness, as if our nudity was a suddenly revealed accident. She reached over and took my hand and held it in her lap.

"I don't mind if you want to kiss me again." Her dark eyes seemed huge, pupils dilated but visible in the darkness.

No cars came by, and we didn't want to put on our clothes until we had dried further. We scooted closer and embraced. I was about a foot taller and even while sitting I towered above her. Her head was back, and eyes closed as we indulged in a prolonged and deep kiss. Her breasts were pressed into my chest, and our thighs rubbed together as we shifted on the front bench seat. That was when I remembered the old cotton sleeping bag I kept in back of the wagon. I usually left the back seat folded down because I rarely transported more than a single passenger. If there were three of us, we usually just shared the front seat.

"I have a sleeping bag in the back. I usually use it as a beach blanket." I decided not to elaborate, to let her pursue the obvious invitation if she wanted. If she didn't, that was okay and our necking session would suffice and more.

She looked at me and simply nodded yes before climbing over the back of the seat. I joined her, unrolled the bag, and we lay side by side. We were still wet and laughing as we began touching each other. I became aroused within seconds and crawled on top of her. She reached down and helped me guide my swollen penis into her vagina but immediately withdrew it.

"It burns, it burns," she said, as if I had tried to enter her with a hot poker.

I could feel it too, but I realized it was the salt water. Sensitive tissue was not compatible with a touch of the brine. I had experienced a similar discomfort when I tried to have intercourse with someone in the ocean a few years earlier. It didn't work then, either. I told her it was the salt and that we would need to at least dry off. A freshwater shower or washcloth would be preferred.

"Sugar would have been better," she laughed.

We sat there, naked, looking at each other's bodies, like curious children exploring sex for the first time. By that time, the passionate mood had passed. We kissed a few more times and dressed, leaving our sandals off, and drove back to the Institute. We parted in front of her dorm. She looked down the lighted walkway toward the jetty and my little white cabin at the end of it.

"Maybe we'll try a real bed sometime, and without the saltwater."

"Sometime, that would work for me."

We exchanged a quick kiss, and she walked up the steps to her building as I walked slowly toward my cabin. I was still reeling from the encounter, at how easy, how fast, and how much pleasure it provided. Was it because of the time that had passed since Sonya and I said goodbye? Was it the magic of the moment, the setting that led to the spontaneity? I had clearly not planned for any of it to happen, not the trip to the beach or the moonlight swim, much less the intimacy in the station wagon. The old saying goes "Not all that glitters is gold." *Sometimes, like tonight, it's better.*

■   ■   ■

ANGELA AND I BOARDED THE R/V *LONGHORN* FOR OUR three-day cruise. Twelve students were signed up, plus two MSI faculty members, Frank, Willie, and I. There was a ship's crew of six, including Popeye, the cook. Most of the students had never been out to sea overnight—a few had never been on the ocean. We shoved off early on a Saturday morning to begin a full schedule of teaching and sampling activities. The 103-foot steel-hulled vessel was relatively new, delivered to the Institute in 1971. She was used for research and teaching and usually made voyages lasting for three days to a week. All the bunks were filled for this one.

The first day out saw gentle swells of four to six feet, scattered clouds, and a moderate breeze. We ran a couple of plankton tows, bringing the nets to the deck and dumping the contents in plastic containers. Two microscopes were set up in a small indoor lab. The students were quickly indoctrinated into the joys of using a dissecting microscope while the water swished back and forth in a petri dish. Several of them took a quick look and hurried back outside to the main deck. We also did several trawls, bringing up shrimp, crabs, flounders, and a few rays. Bucket grabs were lowered to sample a small area of the bottom, including the animals that burrowed in the soft mud-sand substrate. Each sample return was sorted on deck, much to the delight of the students, including myself. There was always something new or exciting to discover as each device returned its payload to the ship. The final sampling regime for the first day involved remaining on station for geological cores. Willie and one of the faculty members supervised this activity, funded by a small oceanographic grant. The cores would be placed in long tubes and returned to the Institute for sectioning and analysis.

That evening, the wind picked up a few knots, and the waves intensified. After dinner, Frank set up fishing stations around the deck. Most were simple droplines to catch snapper, sea bass, and other midwater species. The long lines were run out with a winch and contained about twenty baited hooks. After twenty to thirty minutes, the line was reeled in and the fish removed. Another grant was funding a study to measure red snapper scales for age and population estimates. A few other droplines with a single hook were used for random recreational fishing. Students near the stern were attached to safety lines, and everyone was advised to use one hand for the ship and one hand for themselves.

It had been a full day and we turned in at ten o'clock. By this time the sea was active, with waves averaging five feet. A shower had made the decks slicker than usual, and we retired to our bunks. The gear on deck and overhead kept time with the rocking motions of the ship. One of the problems with the *Longhorn* was the keel configuration—it was round-bottomed, and this exaggerated the impact of the waves when coming to either port or starboard. The crew kept the ship aligned so that most of the wave action came to the bow, but the motion was still very evident to those trying to sleep. I didn't have much problem falling asleep, but others did.

The next morning, bright and early, we were greeted with the strong aroma of frying bacon and pork sausage. The dinner bell called us to the galley where we were served in two shifts. I ate with the first group, along with Frank and Willie and some of the crew. Popeye strolled up and down the galley, smiling and in his element. Although the seas had calmed somewhat overnight, there was still plenty of ship motion to irritate the novices. As the second eating group took their places, it was obvious that more than one of them was not going to sample Popeye's fried specialties. Two of the male students ran out onto the deck and hung over the side. They would wait until lunch.

Angela emerged on deck looking like death warmed over, a Latina with a paler complexion than I thought was possible. No bright eyes, big smile, or bounce of enthusiasm. She made her way carefully into the dining area and asked for a bowl of cold cereal. By this time the odor of fried bacon had dissipated, and the platters of sausage had been discretely placed back in the galley.

It was several hours, almost lunchtime, before the sea-sick-inclined had made, more or less, a recovery. Angela was busy at work, sorting through trawl collections, and I asked her how she was doing. She looked at me like I had asked her how she liked the bubonic plague.

"I'll live, I guess. Although, I'm not sure that's the best outcome at this point." Only a brief smile indicated that she hadn't completely lost her sense of humor.

We were underway, and one of the crewmembers had a rod and reel loaded for bluewater fishing, hoping to snag a sailfish. A yellowfin tuna took the hook, and the fun was on. We momentarily stopped sampling operations to watch Billy, a ship's mate, play the fish. Or, was it playing him? Under the boat, up on the other side, back and forth behind the stern, the tuna provided a welcome respite for the onlookers. We cheered each time he managed to reel it in a few feet and booed when he lost line. Eventually, the fish tired, and Frank gaffed it and brought it aboard.

"Fresh tuna steaks tonight," yelled Popeye as the fish was presented to him.

The line was baited and cast again. In about fifteen minutes, the rod bent sharply, indicating another hardy fighter. The behavior was different this time, lacking the maneuvers under the ship but also lacking the straight-line runs of most billfish. "Might have a shark here," mumbled Frank.

Sure enough, an eight-foot common thresher was brought slowly to the surface and alongside the ship. It required three crewmen to gaff and bring it over the side and onto the deck. As a precaution, all of the students had been moved to the second deck or onto the ladders. The shark looked spent, breathing heavy on its side. The long crescent tail, barely quivering, stretched out behind the body as Frank approached it with a pair of wire cutters to cut the line. He had barely touched the line when the shark suddenly came to life, its tail sweeping across the wet deck, knocking Willie off his feet. He and Frank scrambled out of the way as the shark lunged and twisted. Out of its watery surroundings, it was still a formidable sight, and it was not happy. Thrashing tail and snapping teeth prevented anyone from trying to subdue it long enough to cut the line and return it to the Gulf.

"Should have never brought it on deck," said Billy to Frank.

"I wanted them to see it up close. Didn't realize it had that much fight left." It was a poor excuse and Frank knew it, but he had achieved his objective. We had a close look at the menacing power and primitive beauty of a fabled creature.

The *Longhorn* captain walked onto the deck with a .45-caliber revolver in his right hand. He approached the head of the shark and fired three shots at point blank range. The shark was still alive, but notably less active. Gaffs were used to drag the animal back to the stern, to be slid from the deck.

The captain stood next to Frank and said something to him, quiet enough so no one else heard. Frank nodded and walked away. The captain returned to the top deck with the pistol. We went back to work on less exciting subjects. I later asked Frank what the captain had told him.

He shrugged his shoulders and looked a bit sheepish. "Just what Billy had said. It was a shame to waste a large shark like that, and I should have known better than to bring it aboard. Someone could have been seriously injured."

"Well, it certainly livened up the party." I put my hand on his shoulder and gave him a smile.

Angela was fully recovered by dinnertime. She and I sat on an attached toolbox on the back deck, viewing the sun as it descended to the horizon. The sea was relatively flat and there was again no wind to speak of. Willie joined us and shared some cookies he had retrieved from the galley.

"How is the fair lassie doing this evening?" he asked. She was wearing shorts and a swim bra, displaying a healthy dose of cleavage. I hadn't told anyone about our first night encounter, and both of us had been too busy for an encore. I remarked that beer was an early and often used remedy for seasickness. Unfortunately, American research vessels, funded by government sources, were forbidden to carry anything alcoholic on board. I didn't realize this until years later when I was working on a German research vessel based in Bermuda. They wouldn't think of leaving port without a stock of brew.

"The Party House will take care of those needs and more," indicated Willie, cigarette in one hand, cookie in the other.

"Which hand are you using for the boat?" asked Angela.

"Ship, my dear, this is a proper vessel. If you want to see a boat, the Party House has one in its fleet, right Pete?"

"Right you are, admiral," I replied. I had not forgotten the voyages of the *Good Ship George Dewey* and the St. Melancholy craziness of last month. I looked at Angela, sitting between Willie and me. "Buy you a beer when we return," I said to her.

That night, most of us gathered on the fantail to observe the bioluminescence as we cut through a large patch of surface algae. It formed a large greenish-yellow "V" to aft, the waves glowing brightly. It would have been a perfect time for wine or some pot, but colas and cigarettes had to suffice. Nonetheless, it was a mellow setting, a time to pause and reflect. Angela and I sat together at the starboard corner of the stern. She put her head on my shoulder and I put an arm around her. Once again, the world glittered, in the water, and in a secret place within me.

Angela and I did practice some fencing moves. Correction, *she* practiced fencing moves. I held a foil in front of me, advancing and retreating with all of the grace and agility of a hippo performing ballet (images of *Fantasia*, anyone?). With chest protectors and masks, we must have been a sight, clicking away in the long sterile hallway between the two main Institute buildings. She had professional shoes, and I wore a pair of old boat shoes. She coached me patiently and showed me some exercises to prepare my legs for the demanding posture needed. It always looked so easy in the films, but easy was not part of the lexicon for this sport. Her touches came quick and often, and she easily parried my few attempts to score. She wanted me to try, but each time I did, she was able to capitalize on my clumsy thrust and get the touch instead.

There was, however, a big payoff in pride and bragging rights. Angela wasn't beautiful in the classic sense of the word. Like Sonya, my former partner, she was attractive and sensual, displaying an earthy appeal that left no doubt about her femininity. Fencing wasn't something you saw around the Institute every day. Never, in fact, so we had a monopoly on a bit of drama and fun while others watched. One of those with a wary eye on us was Cindi. As usual, she disapproved of my choice in girlfriends, believing that I should be aiming for something higher and more permanent,

"She'll be gone by the end of summer, Peter. Then what will you do?" She was sitting beside me at the MSI mess hall. She occasionally came over to eat lunch with Carl, but he was tied up, as usual, with a squid, so she selected me as the alternate lunch date for the day.

"It will be before the end of the summer. She's leaving in mid-July," I told her. "I thought you were going to find me someone *suitable*." I put additional stress on the last word, but she didn't seem to notice. "Besides, she's a university student. Isn't that an improvement over a gal from the Party House?" I gave her a hard but not hostile look, inviting her comment.

"Yes, Peter, it is. I don't have anything against her, but if you're going to hang around with a student, why not select someone who will be here year round?" She nodded toward one of the new botany students that was taking summer courses but had indicated she would move down to the Institute and finish her undergraduate degree here.

I looked at the thin blonde, a twenty-something named Jocelyn. She had also been one of the *Longhorn* cruise students. She wasn't unfriendly, but I was not impressed. Maybe it was because of the drama associated with Angela, but Jocelyn didn't trigger any hormones. She was plain and reserved, someone that was sure to garner Cindi's approval. I smiled at Cindi and told her I was too busy in the field to think much about dating at the moment. She knew that was a lie, because Angela and I made it to the Party House at least once a week, sometimes twice, to dance, drink, and be merry. There were few secrets in Port Tarpon.

The merriness didn't include a lot of sex—very little in fact. We occasionally took a nap in the jetty cabin or in her room when our respective roommates were not around. For me, that was most of the time. We slept on a cot, still dressed, necked and caressed, but didn't try to consummate anything. The first botched attempt had created a barrier, not a hard and fixed one, but a hesitation for both of us to pursue an intimate relationship. Passionate, yes, but without full intercourse. We went to the beach a couple of times at night, but the summer crowds made it more difficult to strip down and enjoy the freedom we had experienced earlier. Neither of us wanted it to be an ordeal, an obligation to have sex. Instead, we became buddies, good friends who laughed, drank, fenced, danced, and shared kisses and caresses. In July, we went to the beach and shared a towel, curling up together, sleeping, and kissing. We said farewell the next day, for the last time, and I went back to my crabs, more determined than ever to finish the work on schedule.

CHAPTER NINE

Island Women

FALL 1974

Finishing the work on schedule meant less time drinking and succumbing to distractions. However, while I was watching the courtship activities of my favorite crustaceans, I was also involved, willingly or not, in the courtship behavior of my own species.

Mustang Island females, the ones that live there all year around, come in all sizes, ages, and orientations. Most of them are white-white, despite some heavy tans, a few are Latinas, and there are at least two black girls among the femme fatales. Most of them prefer males as partners, a few are strongly lesbian, and more than a few swing both ways, usually determined by convenience and availability. One common trait is that they come and go when they want to. Feminism was unheard of on the island—they had been there, seen that, and were wearing the proverbial shirt. Exceptions might be a few newcomers that hadn't learned the rules of the game or a few of the terminally meek that would either suffer humiliation from both sexes or leave to marry someone else, somewhere else.

Sherry stated it well during one of her enlightened moments, "You gotta kick ass if you're gonna survive here." She had done that a couple of times, without apology or prejudice, and she was not only surviving but thriving. She was one of the most reliable and gutsiest barmaids at the Party House. She took shit from no one, not the owners, the customers, or her friends. Thing is, she had lots of friends, people she could count on if and when she needed them. She rarely needed them, and that made it even better.

Sherry's sometime old man was a Gulf shrimper. That meant he was out on the briny for about three weeks at a time, loading up a catch that would bring good bucks when he returned. He had his own boat, co-owned by his crew of four. He looked like the classic nineteenth century seaman, straggly beard and long hair, weathered, rough, and full of life, like Sherry. He'd stay in town about ten days, spending his money, loving his woman, and drinking his fill, which was considerable. He and his boys smoked pot and occasionally shot some horse, but they never seemed to be addicted because it was a sporadic thing, never a compulsion. Sherry said that months could go by without any of them mainlining. None of them sported the expected scars of heavy users.

Maggie, Mickie, and Jet were all attractive and in their mid-to-late twenties. Maggie was the outrageous one, a short, freckled brunette who spent a lot of time in the sun, usually topless. Whether at the beach or in the bar, she liked to tease with what she called her "tourist titties." It didn't take much liquor or talking to encourage her to put on a show. Mickie was her companion in crime, often imitating her behavior, but without Maggie, Mickie was often reserved, even intellectual. She was taller, wore glasses, and seemed as comfortable talking with Willie and me as she was playing the tease 'em game. Jet, a tall thin blonde, was a newcomer and most of the guys found her attractive but distant. She definitely preferred the female side and only partied with the guys when it was a mixed crowd and there was no danger of her pairing off with a "beefy," as she called anyone with more hair on their chest than she had. The three ladies often caroused together, hopping from bar to bar, dancing with each other, and making the men who didn't know them feel uncomfortable and unwanted. They had it right.

Some of the island women were married, either formally or informally, but they assumed the same independent attitudes as the single ones. Although Sara and Willie were a couple, she spoke for herself and wasn't afraid to flirt or make a midnight visit when the occasion called for it. Darla was Randy's legal wife, and they had children, but she mixed readily with the guys she knew around town. She especially liked to pal around with Henry, but the nature of their relationship was vague. In other places, she might have been labeled with epithets like slut or whore but not in Port Tarpon, or at least not by the guys and gals she ran with. It was still the seventies, and terms like free spirit, hippie, or, simply, independent, were more appropriate descriptors.

Toni and Nick were also married, but no one was sure if they ever had a license or a formal ceremony. They had been together for at least fifteen years, well before they had arrived in PT in 1968. But both of them exercised their island rights to gander, wander, and feel nary a twinge of guilt. Nick occasionally hit the road for a few days on his Harley, not saying where he was going or when he would return. Toni never did anything outrageous during his absences, but occasionally she would kiss one of her male friends at the beach, or while dancing, or during a beer party. Possessiveness just didn't seem to be in vogue, for either the guys or their ladies. When Mitch was asked if he ever got jealous about Moonshine when she was drunk and putting on a show for the guys, his reply was, predictably, "Tain't nothin' to me."

The situation with the local girls was quite different from that with the nonresidents. There were two kinds: women who no one knew and who arrived with the spring break and summer crowds, and women who didn't live full time on the island but made occasional or frequent appearances. This latter group included some of the women associated with the Institute, families with condominiums or businesses on the island, or just people that showed up every so often for whatever reason. The first type, generally regarded as tourists, were fair game for the hustles, parties, and debauchery that highlighted the visitor seasons. They came and went and unless they were friends with or attached to one of the local guys or gals, the men treated them like they treat women almost everywhere: with little regard for their feelings or welfare. Some men, as in other places, were exceptions. They weren't above taking a slow ride on the beach, but they generally acted with restraint and respect. It wasn't always obvious or predetermined what a first-time visitor to the Party House or any other watering hole in Port Tarpon would encounter.

It took me a while to sort this out, the hierarchy and classification of female genres and the behavioral expectations of each type. But I was a biologist; I specialized in courtship behavior and systematic classification. Should have been a snap, but it wasn't. Just when I thought I had figured someone out, I would often learn that it wasn't that way at all, and I had been wrong again. So it was with the prospective girlfriend that Cindi had determined would be "just right" for me.

I met Diana at a dinner hosted by Cindi and Carl. To give credit to the Canadian couple, they alerted me ahead of time that this particular dinner in late September 1974 would be different because there would be a special guest for me to meet. You'll love her, Cindy told me on Tuesday. She was excited and wanted me at their house by six o'clock on Friday so I would have "enough time to get to know Diana" before the evening was finished. Attempts to find out more from Cindi about my blind date were unsuccessful, and no one else among my friends knew who she was. Must run in a different crowd, remarked Willie. He asked Sara, his partner, who knew everybody on the island it seemed, but she also drew a blank. Must be new to Port T, reported Sara.

I put on a collared shirt and clean pants, wore shoes and socks instead of sandals, and brought a bottle of semi-expensive wine to dinner on Friday. Diana was of average height, had brown hair, medium length, and was wearing a dress with full skirt, rare in Port Tarpon even among the academic set. Cindi was dressed in a similar fashion, as if the women had carefully coordinated their outfits. Carl looked somewhat abashed by it all, as if he had been dragged into the matchmaking scheme under protest. His eyes met mine for only a second as Cindy proudly introduced her friend.

Diana was indeed new to the island, having arrived in the middle of the summer. Her father was a yacht broker, and he decided to set up shop on the island. The family bought an expensive condo in one of the new high towers along the beach. From the description Cindi related, it made Fran's apartment (remember Fran, my early under-grad research charge?) look like a slumlord special. Diana belonged to an embroidery group with Cindi and several other of the island's more refined (read: respectable) ladies. I knew many of them by reputation (mayor's wife, one or two school teachers, pastor's daughter), but none of them personally.

Diana seemed personable, that is not shy or unsociable, but she also lacked any spark or evidence of passion for anything. She sewed and cooked, was educated in the domestic duties of a prospective spouse, but identified no hobbies, didn't participate in sports, and appeared uncomfortable in an outdoors setting. Her pale skin after two months on the island provided ample proof that swimming and sunbathing were not among her favored pastimes. After a cocktail (she drank, but only enough to meet the minimum social obligation), we sat down to dinner. It was a pot roast, and it was only after we were finishing a cherry cobbler a la mode that Cindi announced Diana had fixed everything they were eating. Diana blushed and lowered her head, but Cindi beamed as if she had just discovered the greatest chef in Texas. Carl and I murmured some words of gratitude for a great meal, and we adjourned to the living room.

Cindi brought out her daughter for the mandatory admiration ceremony, and Diana held her for several minutes, cooing over her like she had never seen a baby. Carl poured Irish creams for the men, and we sipped them silently while watching the women's tableau play out. Diana was sitting on the couch with me—Carl and Cindi had strategically placed themselves in the two chairs facing us. Diana and I were about three feet apart, but Cindi had contingency plans. She grabbed an album of family photos and sat to Diana's right, forcing her to the middle and closer to me. After showing us a few photos, she announced it was time to feed her daughter and would we excuse her for a few minutes? As she left the living room, I noticed her finger signal to Carl to follow her into the bedroom, leaving Diana and me alone and sitting only a few inches apart. I fully expected she might shift back to her former place on the couch, but she remained in the center.

"Does that taste good?" she asked, indicating the last bit of my liqueur.

"Never had Irish cream?" I said, holding it out to her to smell.

"Umm, smells yummy. Can I have a taste?"

I handed the glass to her, and she took the daintiest of sips, barely wetting her lips. "Sweet, almost like candy," she said, passing the glass back. "Maybe I will ask Carl to pour me a little."

"Sure, he'll do that," I said, relishing the first spark of interest Diana had shown in anything beyond domestic household skills.

We made small talk about the island, and she asked me about my graduate studies, but I decided not to bore her with details. After I mentioned crab social behavior, her eyes seemed to fog over, and I knew her interest had been sated. Our host and hostess returned to the living room and I could tell Cindi was pleased that we were still sitting next to each other. I asked Carl for another shot of liqueur and indicated Diana would like to try some. Cindi looked at me and then at Diana, as if I had proposed something immoral or worse. Carl immediately returned with the bottle and a glass for Diana.

Cindi was drinking iced tea, but she proposed a toast "to friends," and we raised our glasses and drank. I was certain Cindi had more than friends in mind, but I couldn't read Diana. Once again, Diana remarked about how good the liqueur tasted and how she could get used to something alcoholic that tasted so nice. Cindi still looked concerned but smiled at us encouragingly. To provide further opportunity, she invited Diana and me to a larger get-together during the following weekend, a birthday party for one of the academic wives at the Institute. It would be an after-dinner affair with dancing and what Cindi called "fun games." I had heard about the get-together but had not been specifically invited. I only knew the wife from a couple of encounters during the past year. Her husband was a staff investigator studying sea grasses. Jocelyn, the student Cindi had mentioned earlier in the summer, was one of his students. They were not among my favorite people. No hostilities, just nobody to go out of my way to cultivate as friends. Diana lit up and said she would love to go. Cindi looked at me. By this time, the drinks had worked their magic and I was relaxed and compliant.

"Works for me," I said.

Cindi clapped her hands together and said, "That's Pete's favorite expression. He probably says it a dozen times a day, don't you Pete?"

"I guess, if you say so." I drained my glass and stood up, preparing to go. I had another date with my animals in the field the next morning. Even though I often partied into the late hours on Friday, I knew that eleven o'clock with the Canadians was pushing the boundaries. I wasn't sure what Diana's usual regime was, but I didn't figure it included wild nights of drinking and dancing.

"Saturday, a week from tomorrow, about seven at Paul and Nan's place. Right?" Cindi was determined that I wasn't leaving until I made a firm commitment, so I did. I thanked her and Diana for the dinner and good company and made a gracious exit, knowing I might be paying a big price for the meal in about a week.

Diana was twenty-four years of age. She had two younger brothers, one in high school and the other in middle school. She had worked as a clerk in an insurance company in Houston and had grown up there as her father developed his boat business. He was now semi-retired, having made enough money to work primarily as an ongoing hobby. In addition, he had made some shrewd investments in real estate and in the stock market. Sara later told me she hadn't known Diana, but she knew quite a bit about her father, Lionel. It seems the McKenna family had done quite well, and that Diana and her brothers would be worth a great deal of money. Most of her money was still in a trust, but she could draw it out whenever the need arrived, or when she got married. Cindi confided to me a few days later about Diana's financial status, indicating how fortunate I would be to land someone like her for a girlfriend, perhaps something more serious.

"Huh, Pete, what do you think? Is she a good one or not?"

"She can cook," I ventured, although pot roast wasn't one of my favorites.

"Go easy, Peter, she is delicate and refined, not like most of the girls on the island." She smiled and walked away, satisfied with her progress toward my domestication.

I smiled also, thinking about her and the other island women I had met over the past year. Yes, she would be a different breed, and I would go very easy, tiptoeing in fact, because I knew my tastes in friends and social activities had undergone a transformation. As much as I liked Carl and Cindi, I was finding it increasingly difficult to spend more than an occasional hour or two with them. The baby goo-goo and the marital bliss could only hold my interest for so long, about two hours tops. I doubted that the intricacies of embroidery would be entertaining for more than two minutes. Poor Diana, not your fault. Cindi made the wrong match for you.

Sitting at the Party House bar on Tuesday night, I related the account of the dinner party and my new "girlfriend" to Mitch and Willie. I told it straight, neither sarcastically nor with bitterness, just what had transpired and what was looming at the Saturday night birthday bash at Paul and Nan's place. My friends knew them well and had a similar opinion about Paul. He's an okay guy, offered Mitch, but boring, terminally boring. Willie wasn't as charitable. He might have been okay if he hadn't married Nan, he told us. She's insufferable and thinks that somehow high society is present and thriving in Port T. What's worse, she thinks she's the grand dame of the debutante ball.

The three of us were chugging beers, and we had a bottle of Black Jack for shooters. Neither of you going? I asked. They confirmed they were not, and Willie told me the Party House had hired a band from Corpus to close the summer out. Gonna be a blast, Pete, you shouldn't miss it. *Damn it! If I had known that a live band was playing and it might be the last big shindig for the summer, I would have never agreed to go to the birthday party.* There didn't seem to be any honorable way to renege, so I resigned myself to duty—I was still an honorable, well almost honorable, person in those days.

Saturday evening arrived and, as arranged, I picked Diana up at her condo. Her parents were away, so I escaped the big introduction. Her younger brother gave me a quick hi before returning to the television. I was dressed about like I had been at Cindi's the week before, but Diana had on a very revealing and tight-fitting satin dress, dark green and glimmering with every step she took. It was a complete contrast to how she looked last time. Her hair had been done in a perm, she was wearing lipstick and a light touch of rouge and sporting a perfume that could only be described as intoxicating. The Diana light bulb had attracted a moth, and the glare was blinding.

We arrived after the party had started and from the number of cars parked along the street, there had to be at least fifty people inside of the well-lit bungalow. She took my hand as we walked up the steps and greeted a couple of the guests, then the hostess Nan.

"So glad you two could make it," she said, hugging Diana, then taking my hand. Paul stepped up beside her, looked appraisingly at Diana and her shimmer, then shook my hand and with a simple welcome, we were in.

A couple of kegs had been set up in a corner and the bar seemed busy. A man and a woman, both in white uniforms, were pouring drinks for an enthusiastic crowd of guests, about half of whom I recognized from MSI. Cindi and Carl waved at us from across the room. Carl's stare at Diana confirmed my suspicion that this wasn't Diana's usual type of attire. As I looked around at the noisy room, I realized almost everyone was better dressed than I was—many of the guys were wearing buttoned shirts, many with ties, sports jackets, and slacks. I wasn't totally out of place, but I wasn't going to make anyone's best-dressed list. On the other hand, the girls were wearing cocktail dresses, fashionable slacks, and were made up as if for a pageant. Diana out-spectacled most of them, and men's eyes followed her as we mingled. Jocelyn was also in the crowd, talking with another MSI student. She was dressed nicely but nowhere near the pizazz that Diana displayed. Her eyes followed Diana and me. *Does she know about Cindi's suggested match with me?* After a few greetings and introductions of people to Diana, I suddenly developed a thirst and we edged our way toward the bar.

"What can I get for you?" I asked, hoping they had soft drinks available. Considering the guests, I was sure they did, but Diana surprised me.

"I'll have whatever you're drinking," she said, staring into my eyes as if throwing her life into my hands. Thinking later on what happened that night, I suppose she did just that.

"Are you sure you want to do that?" I was still trying to decide whether I wanted to go with beer or hit the hard stuff in an attempt to forget the real party taking place about a mile away at the marina.

"Yes, I'll trust you to get me something I can drink." She smiled and squeezed my hand.

I stepped up to the bar and thought quickly. When my turn came, I asked for a whiskey on the rocks and a brandy Alexander. "Can you make that?" I asked. The bartender nodded her head yes and turned to mix the sweet concoction. I took our drinks, tipped her, and headed back toward Diana, who was now in heated conversation with Cindi.

Handing Diana her drink, I said hi to Cindi and raised my glass. Diana took a sip, smiled and took another, as Cindi looked on, obviously horrified. She started to shake her head from side to side but stopped when Diana exclaimed that the drink was great and wanted to know what it was called. Cindi gave me a hard stare, turned on her heels and walked back to Carl, who was engaged with three other MSI guys in conversation.

"I take it Cindi doesn't approve of my choice of libations," I said, sipping on my whiskey.

"What does that taste like?" she said, pointing at my drink.

"You probably won't like it," I said handing her the glass.

A quick sip, a grimace, and she handed it back. "I guess I'm not ready for that, yet."

Yet? Oops, what have I created? Where is this going? We sipped and mingled again, chatting here and there. Diana introduced me to some of Cindi's friends and members of her sewing circle. They looked at me appraisingly. *What had Cindi and Diana told them about me?* Some soft rock music started, and a few people began to dance in an attached external patio. It was a nice evening, not too warm, with an ocean breeze. After the first few numbers and the initial conservative dance floor maneuvers, a couple of funk pieces played, and I asked Diana if she wanted to dance.

"I'll need another one of these," she said, indicating her empty glass. "Or maybe something stronger." She had assumed a different appearance, a facial glow and slightly seductive look in her eyes. Her stance and movement emphasized her hips. I was now Port T-educated enough to read the signs. I took her glass and returned to the bar.

"Double Alexander and double whiskey straight," I said. The barmaid smiled and looked across my shoulder at the shimmering green dress.

"Good luck, sailor," she said, turning to fix my drinks.

"I'm not a sailor," I said, "just a student." I dropped a couple of ones into the tip jar as she handed me the two glasses.

"Tonight, everyone's a sailor," she replied, giving me a knowing smile.

Diana and I consumed our drinks and a few minutes later we were on the floor, doing our thing. I had learned to dance with a variety of partners, starting when I was fourteen. I wasn't shy about dancing, letting the music take me where it would. At first, Diana just shuffled her feet, but the liquor must have taken hold because about halfway through a James Brown tune, she began to loosen up and let it go. Cindi and Carl were also on the floor, doing a slow jitterbug to Brown's "Sex Machine" (a surprising tune for a party hosted by Paul and Nan—maybe there were things I and others didn't know about them). The look of dismay was once again evident from Cindi. She must have believed I was seducing her friend, plying her with the evil spirits, both liquid and otherwise.

Diana had some great moves and after we had finished a couple of numbers, she asked me if I wanted some fresh air. I nodded yes and we stepped off the patio and out of the light. *What now?* I was feeling very relaxed and increasingly satisfied with my very sexy partner when I spied Cindi walking our way with a look that could kill. I knew who her intended victim would be.

I thought quickly and spoke even faster. "There's another party here in town. Would you like to go and meet my friends?"

She smiled and nodded in the affirmative. I grabbed her by the shoulders, and we moved around the house and to the street. We were in my car before Cindi knew we were leaving. Fortunately, Diana hadn't brought a purse and we hadn't left anything behind. A few minutes later, we pulled up to a very noisy Party House. I parked in the back, on the marina side, and we walked into the poolroom, behind where the band was set up and playing very loud Lynyrd Skynyrd-inspired southern rock. People had filled the bar, and there were many more outside, on the porch, along the side, and in front, listening to the music through the open windows and doors.

As I looked at my friends, I realized that we, but especially she, were way over-dressed for the place and time. Shorts, cut-offs, swimsuits, beach shirts, jeans, everything but cocktail dresses, were on display. As Diana and I passed in front of the band, the song came to a dead halt and the boisterous crowd stopped and stared. Diana looked around and realized immediately that she was the cause of the musical pause and stony silence. I turned to the band but yelled so everyone could hear, "Is this a fucking party or not? Start playing." The crowd laughed, the band resumed, and we made our way over to a table where Willie, Arnie, and several other friends were having a dice and chug contest.

I introduced Diana, they all said hi, Willie stood and kissed her hand, and Mitch said, "Damn, Pete, you sure know how to make an entrance." Arnie's eyes were focused on the top of Diana's dress, which showed only a bit of cleavage, but the sweat running down to it from her neck must have been an irresistible magnet. Sherry yelled across the room to see what we wanted. Mitch pointed to a bottle of Mexican rum and yelled back at the barmaid. "Set-ups, Sherry. Coke and… what would you like Diana?"

"Whatever Peter is having," she said, clinging to my arm with both of hers, as if we had been inseparable lovers forever. Despite her closeness, she didn't seem at all threatened by the people or the atmosphere.

"Just Coke and ice, then," Mitch yelled and we sat down. The setups came, I mixed Diana and me a drink, and Arnie produced a fresh lime.

"Cuba Libres, it is," I said raising my cup to Diana and the friends around the table.

"Will I like this?" she said, raising her cup tentatively.

Willie couldn't resist. "Like it? Why lassie, you'll learn to love it. And us."

We toasted, talked, danced to the band, and the evening wore on, approaching the forbidden hour of two when bars were legally supposed to close. The band had left, and much of the crowd had cleared, leaving the hard-core regulars to nurse a few more for the road or whatever. Diana was feeling no pain, relaxed in my lap with an arm across my shoulder. I was well on the way to imagining a moonlight drive to the beach and a deepening relationship when the front screen door slammed open and a burly man in slacks and an open collared white shirt burst in. His face was not friendly, and he stormed up to our table with clinched fists. Diana sat up with a start, jumped out of my lap and said, "Daddy, we were…"

That was all she got out before he grabbed her and placed her behind him. His attention was solely on me. "Are you Peter Gilbert?"

I stood and the other guys stood also. Arnie quietly walked to the other side of the bar. "I am," I said simply, waiting for his next move. Diana was quietly crying, and I could see her shoulders shaking.

"What the hell do you think you are doing with my daughter, you son of a bitch?" He was standing close enough so I could feel moisture in my face as he spat the words out, leaving no doubt about his mood.

I took a step backward, remaining wary, but the others held their ground. They knew I wasn't a fighter, and they were not about to let someone they didn't know beat up someone they did.

"Daddy, I went with him, it was my idea, he didn't mean anything, we didn't do anything…" It was a babble of desperate pleas as she held onto his shoulder. He ignored her and shook her off, continuing to stare at me. Finally, I had to say something.

"Mister McKenna, I apologize if there is a misunderstanding. It was my fault, I brought her here and she didn't know what…"

"You sorry son of a bitch, there is no misunderstanding. I know what you are up to. Do you think I'm stupid, boy? Do you?"

He sounded like a drill sergeant I had encountered during basic training in the military, taunting and daring me to throw a punch, to start something I knew only too well he would finish. I held my ground but kept my arms at my side, my hands relaxed.

"Your daughter is of legal age, Mister McKenna, but I take full responsibility. Don't be angry with her."

For the first time, he turned and looked at Diana. "I'll deal with you when we get home. Go to the car." A brief pause while Diana stood transfixed, afraid to look at me. "Now, damn it, now," he bellowed. She took off for the door and just before exiting, she cast a glance back at me, a brief one that said all I would remember about her being hurt, my being sorry, my being helpless to do anything. Then she was gone.

McKenna turned back to me and looked quickly around him. My friends had remained ready but silent. All of them were staring at the bull in the room, waiting with me. "I should kick your skinny ass for this, but I guess your buddies here would have their say, so I won't. If one of your friends at the other party hadn't told me where you and my daughter might have gone, I'd probably have the rangers out looking for you right now. And I'd be either kicking your butt or pressing charges."

"Charges? For what, being friends with your daughter? I haven't touched her, we haven't even kissed, for your…"

"Shut the fuck up."

Bart stepped forward, displaying his familiar bull charging countenance, fists doubled up, biceps pumped. I glanced at him and Willie put a hand on his arm.

"Let Pete handle this until he can't," whispered Willie. Bart nodded and stepped behind me.

McKenna wheeled on his heels and stormed out the way he came, slamming the door. A few seconds later the car started, and we could hear the tires squeal as he peeled down the street. I stood there, visibly shaken, wondering what waited in store for Diana. My friends gathered around and consoled me to the best of their ability. I was still distressed, disappointed at my lack of ability to intervene. Willie reminded me that it was Diana's choice to leave with her father and there was nothing I could do about it. At least he hadn't thrown a punch. I probably had Bart to thank for that. Another Cuba Libre, heavy on the rum, helped ease my way back to MSI. I would have some harsh things to say to Carl and Cindi because I was sure that they were the ones who directed the angry father to the Party House.

I didn't see Carl until Monday. I decided not to confront either of them on Sunday, giving me time to cool off and attempt to be more rational. I was more concerned about Diana and I needed to question Cindi before I pissed her off forever. Carl was in our office at nine. The summer meal service at the Institute had stopped, and I had eaten breakfast at the Island Cafe. I walked in and sat down in my chair. Carl looked up and bid me good morning.

"Good morning, Carl." I waited, hoping he would say something about Saturday night. He didn't.

"What happened Saturday, after Diana and I left Paul and Nan's?"

Carl put down the book he was looking at and leaned back in his swivel chair. He clasped his hands in front of him and he cleared his throat twice before answering.

"I'm sorry about that. Cindi was worried about her friend and she knew she had quite a bit to drink. She was going to ask her to slow down, maybe go home with us." He stopped and fumbled with his thumbs. "She doesn't hate you, Pete, she just thought that Diana wasn't aware of what was happening and that maybe you were getting carried away. I mean, she was very attractive in that dress and I can hardly blame you, but you know how women are, and Cindi can be… well, difficult and stubborn at times. I tried to stop her from interfering, but…" He stopped, at a loss for words. I nodded and smiled at him, trying to provide some reassurance.

"It's okay, Carl, I understand. Right now, my main concern is for Diana. Has Cindi talked to her? Is she okay?"

Carl could see I was sincere and worried. He leaned forward and told me Cindi was supposed to talk to her that evening and he would pass along any information he could get. I thanked him and left.

I was distracted during my Monday fieldwork, trying to concentrate on measurements and observations. I needed to get in as many as I could before the summer ended. After my first summer in Port Tarpon I had returned to Austin and the main campus to consolidate my notes, take a course or two and resume the true academic life. My decision to stay on the island during the coming year had cost me my housemate. The debacle over Diana created reservations about staying. I didn't want to return north because most of my friends were now on the island and some of the ones in Austin had graduated, left, or drifted on to other things. Despite the slowdown in the pulse of life during the winter, the island still seemed a more enticing place to be. My cabin on the jetty was mine for as long as I was in good graces with the MSI administration, Chun was still an agreeable roommate, and the bar scene loomed ever larger in my everyday cycle of activity.

Wednesday morning, Carl informed me of Diana's fate. Her father had been angry but did not physically assault his daughter. She told Cindi that she was forbidden to venture within a mile of the Party House and to have no further communication with me. She asked Cindi to tell me thank you and she hoped I would understand that we could never see each other again. She would be leaving the island on Friday and returning to Houston to resume her job and stay with an aunt. Carl told me his wife was very sorry she had gotten her friend into trouble and hadn't realized that Diana was as fond of me as she was. Diana's farewell was thus passed on, and I thanked Carl for the information. He asked me if I would also forgive Cindi, and I told him it was all right and I would look forward to our next dinner engagement.

"But," I warned him, "no more attempts at matchmaking, okay?"

"You got it mate, I'll make sure Cindi understands. And, again, I'm sorry."

I thought about Diana during the next few weeks and what might have been if our relationship had developed. Mitch had one view on it. Might have had me hook, line, and sinker, he mused. Arnie and K.C. kept reminding me about that bright green dress and the provocative cleavage. I couldn't forget that she sat in my lap and had me considering a drive down the beach. Would she have gone? Would we have regretted it if she had? Considering the reaction of her father, we probably avoided a bigger confrontation, but I will always remember we never had the opportunity to say our farewells in a more appropriate manner. The ill-fated friendship, nipped in its infancy, was another reminder of my ineptitude or bad luck, maybe both, in affairs of the heart.

CHAPTER TEN

Randy, Mitch, and Moonshine

1972 TO 1976

Mitch lived in a small cabin a few blocks from the Institute: one bedroom, a small kitchen, bath with shower, and a shed to store a few things. He had arrived in Port Tarpon in the spring of 1972, searching for work, any kind of work. He had a biology degree from a small Indiana college and had tried to get a job on one of the deep-sea charter boats. There were many others ahead of him, hoping to work at what they liked doing best. Failing that, he signed on with a bay trawler, but three weeks convinced him the commercial fishing and shrimping business was harder and more dangerous than he had anticipated. It was also mind numbing and didn't provide the desired working colleagues. When a position opened up at the Marine Science Institute, he applied, was hired, and assigned to help in one of the fisheries labs. He also enrolled at the university to take an occasional course and make some progress toward a master's degree, but he was not officially considered a graduate student. Compared to bay shrimping, the job was ridiculously undemanding and allowed Mitch to settle into a Port Tarpon lifestyle of minimal material needs.

He soon met Randy, a biologist with the Texas Parks and Wildlife Service. TP&W had a lab on the island that specialized in monitoring red snapper populations, an important commercial resource for the coast. But Randy had his own dream. He had contacts with several universities and was aware of the demand for certain types of live fish for research. Especially in demand by several West Coast research laboratories were electric rays, which were not only abundant in the nearshore Gulf, but were considered trash fish by the trawlers. Nets often came up with several rays that had to be separated from the commercial haul and carefully kicked back into the ocean.

In 1974, over a beer with Mitch, Randy proposed they start a small commercial specimen lab. Randy was certain he could talk some of the Gulf fishing boat captains into letting them put a live box aboard. Instead of kicking the rays back into the ocean, Randy would encourage the boats to retain the rays by providing the boats with a rubber-handled net, a large Styrofoam container, and a small motor with an aeration tube. This would keep the rays alive until the boat returned to the pier, where Mitch or Randy would unload them and pay a small amount for each live ray collected.

Randy also had his eye on a vacant building bordering the marina, complete with a back dock. It had been a bait and tackle shop, but he felt it would be ideal for his scheme. About this time, Willie showed up in town and he joined them. By pooling their money, they secured the building on a long-term lease, bought some large glass tanks and several deep holding containers, and set up shop as Tarpon Marina Laboratories. Since all three had full-time day jobs, it was a moonlight affair, with much of the labor expended on weekends. They managed to con a few friends into helping meet the departing and arriving boats when they couldn't get away from work. They started with the small electric rays, but soon added eels, crabs, and a few species of hardy fish to their inventory. Randy contacted the universities, he printed some impressive catalogs and brochures, and they soon had a modest but successful enterprise. As a bonus, TML was only two blocks from the Party House.

Once Willie began cultivating the magic weed in earnest, Mitch became a faithful consumer. Randy occasionally joined them, but his job with Texas P&W demanded a cleaner life style. Mitch let his curly hair grow long and developed a full beard. Neither he nor Willie would ever win a best-dressed award, and much of the time they were either in sandals (on the job) or barefoot (the rest of the time).

That fall, one of the local town girls took a liking to Mitch. She was a real flower child, a hippie that had dropped out of high school at fourteen and never looked back. She had been in and out of town several times, chasing one dream or another. Finding little to sustain her in the mean world off island, she made her way back to Port Tarpon. Her folks had cast her to the wind when she left school, so she made her way around town, doing odd jobs and staying with friends, until they too showed her the door and asked her to bless someone else with her presence. Sometimes she left on her own, seeking another place and another face. Often this happened at night on a full moon. Lunar light gave her the power to make good decisions, she claimed.

Her real name, when she was a real person, was Pamela. But she called herself Moonshine and the name stuck. By the time she was eighteen and decided to become Mitch's special friend, hardly anyone knew her real name. No matter, she was friendly, cheerful, short, thin and light on her feet, wore as few clothes as possible, and seemed to dance even when walking down the street. Mitch thought of her as his pixie, a diminutive Tinker Bell without the magic dust. Their living arrangement was simple: she stayed with him when she wanted and somewhere else when she wanted. They cooked for each other and she kept his place tidy, no big effort required since it was small and furniture and other material possessions were minimal. They shared his transportation, an old, one-speed bicycle. She also liked pot, beer, and anything else being passed around. Moonshine was a Party House and Port Tarpon presence, even when she was mentally absent, which was a great deal of the time.

At first glance, Mitch and Randy seemed like the odd couple. Clean-shaven Randy was well spoken, well read, and wanted to get ahead. He and Darla owned their brick house a few blocks from MSI and he occasionally helped some of the Institute biologists by providing specimens and data from TP&W. Although he smoked the good weed only occasionally, his wife indulged often, and she was one of the Party House in-group. Their two pre-teen children were clean cut, and, except for Darla's rough edge, they could have been the All-American family.

Mitch worked hard, knew his stuff around the lab, and was considered one of the better boat handlers in town. Mary Jane, however, was his true girlfriend. Supplied mostly by Willie, Mitch was rarely without a joint and when off work, his buzz was almost continuous. This did occasionally produce problems. Several times, he walked out of his small bungalow leaving one or more stove burners on. Other than wasting some gas, he had been lucky, and nothing had caught fire. He also misplaced his bike more than once, and he would scurry around asking everyone if they had seen it. After a while, we made ongoing mental notes of where we had last spotted the rusty blue Schwinn. There were no locks on the bikes and very few on the doors of most Party House people. Despite the summer influx of students and tourists, the main part of the island was relatively crime free. Burglary seemed to be confined to the condos and better motels.

After Pete arrived on the island, Mitch and he became good friends. Although Pete never became the heavy weed connoisseur that characterized Willie and Mitch, he participated socially and the three of them often partied together. Pete also became interested in the Tarpon Marina Laboratories and began volunteering his time there. He also donated a display terrarium featuring several fiddler crabs.

The most famous inhabitant of the lab was a small brown octopus one of the trawlers had netted and brought to Randy. A large and well-aerated tank had been set up, and Herman the octopus became the star attraction. The school kids loved it, and visitors made a special effort to come by and watch it crawl around on and among the rocks that were provided. Feeding it live shrimp became a show unto itself, attracting additional visitors after a few newspaper articles and local television coverage. Although TML was occasionally offered money to sell it, the owners knew that few aquarists, even experienced ones, could keep an octopus alive. The input of filtered circulating seawater was a critical key to their success. There were also several displays of various fish, crabs, shrimp, and a few of the eels and rays. In a large bathtub-sized tank, they kept a small nurse shark.

Moonshine would stare at the fish for hours, sitting on a stool, lost in another world. One day, Willie brought her a costume he had picked up in Corpus Christi. It was a mermaid outfit, a bikini top and a lower section complete with tail. After a bit of grass and a few margaritas, they had her sitting on a stool by the open door as tourists wandered between restaurants along the marina. Sure enough, most of them, especially the guys, couldn't resist. Moonshine had the build of a young girl, but she had an attractive smile and a way of throwing her hips to one side that belied her innocent waif image. After a few Saturdays of posing, she grew bored and made one of her periodic exits out of town.

One morning toward the end of the summer, Randy opened the TML door to begin work. One of his first jobs, or the first task of anyone opening the lab, was to survey the tanks, make sure the water circulation and aeration were working, and feed the animals. He glanced in the octopus tank and didn't see Herman. Sometimes the slippery one wedged itself behind a rock and you had to look carefully. Randy did, but no Herman. A lid over the tank was still in place, but there was a very small gap, less than a quarter inch, in a rear corner, as if it had been pried loose. A few spots of salt from dried seawater behind the tank provided the essential clue—Herman had escaped. Randy was searching frantically along the wall, behind aquarium stands, boxes, and other barriers when Mitch entered. Randy told him about the escape and a few minutes later Mitch found Herman behind a refrigerator, thoroughly desiccated and thoroughly dead. Randy picked up the small stiff body and placed it in a jar of preservative. The animal had probably been out of the tank for ten hours or more. They had forgotten how little space is required for the rubbery body of an octopus to squeeze through. When Willie and Pete joined them later that morning, they reflected on the tragedy of the escape, the amazing agility of the animal, and the drive for freedom that often demands a high price.

■　■　■

ONE AFTERNOON IN 1976, WHILE WILLIE, MITCH, AND Pete were nursing some cold ones at the Party House, Willie asked Mitch what he and Moonshine talked about. Willie could talk to anyone about anything and often did. Mitch didn't say a lot unless he was wound up about something, but we were intrigued with what might pass for conversation between Mitch and his flower power girl. The couple didn't have a television, neither of them expressed any interest in politics or world affairs, and neither of them were deep readers. In fact, we believed Moonshine might not be able to read at all or only at a lower grade level.

"How about it, Mitch? What does Moonshine like to talk about? Anything you can tell us that isn't too secret or intimate?" Willie was on his fourth beer, had probably done a joint or two earlier, and was slouched over the table, almost nose to surface.

Mitch was still relatively sober, as was I. "Intimate? I don't think she and I have ever said anything intimate." Mitch took another swig and Pete followed his example.

"Oh, c'mon now, you mean you and your mermaid have never done the deed, in all this time you shared your shack?"

Mitch put his mug down. "I didn't say that, I just meant we never talk about it. We just do it." No further details were forthcoming—that was Mitch. Whether playing poker, drinking, smoking, whatever, he didn't discuss his exploits with the ladies, Moonshine or any other.

"Get him another beer, Pete, we need to loosen him up."

Pete started to rise and go for the tap, but Mitch finished his mug and stood up. "Fuck you, Willie, I'm outta here." And he was, just like that. It was very rare for Mitch to curse at anyone, unless he was joking. He wasn't.

"Don't think he likes to talk about sex," Pete observed. "Some guys are just like that. Go easy. Maybe there is something going on and he's sensitive about it."

"Maybe," said Willie, "maybe not." His head went down,

and his face kissed the table. Not for the first time, Willie passed out before six in the evening.

There was something going on. Moonshine was pregnant. She confided to Sara and Darla and they told Willie and Randy, respectively. Two days later, everyone in the Party House and half of the people in town, even those who didn't know Moonshine, knew about her condition.

"What the hell am I…, uh, are we, going to do?" asked Mitch. He was cold sober and worried. Moonshine was at his place, taking a nap. Randy and Darla, Sara and Willie were gathered around him at the TML, sitting on the back dock. After retrieving a cold longneck from the cooler on the back porch, Pete joined them.

"Is it yours?" asked Randy. Darla gave him a dirty look, but Mitch shrugged his shoulders.

"I don't know. Could be, I guess. She and I haven't talked about it that much, but it could be someone else's. I just don't know."

"Does she want to keep it or have an abortion?" asked Sara.

Mitch looked at her and paused before answering. "I think she wants to keep it. She hasn't made a final decision, but she is talking about how she might look pregnant." He looked at Willie. "She said she might finally get breasts big enough to notice."

Darla laughed and put her hand on Randy's knee. "Greatly overrated, I'm afraid. Sara, let's have a talk with her, just us. I don't know if we can be of any help, but I'm sure you guys won't be."

"Amen," said Willie, only too happy to duck out of this one. The ladies got up and left the lab.

Mitch looked at Pete. "Ever have any experience with this kind of thing?"

"Not really. I had a girlfriend that missed a period and we thought she might be pregnant, but it was a false alarm."

"If it hadn't been, what would you have done?" asked Mitch.

"I was really young. She and I had both just turned twenty-one. I did mention the possibility of marriage before we found out it wasn't going to happen."

Willie took a drag on his cigarette, exhaled, and said, "And…?"

"She didn't seem very excited about the prospect, either of being pregnant or getting married. I guess we were lucky." Pete took another sip of beer.

"Luck, in poker and life, is the best you can hope for," said Willie, always the philosopher.

Mitch never did find out if the baby was his, and he never found out if it was a boy or girl. Not that its gender would have mattered. He seemed prepared to take responsibility and even talked to Willie and Pete about marrying Pam. He was no longer using her nickname, and we could tell his relationship to her had changed dramatically. Whatever, he never got the chance to prove his honorable intentions. Moonshine called her mother one night and two days later, Sara dropped her at a bus station in Snapper Pass and she was gone, home to mom and to start a family. She left with minimal fanfare—that is to say, none—and she barely said goodbye to Mitch. He didn't know she had left permanently until Sara told him.

That night he got drunker than anyone had ever seen him. No pot, just straight tequila, until he passed out at a corner table. Randy and Willie carried him home. Darla stayed with him at his bungalow all night, an unusually bright full moon providing the only light, as if our lonely satellite was commemorating Moonshine's departure. Mitch didn't wake up until ten the next morning. Hungry as a bear waking from hibernation, he shook off what had to be a hell of a hangover and indicated he didn't have any food in his house. Darla took him home and watched him consume ten pancakes and three eggs. Afterward, he seemed to be his old self, helping Randy at the lab, working hard at MSI, doing his fair share of weed, and joining in the Party House banter. Under it all, however, his friends sensed the hurt, a deep lingering pain he suffered quietly by himself.

Mitch without a girlfriend attracted interest and a few offers from some of the island ladies, but the prospects didn't seem to interest him. I suspect that if one of them barged into his bungalow and threw herself on the bed, he might have gone along with the program, but it didn't seem likely he was going to initiate anything soon. He became a more frequent dinner guest at Randy and Darla's, but, otherwise, he seemed the same old Mitch we all loved and cared about.

CHAPTER ELEVEN

Captain Ahab's and Bruce

SPRING 1973 TO LATE FALL 1975

Other people and other places played significant roles in Port Tarpon during the nineteen seventies. As in any community, individuals and groups large and small had their own tales to relate. In some cases, there was little or no connection with events at the Party House, but there were exceptions.

Bruce was in his early forties but could have been much older. He was about seventy pounds overweight, most of it wrapped firmly around his middle. He had dark hair and a dark mustache, almost a handlebar, but never that well-groomed. He hailed from the Midwest and showed up in the spring of 1973. He worked around the docks, cleaning fish, mopping up messes and any other menial work that became available. He wasn't particular, and his needs were simple. He wore old army fatigues and sometimes an olive-green jumpsuit. When it warmed up, he changed to cutoff jeans. Long or short—his pant edges were as ragged as he was. Strangely, despite cleaning fish and sleeping on a soiled mattress in the back of Arnie's garage, he never really smelled bad. He took a shower every day—cold water from an outside standing pipe with showerhead—and used generous amounts of soap. But he looked like a bum and he mostly kept to himself. His major purchase every day was a half-bottle of Mogen David wine, MD 20/20. Bruce and everyone else called it "Mad Dog" and most of the locals thought you had to be a rabid canine to enjoy it, although they never observed any of the island dogs drinking it.

Bruce sometimes worked nights and slept days. Depending on his schedule, you would see him walking along the streets, slumped forward with plodding short steps, the bottle hanging from his side pocket like an inseparable friend. He swore by the stuff, attributing his good health to the red juice. People were amazed that anyone who looked like Bruce could speak of good health. Not much changed for him during his two years in Port Tarpon. He had few friends, but he was friendly and, when in the mood, he could talk and reminisce with anyone. He rarely came to the Party House and no one ever saw him at the beach. It wasn't his place. Occasionally he would splurge and buy a bottle of Four Roses or Smirnov or something else to break the routine, but he always went back to Mad Dog.

By the summer of '74 Bruce had grown a shaggy beard to match the shaggy mustache and his hair was long, uncombed, often hanging in his face. At the end of the summer, one of the tourist bars and nightclubs, Captain Ahab's, was closing down. It was usually open only during the spring-summer student season, catering to a younger crowd of mostly legal-aged college students. The music was pop-rock, the liquor flowed fast and furious, and the PT police had their hands full keeping order and checking IDs. The bar was isolated, located three miles south of town on the Island Road. It was not a pretentious building—no bright neons or razzle dazzle. It was wooden, like much of the island architecture, a simple bar, a couple of pool tables, a floor big enough to dance on, and several round tables. It had a large parking lot, was not far from the beach, and it attracted crowds, including numerous unattached women looking for good times. After Labor Day the bar closed down and locked up. In 1974 the bar changed owners and they decided to keep it open during the winter. They didn't expect much revenue and they didn't want to pay much for employees. They removed the liquor, keeping beer and setups during the winter. They hired Bruce, who indicated he had tended bar in his illustrious past. Maybe he had, maybe not, but it didn't take much skill to pop a cap or pour a draft. Bruce wasn't athletic, but he was strong and could lift a keg or turn away a problem drinker. As the nights got colder and darker, Bruce moved into the back of the bar and kept it open from early afternoon until closing time, which by tradition in PT, varied with the whims of the bartender on duty.

The next event in Bruce's tenure at Ahab's was the arrival of Donna, a seventeen- year old runaway from Fort Worth. She was pleasantly overweight, an oversized version of Moonshine—cheerful to a fault but just what the usually morose Bruce needed. She moved into the backroom with him, sharing a cot, skimpy meals, and, of course, Mad Dog. Apparently, no one in Fort Worth had a clue where she was, and she kept discreetly out of sight, inviting no inquiries from the local authorities. She became a fixture at Ahab's that fall and often she and Bruce were the only ones in the bar.

Pete and Mitch stopped by one evening to say hi and grab a quick beer. The place was essentially empty, and only Bruce's rusty bike on the porch next to the door gave any indication that someone was in the building. Bruce was sitting at a table with his favorite bottle in front of him. Donna was in his lap, naked as the day she was born. Neither of them was feeling any pain, so Mitch and Pete gave them a wave and went on their way.

The summer of 1975 brought the largest crowd of visitors in Port Tarpon's history. The beaches were overflowing. Motel rooms, never adequate for a destination beach resort, were filled, and the bars and restaurants were doing a landmark business. Although many of the nightspots catered to particular tastes during the off-season, in the summer most places enjoyed an eclectic clientele. The young, the retired, the sportsmen and women, casual family vacationers, college students, high stakes business people, inland hippies, and of course, the locals, all joined together to drink and make merry. Most places did have preferred customers, and Captain Ahab's was the bar of choice for the younger dancing set. Because many of the locals, although a tad older, also liked to dance and party loud, Ahab's was also a popular spot for them, especially on weekends.

There seemed to be a different dynamic at Ahab's. The party could get loud and raunchy at the Party House or at the Gun 'n Reel, but it rarely had the sense of festivity, of wild abandonment that emanated from the bar down the road. With the summer, the owners had reopened and hired additional bartenders and waitresses, but from some unexpected sense of loyalty, they also retained Bruce, as a bouncer.

There was no outside sitting area, no marina with moonlit waters, and no other bars nearby to hop to. Ahab's was surrounded by dry sand flats, nothing else. The generous parking lot was lit, but otherwise, it seemed like a desolate place to party. That was also one of its attractions. The isolation meant no complaints about noise and fewer visits by the city police, who regarded it outside their jurisdiction except for emergencies.

Angie had just turned twenty, and she could legally drink alcohol, including the hard stuff. Texas had lowered its minimum legal drinking age (MLDA) from twenty-one to eighteen the previous year, and the party for college undergrads was on. But Angie had more than that going for her. She was small, slender, had natural blonde hair, and she was cute. She also liked to wear hip huggers and semi-transparent blouses that left an exposed midriff. Sometimes she wore lacy bras, sometimes she was braless, and when she was at Ahab's, she was an all-star attraction. But, as the TV commercials say, wait—there's more. She could shoot serious stick.

No one was sure where she came from, but someplace from outside the coastal area. She showed up that spring with a couple of other foxy girls, rented a two-bedroom condominium at the beach, and began making the rounds. This included several taverns, each of them with pool tables. Most of the tables were the three-quarter sized, coin-operated types, but one of the nicer places in town had two full-sized regulation tables. Most of the locals didn't go there. The prices were high, and they weren't especially welcome, but every place in town put out the welcome mat for Angie and her friends. They drank, they flirted, they danced with the men, and they shot respectable pool.

Angie was the best of the three, and the locals quickly learned she was a prime hustler. She played the game to the max, slopping through a game or two until some guy raised the stakes to something reasonable. Most games were played for beers, a round of drinks, or a couple of dollars. Even with stakes at five or ten dollars, Angie would lose but usually by just enough to seem competitive. Twenty dollars defined the magic line. She would beat her mark, but again, just barely. This almost always resulted in a rematch and sometimes a third game before the guy finally realized he had been suckered by the sweet young thing who didn't look like she knew which end of the stick to hold.

We sometimes shot a game or two with her just for fun and to give her a chance to make her play. During the summer—and especially at bars like Ahab's—there were always strangers, new meat for Angie and her friends. There were also enough of us to protect her if some of the marks got nasty after being hustled. She was only a summer lady, but we treated her as if she was a local and she never took money from any of us.

The other difference between Ahab's and the Party House was their license to serve liquor during the summer months. While most men and the few women who regularly played on the green felt table drank beer, Angie preferred margaritas. For her age, she tossed them down with surprising impunity. Even after a night of steady drinking, she seemed to be in control, but she was an experienced actress and didn't make that apparent.

One night approaching eleven, she is playing slop ball with Nick. They are laughing and fooling around, missing a fair number of shots. She is sipping on a salt-rimmed glass and having a good time. A quarter appears near the coin slot, indicating the next challenger for a game. Nick looks at Angie as he lines up for the eight ball shot, one he rarely misses. He misses it and she laughs, punching him in the arm. Nick withdraws with a satisfied smile and joins Toni at a table to watch. Several of us look on as the stranger, a tall guy in his late twenties or early thirties, wearing jeans and a straw cowboy hat, saunters up to the table, drops the coin in the slot and racks the balls.

"How ya doing darlin'?" He says this a bit too loud as he removes the rack, giving a slight lift to his hat. "You playin' for anythang, dear, besides your smile?"

Angie stands straight with her stick, actually just one of the plain beat-up bar sticks. She gives him a coquettish smile and replies in a quiet, shy voice, "Usually I just play for a drink." She nods toward her almost finished margarita, "But I don't mind if we add a little spice, if you promise not to be too tough on me."

We almost can't keep ourselves from breaking up. Angie is usually more subtle, more nuanced in her approach to the hustle. If you want a big fish, you have to know when and how to set the hook. But Cowboy is anything but subtle. The way he struts, holds his stick, and leans close to Angie signify a confidence badly misplaced.

"Pete, I don't know if I can keep a straight face," whispers Willie.

"Try man, try," I reply softly, not wanting to give Angie's play away.

"I'm never tough on a sweet thang like you," Cowboy says, butter rolling off his tongue. "How about, let's say a five-spot? And, I'll buy you a fresh drink right now." He whispers something to a guy standing behind him and the guy walks to the counter to get Angie's drink.

"Well, aren't you just about the nicest ever," she drawls and leans over to break the rack, drawing the stick back and exposing her bare chest beneath the flimsy blouse. The view isn't lost on Cowboy, and we can see his fingers grip his stick just a bit tighter. She slams the cue ball into the set but without any balls sinking.

"Nice break, darlin'. Mind if I take over for a bit?" She stands back and watches him walk around the table until he lines up behind a solid and puts it in the side. He knocks in a couple of more before missing, and she gets a few stripes. As we could easily predict, she keeps it close, but he sinks the black one while she still has a stripe on the table. Her drink arrives, and she quickly puts a quarter on the table along with a five-dollar bill.

"What'cha drinking, cowboy?"

"Well, I'll just have one of them thangs you're having, if ya don't mind." He signals to his friend, and Angie hands him a few dollars for the drink. The game is on, and Angie drops the coin in the slot. The balls fall into the chute, and she grabs the rack and puts the balls, a bit clumsily, into the triangle.

He watches her carefully, staring hard at her blouse. "Same stakes, darlin?"

"Oh, I just barely lost. Let's double down so I can get my money back."

Cowboy nods, "Ten it is." He leans down for the break, a bit more serious but still enjoying the banter. Willie pokes me in the arm with his elbow and we watch in silence, enraptured by Angie's skill.

Cowboy sinks a stripe and a solid and takes the latter. He isn't a slouch, and he makes two more before missing. Angie has a nice small run and they duke it out for the eight ball. He leaves her with a decent shot, and she puts it in.

"You're something else, you are. Where'd ya learn to shoot like that?" By now they are both sipping tequila and lime, licking salt. He racks the balls. No one else has approached the table because now two twenties lay on the edge. She shrugs and gets down to business.

They play four more games, each for twenty. He can't believe he is losing, although it is never by much. She keeps it close and he keeps buying her drinks. He also doesn't understand why she isn't getting drunk. She's so small, so sweet, such a darlin'. The crowd follows every shot, clearly cheering her on, but he is unperturbed, almost dismissive of them and of the skill in which she pulls out every game. Finally, his friend comes over, puts his arm on Cowboy's shoulder and whispers something in his ear. Cowboy turns and looks at him and then at Angie. The muscles in his arms tighten and he puts his stick down on the table.

"I believe I've been hustled. That's right, ain't it darlin'? You've just hustled the shit out of me?"

Angie looks him directly in the eye as she picks up the twenties. "Not shit, darlin', just some green stuff and a couple of nice drinks. I do thank you." She says this without hostility but with a no-nonsense firmness, as if thanking a customer for his business.

It doesn't please or appease him and he takes a step toward her with his fist cocked. That is all Nick needs. He steps out of the shadows and plants himself firmly in front of the cowboy. Nick's hands are open, and his arms hang limply at his side, but his jaw is tight, and his nose is less than six inches from the cowboy's nose. They are about the same height, but Nick looks like he has a lot less to lose than the cowboy. The other must sense this, because he backs up a step and looks over at his friend. The friend steps forward and to the side of the cowboy, but three of the locals line up behind Nick. Everyone in the crowd holds their breath, but it's over. Cowboy looks around the bar and realizes he is out of his element. He looks at Angie one more time. Without another word, he puts his head down and leaves Ahab's with his friend.

Angie looks over at us and smiles. "Thanks, guys. Anyone want to play some slop ball? I need another margarita."

■　　■　　■

A LOT OF WEEKENDS WERE SPENT DANCING AND DRINK-ing at Ahab's. A few underaged kids were thrown out, some over-aged kids threw up, and through it all, the events and relationships of the summer of 1975 passed. I continued to work in the fields during the day, occasionally at night, gathering data for my dissertation. Most nights, however, took place in a different universe. Despite the earlier warnings from Carl and Cindi about the locals and their dubious deportment, I felt increasingly at home among the residents of Port Tarpon. It was no longer just research. Living beside the jetty with the Taiwanese roommate I rarely saw, I had settled into a balanced routine of academic study and alcoholic debauchery. Perhaps "balanced" isn't quite correct. Despite my best intentions, I had fallen somewhat behind schedule in gathering data.

I made a few dollars here and there helping at the Tarpon Marina Lab, bartending at the Party House, and washing dishes for three weeks at Blackie's, the Cajun restaurant. I smoked jays with Willie, Mitch, and some of the others, played poker with the same, and occasionally went on runs to Mexico for vanilla, tequila, and black beans or to Austin to see old friends and visit my advisor. It was a full life, but the fall arrived and the darkness descended, tipping the scales toward debauchery.

It was colder and the streets became increasingly deserted. Most of the tourist haunts shut down and motel vacancy signs transformed into "closed for the winter" signs.

Ahab's rehired Bruce as sole bartender to keep the doors open as a beer bar, but few people came. The students were gone and with them, most of the music and the party atmosphere. The bar became a hollow and lonely caricature of itself. Bruce and Donna again lived in the back with Mad Dog to keep them company.

■   ■   ■

I STOP IN ONE EVENING IN OCTOBER. IT IS MODERATELY COLD, about forty degrees, and the Island Road is silent. Donna has left for the weekend to visit Corpus with another girl and Bruce is in the mood to talk. He mentions his ex-wife and how he had wanted to call her and see if there was a chance to get back together. He admits his lifestyle is not much of an attraction for her or anyone else. He enjoys Donna's company and her youthful sense of humor, but he also realizes there is no future for him or her. He feels like he is approaching a breaking point, that he has to do something to shake himself out of the present if he is going to have a future.

Bruce and I sit at a table sipping on a bottle of whiskey I had brought, chasing it with Coke. I listen attentively, hoping to provide some advice, something to encourage Bruce to take action. I also think about my own life. *Have my academic aspirations been derailed? Is this just a temporary slip into darkness or is it more insidious, the start of a downhill ride into oblivion?* We talk quietly in the dark, the bar lit only by the parking lot lights, the open sign in the window, and the neon beer signs over the bar. Bruce is relaxed and thoughtful, but chain smoking nevertheless. It is clear he appreciates my company, and I keep thinking about Bruce sitting in the bar by himself, waiting for customers that aren't going to come.

I'm the first to hear the growing rumble outside, the unmistakable throaty growl of highway hogs. Nick and Bart ride Harleys, as do a few of the shrimpers on the island and from Snapper Pass, but this is a big growl, the kind made by a dozen or more choppers. The sound of scraping gravel and the sudden quiet as the engines die heralds the arrival of Captain Ahab's unexpected guests, a large party of them.

Bruce and I get to our feet as the front door swings open and the first black leather jacket enters. The first jacket is followed by thirteen others, all worn by burly bikers in outlaw leathers. One of the bikers is an older woman, and the men vary from early twenties to graybeards that could be in their fifties, possibly older. With them are two young girls. Everyone seems to be in a good mood, laughing and smiling, including the girls. Bruce quietly speaks to me as the group crosses the room.

"Let them do or take what they want, it's not our money."

I silently nod. Bruce walks behind the bar and I stand several feet away, partly behind the counter and partly blocking the opening. I'm not sure why, because I am not likely to prevent anyone from going where they want, but it keeps me closer to Bruce.

Bruce starts to pull some mugs out of the cooler, but one of the bigger bikers, sitting in front of him, tells him not to bother. They want setups for their own booze. I notice several of them have bottles: whiskey, vodka, and tequila, lots of tequila. Most of them find a table and sit down. The two girls, obviously underage, are sitting with two of the younger bikers. The girls laugh a lot and speak with excited enthusiasm, as if this is the biggest adventure of their lives. I look at Bruce and he shrugs, like, what are you going to do, ID them? Bruce lines up a bunch of plastic cups and begins filling them with different soft drinks as each guy orders. Only one guy wants beer. The biker woman doesn't want anything—she drinks her tequila straight from the bottle. A couple of the bikers put coins in the pool tables and several of them start playing eight ball. Another punches up some country and western tunes on the jukebox. A couple of twenties are lying on the counter.

"Let me know when that runs out," says one of the bikers.

As the group settles into its own party, largely ignoring Bruce and me, we stand close together and exchange a few quiet words.

"I know the Hispanic chick on the right," whispers Bruce. "Her name is Lucy, and she is only fifteen. Her mother works at the store where I get the Mad Dog." Lucy is sharing a cup of tequila and 7UP with one of the leathers.

"Shit," I whisper back. "If the cops come in, we'll all be busted."

"Not to worry," says Bruce, "no cop in his right mind is going to enter here with that many hogs outside. Just be cool and hope they'll have their fun and move on down the road."

We watch, wait, and pour. About eleven, the two girls are drunk and their clothes come off. Lucy is face up on the table, spread and naked. One of the bikers pours tequila on her crotch and another kneels in front of her and laps it off. Lucy giggles and another one of the boys in black waits in line for his turn. The other girl has disappeared into one of the two bathrooms with the woman and one of the gray-beards. Hard to know what they are doing but I remain at the bar with Bruce. He fully expects that one or more of the bikers will have sex with Lucy, but no one does. I can't tell whether this disappoints her or not. For her and me, the night has become hazy, losing definition and direction. The outlaw gang seems satisfied to play around and enjoy themselves. The other girl comes out of the bathroom and retrieves her clothes. Graybeard and the woman follow a minute later.

"I need a Coke for Juicy Lucy," says one of the bikers. "Need to sober her up before we drop her back in town." He stops and thinks for a second. "Got any coffee?"

Bruce shakes his head no, sorry, and pours him a Coke. Bruce makes change with the money on the counter—more has been added but still plenty left. So far, the bar has sold more than fifty sets ups, and the pool tables and jukebox have taken in several dollars. This is more money than Ahab's has earned in all the days and nights of fall combined.

At two thirty, the leader signals to his boys that it's time to leave the premises. "Don't want to get our friends here in trouble with the law, do we?" he laughs and looks at Bruce and me. The gang and the two girls leave and a minute later the rumble disappears down the road toward town. They leave the bar cleaner than is usual during a summer night. No damage, only a few minor spills, and a sense of relief as we lock the door and turn out the lights.

A few minutes later, I get in my car and slowly drive back to town, careful not to overtake the choppers and my new "friends." I'm sweating on a cold winter night as I enter the MSI parking lot. I can't believe that we have miraculously escaped an encounter with one of the most notorious biker gangs in South Texas. It will give me food for thought in the dark days ahead. Bruce, Donna, the Party House gang—is this what I came to the island for? It is the last night I spend with Bruce. I see him once or twice on the street and we exchange waves. Another summer will finish my dissertation research. Then what? The future looks as dark and unfathomable as the Gulf on a moonless night.

CHAPTER TWELVE

Baseball of the Amateur Flavor

SPRING AND SUMMER 1975

You might think that Port Tarpon was only about drinking, playing poker, and chasing skirts.

You'd be wrong, pardner. Sports were also a big part of the scene. In addition to barroom bicycle racing, swimming, and sun bathing while drinking, there was baseball. The local middle school had an impressive field situated near downtown, along a main street paralleling Island Road. Softball games were held between some of the churches, teams of school kids, and among the attendants of a few family reunions. Some anonymous donors had provided a metal backstop, decent bleachers, and nightlights on tall poles—some semiprofessional parks would have been envious. Naturally, a field of this magnificence begged for a league to schedule competitive games with teams of designated players. The Coast Guard station, the Marine Science Institute, a number of different stores and restaurants, and the Catholic Church were represented and had been playing for several years, to the delight of crowds of up to two hundred for the night games. The league paid for an umpire, and a couple of volunteers helped staff the field. Sponsors added their blessings on the outfield signs, and a manual scoreboard graced centerfield. A cinder infield, well-maintained outfield grass, and bright white chalk base lines presented an attractive setting for the national pastime. Of course, we all know that football is the national pastime of Texas, but, remember, Mustang Island was only nominally a part of the Lone Star State.

In 1975, a new team was announced for the Port Tarpon Community Softball League. The Party House decided to field a team and Bart, our once-upon-a-time minor league ball player, was our ringer. He had been playing for the Island Cafe team, but once we organized, he was solidly in our camp. He also became our manager-player. He could play any position, but his favorite was third base, and he could hum the ball to first on a tight rope. Despite his frequent bouts of drunken excess, Bart knew how to play, and he was willing to teach us.

As before, with the *George Dewey*, Willie took charge of selecting a name for the team. Most of the teams sported tags like the Tarpons, the Seagulls, the Tsunamis (as far as we knew, there had never been a Tsunami on the local beaches), and other nautical themes. The MSI team was, of course, the Longhorns. We decided that an armadillo was a more appropriate mascot. Connie, Bart's live-in unofficial spouse, suggested the Road Kill Armadillos, but we reminded her that a one-word name sounded spiffier. Moonshine, in a rare moment of clarity, came up with the winner. I think she simply misheard the original suggestion, but she proclaimed, "Armadildo, great name." We looked at her for a moment and then the laughter started. Armadildo, it was.

Someone wondered if the name would fly in a league containing a church team and with an audience composed of families with young kids. Mitch replied that we would just tell folks it was an unfortunate typo on the shirts, and we would change it next year. The bright purple shirts with the team name and Party House designation were ordered, and we settled down to team tryouts and practice under the occasionally sober eyes of Bad Bart.

Bart brought the prospective players together in mid-April. He had hoped to narrow down the team to about fifteen-to-twenty players, but only eight of us showed up, including Bart. That gave us the minimal team, leaving no one to substitute for injuries, absences, or pinch-hitting. Darla, game for just about everything, also wanted to play, but Bart said that if she played, Connie would also demand to play. "Ya can't have women in a men's locker room, can ya?"

We reminded Bart that we didn't have a locker room and that the women and men often shared the lavatory facilities in the Party House without so much as a blink. He thought about it and relented, and we ended up with Darla, Connie, and Debbie, Frank's spouse, on the team. Darla and Debbie were short, and Darla didn't have much arm power, but the three women weren't in bad shape, and they could run better than most of the men.

Bart's game was real baseball, that is, hardball, but he had made the adjustment to slow pitch and was ready to show us how to play the unofficial national game. The first question was, who can pitch? Slow pitch doesn't require a lot of finesse or power, but you do have to get the ball over the plate. Runs walked in count just as much as those batted in.

Jimmy demonstrated that he had the control we needed, and Mitch was selected as a backup on the mound. Frank had played for the MSI team the year before, and his size awarded him first base. Henry was small but fast on the draw and he made shortstop. Bart took third but was prepared to shift if and when needed. Mitch played left field when not pitching, and Nick took center. He had a great arm, second only to Bart. That left second and right field. These were usually considered the weakest two positions, and Bart tried out Arnie and me at both. Arnie had a better throwing arm, and I was always bothered by high pop ups because of eye operations when I was little. Bart put me at second. The girls would come in as runners when needed and play wherever they could do the least damage. Or so Bart thought. After we had been practicing for two weeks, Randy volunteered to join us, probably shamed by Darla. He also played outfield, rotating with Mitch and Arnie.

Bart was a driver on the field, barking orders, overseeing every play, showing everyone how to hold the bat and swing, and how to appraise the strike zone. "The umpire has a big strike zone," he said, "so don't let anything close get by you." Although all of the guys had played softball at some time in their lives, we appreciated Bart's efforts. Miraculously, he managed to remain reasonably sober, even during the evening parties after practice. This was his element, and he was as serious as sin. Bart vowed the Armadildos were going to win the League Cup. For some reason, he especially wanted to beat MSI and the CGS.

I was a bit nervous about my role at second. Most of the time when playing, I was assigned to right field, relegated to the place where the least harm might be done. I didn't have a very good arm, I wasn't accurate, and my fielding skills were suspect. Fortunately, most balls were hit to the left side of the infield or outfield. Bart did have me practice double play combinations, but he told me not to worry about it. He and Henry would do most of the work. "Just don't get wild and throw the ball across the street," he said.

"Don't worry," I told him, "I can't throw it that far."

Debbie was the surprise for Bart and the rest of us. Small in size, yes, but big in heart and determination. She could flag a ball on the run and get it back into the infield about as well as anyone. He had her also try out at second and shortstop, and he was satisfied he now had some flexibility in positions. We shouldn't have been surprised at Debbie's skill after she won the women's barroom bicycle race the year before.

The first game in our eight-team league came on Memorial Day weekend. Friday night lights in Port Tarpon brought a big crowd, including a sizeable bunch of Party House supporters. A large banner across the third base line bleachers proclaimed "Go Dildos." Sherry, Mickie, and Two-Ton Kelly had donned short skirts and team shirts to form an impromptu cheerleader squad. Willie and K.C. had volunteered as base coaches and helped during team practice.

"Who's minding the store?" I asked Willie.

"That'd be Janet. She doesn't care much for baseball, and she volunteered to keep the place alive until we finish the game."

Our opponent was the Catholic Church team, the Cardinals. Although they sported a red bird on their shirts, we suspected that the animal had little to do with their name. Most of their guys were young and played hardball on the high school team in Corpus. Port Tarpon was still trying to organize its own high school, and bonds had been proposed and rejected several times. Meanwhile, the high schoolers were bussed into south Corpus Christi, a thirty-minute trip each way. The Cardinals had been playing for several years, their manager was a young, athletic-looking priest, and their morale was sky high. I don't believe it was lost on them that they were playing against the only tavern team in town, and with one of the most disquieting reputations to boot. The crowd anticipated a holy war, and our team name did nothing to alter that impression.

Our games lasted seven innings, and most were relatively high scoring, definitely not pitcher's duels. Most of the batters connected—strikeouts were relatively rare, walks more common. This created a lot more entertainment for the crowd, that and frequent errors, not only in the field but with base runners as well. Alcohol was not permitted at the park, but a hotdog stand and soft drinks were available behind home plate. Nachos, chips, and soft cone ice cream completed the food inventory. Not bad for a small town. The crowds would swell further, filling the bleachers and the grass along the foul lines when summer arrived.

We were the home team, and I took up my position, made the customary practice throws to first base, and waited for the first batter. Not a single ball came my way during the first three innings. We were behind five to four when we started the fourth. I was both relieved and frustrated by the lack of activity at second. The most I had to do was stay near second with a runner on, but no one attempted a pickoff or a play to force a runner. Bart knew I wasn't the one to trust with a close play. With one out, the second batter hit a soft grounder directly at me. Forcing myself to relax and place myself directly in front of the oncoming ball, I snagged it in my glove and tossed it leisurely to first. Out by three steps!

"Way to go, way to go, Pete," yelled Bart, echoed by several teammates. The cheerleaders and Party House crowd added their support, and I felt like I had just completed an unassisted triple play.

The game went on and we played well enough but lost twelve to ten. I batted four times and got on safely twice, with a walk and an infield single. Not an award-winning performance, but I hadn't let the team down. Bart knew when to praise and when to bitch. He was mostly praise as we adjourned to the Party House and some well-earned brew. "Practice tomorrow at two," he said, "we can do better, and we will."

The bar was full, and Janet was running, trying to serve beer and make pizza, sandwiches, and maintain order. A number of barely legal, or not, kids were dancing, drinking, and having a good time.

"Did you check IDs?" asked K.C.

"Haven't had time, but I suspect the group on the back porch might not pass muster," she replied.

K.C. nodded, and Arnie joined him to start the routine, asking for photo IDs. Three of the girls and two of the guys were asked to leave, but several others with them also vacated and the bar was a bit roomier. Willie spelled Janet, and I helped until we caught up with back orders. By ten, the crowd had thinned, and we were mostly left with the regulars, including most of our team. We were still wearing our shirts and our cheerleaders had joined us. Sherry had on a bright yellow bikini bottom and the purple shirt. It was obvious she wasn't wearing a bra, but then she rarely did. Kelly, our hefty blonde bundle of joy, was shooting stick and yelling "Go Dildos" before each shot. Bart was still coaching, talking to individuals about what went right and what went wrong. He sounded like a real manager, all business, most un-Bart-like. My turn came, and we sat down at one of the back tables. We were drinking drafts, but Bart was as straight and sober as I could remember.

"Pete, you did real good tonight. Not a lot of chances, but you hung in there, made your plays, and did a respectable job at the bat. All I can tell you is to keep your focus, get used to the razzle-dazzle of some of the other teams—they'll try to confuse you when running bases —and we'll be fine." He slapped me on the shoulder and went looking for Mitch.

I sat back and enjoyed my evening of quiet triumph. I had met the challenge, and now I was looking forward to the next game, Tuesday against the Island Cafe. A Saturday day game against MSI would be the third game on the fourteen-game schedule, and that would be one we had to win. CGS and MSI were the most frequent champions of the league.

We beat Island Cafe handily, thirteen to three. Bart's former team was not happy that he had deserted them, and Bart was pleased as punch to beat them. Our practices were beginning to gel, batting was getting better, and the fielding was improving noticeably. The first game loss had awakened our competitive juices, and Bart's enthusiasm drove us on. Now we were one and one, looking toward the MSI game on the weekend. They had won their second to remain unbeaten, so we put them in our crosshairs. Frank and Debbie were especially anxious to show them up. Very few of the MSI staff and students had turned out for the bar-room bicycle race, and the winning couple was not going to forget or forgive their colleagues. Beating the Longhorns became the battle cry for the rest of the week.

A couple of the MSI students approached Willie and asked him if they could play for the Dildos.

"Why not the Institute," he asked.

"Dildos are a much cooler name and MSI already has a team," they said.

Willie referred them to Bart, and they joined the team. They must have wanted to beat their own group as much as we did, but because they had the chance to practice for only a couple of days, Bart decided to play them as pinch hitters or subs.

Two o'clock on Saturday was overcast but no visible threat of rain. The bleachers filled up early as we took our batting and fielding practice. It was hard to tell who some of the crowd was rooting for, although Carl and Cindi, wearing Longhorn shirts, left no doubt. A number of the administrators were also there with their families. Jimmy had sprained his arm and was having trouble putting the ball over the plate, so Mitch took the mound duties. Debbie was in right and Frank on first, Henry in left, and I was at second. Dildos or not, MSI was well represented on our team. The two new students sat on the bench, wearing our purple shirts. We now had a full team with reserves. The coin toss determined we were the home team, so we took the field and Mitch settled in to face the first batter.

He hit a home run over the left center fence, one that looked like it might make it to the Gulf a half-mile away. The crowd oohed and aahed as the MSI chemist, big and athletic, rounded the bases. Mitch had his head down, waiting for a replacement ball because we weren't going to find the last one anytime soon. Bart and the rest of us yelled encouragement, and Mitch received another ball from the umpire. I didn't know how many he had brought, but it was the first homer I knew about that cleared the field entirely.

They scored three runs in the first inning, and we got one back in the bottom of the first. After three completed innings, they were ahead eleven to two. The clouds, in the meantime, had become darker, denser, and a strong offshore wind brought a faint hope to our team. "Rainout! Rainout!" Our fans yelled and Sherry was stomping around like an Indian, appealing to the rain gods. We started the fourth and the skies opened. Rain, hail, and a strong wind cleared the bleachers and had us running for shelter. It lasted over an hour, and the infield was drenched. No tarps in Port Tarpon. Several of us sat in Nick's VW van, smoking, drinking beer, and waiting. Finally, at five, the umpire called the game and our huge deficit was history. We would reschedule toward the end of the season. As we made our way off the field, one of the MSI staff yelled at Willie and me.

"Lucky guys, but the weather won't save you next time."

Willie flipped him the bird, and we adjourned to the Party House. Bart was unhappy, and he was worried. It wasn't all Mitch's fault. Although he walked several batters, the field play was sloppy, and we just couldn't hit their pitcher. I had made one error, but it didn't lead to a run. Willie summed it up.

"We are still one and one, and we still have a shot at beating them. Drink up lasses and laddies." That we did.

The season progressed and we won two more games before facing the Coast Guard boys on a Wednesday night. They were young, fit, and had a lot of time to practice. It would be a tough game, but we had regained some momentum after the disaster with MSI. In the fourth inning they had two men on, at first and third, with two out. One of the night-lights had blown, leaving a shadowy area between first and second. Crack went the bat and a sharp grounder came my way. The runners were going, and I didn't have much time to make the play. I reached down, grabbed something solid and hurled it to Frank at first, right on the mark. Unfortunately, what I threw wasn't the ball, it was a rock that hadn't been cleared from the back of the infield. Frank ducked just before the rock reached his head. The man on third scored, and the batter rounded first and was headed my way. I found the ball, grabbed it and managed to tag him before he reached base. Bart didn't know whether to laugh or cry, but we got out of the inning with only the one run scored. It was my first unassisted putout. We beat CGS nine to six. I hit a double and drove in one of the runs, my first RBI for the season. Bart was the first to buy me a beer later. Frank never let me forget the rock—he would duck and put his hands in front of his face whenever we met at the institute or in the Party House. We'd both laugh and shake hands. Reputations are easy to make and hard to overcome.

The two teams with the best records would play one game for the cup, regardless of their wins versus losses. We lost the make-up game with MSI but beat them in the second faceoff. Their record was twelve and two, ours ten and four. The championship game was set for a Saturday in mid-July.

It was hotter than blazes as we took the field in the top of the first. Umbrellas, swimsuits, a garden hose, and lots of lemonade were on hand. A dark purple shirt didn't seem like a good idea on a day like this, but the burnt orange shirts of the Longhorns weren't that much cooler. By the third inning, everyone on the field and most of the spectators were drenched. The smell of coconut butter hung over the field, and new sunscreen was added every other inning. Instead of our usual many run games, it turned out to be a pitching duel. Jimmy was in rare form and their pitcher, as expected, was tough. Only a few people from either team reached base, and by the end of the sixth, it was tied one all. Bart was intense, and I knew he wanted this game in the worst way. I didn't want to think about his mood if we lost, especially since it was so close, the cup almost in our hands.

MSI didn't score in the top of the seventh, and it was our turn to break the tie or go extra innings. Everyone wanted it to end. Unfortunately, the bottom of our lineup was due, including me, Mitch, and Debbie. None of us were dependable hitters, and Bart was seriously considering pinch-hitting for one or more of us. The two students hadn't shown a lot of promise in the field, however, so Bart was afraid to sub us out if the game went extra innings. His instructions to me were short and clear.

"Get them to walk you, Pete, just get on base." I knew if I could, he would probably sub for Mitch or Debbie.

Fortunately, their pitcher was as tired and dehydrated as we were. After an initial strike, he threw three in a row outside the zone. Even with our generous umpire, I was ahead in the count and needed only one more. Bart had taken over third base coaching from Willie and he made it very clear he didn't want me swinging. I didn't. Strike two!

Bart called time and hurried down the line so we could confer.

"Guard the plate, Pete. Don't let him get it by you. Good eye, Pete, good eye."

He hurried back to third and I took my place in the box. The crowd was roaring, despite the heat. Several of the girls were promising me kisses all night if I could connect. The pitch came down the middle and I swung, fouling it off. Another pitch, same result. My team kept yelling encouragement, and Mitch stood on deck, wondering if he was going to bat or not. The next pitch almost clipped the corner, but it was out.

"Take your base," said the umpire.

The MSI manager yelled at him. "You've been calling that a strike all season. What's different today?" Some of the Longhorns were also protesting, but the umpire waved them off.

Now Bart had a problem. Did he bring in a hitter for Mitch, and did he get someone faster on the bases for me? He talked to Mitch briefly and walked back to the coaching box. Mitch stepped up. He struck out on four pitches. Debbie was on deck and Bart stayed with her as well. I think everyone was surprised he didn't sub for one of the MSI students. On the second pitch, she connected with a sharp grounder to shortstop. I was on the move, making sure I didn't get doubled up. Their player, usually with a sure glove, hesitated just a moment, all I needed to reach second. Two on and one out. Bart put one of the students in for Debbie to run and Frank, our lead-off, stepped to the plate.

Frank and the pitcher, a new professor down from Austin, didn't particularly care for each other. Stan was a Christian teetotaler and had made it clear on more than one occasion that he thought Frank and Debbie should pray more and drink less. Stan stared in at him and Frank returned it, with all the evil eye he could muster. He gripped his bat and twirled it slowly. He hadn't had a hit during the game, and he was itchin' to put one in play.

After four pitches and a two and two count, the big fat ball came down the centerline and Frank got all of it. I tagged and stopped halfway to third to make sure it wouldn't be caught, and it bounced off the wall. I rounded third while Bart was windmilling and going crazy. When I crossed the plate, the bleachers erupted. Debbie was on third, Frank, her loving husband, on second, and the game was over.

We had beaten MSI and CGS during the course of the season, and we had a piece of hardware to put on the top shelf overlooking the bar counter. Sherry grabbed the hose and doused the entire team as we celebrated at home plate. Bart and the MSI manager thanked the umpire, the team members shook hands, Frank and Stan glared at each other, and we departed for our watering hole. It was Saturday night, and the drinks flowed until three in the morning. The cops had been on hand during the game, and they didn't stop by after two in the morning to close us down. Something about having to check out a prowler call somewhere.

The next year was different and we came in fourth place, but none of us would forget the sweet victory in 1975, when we took our rivals down. Bart said it was the best win he had ever experienced, including his time in the minors.

CHAPTER THIRTEEN

Playing the Pimp Game

SUMMER 1975

I'm pretty sure it wasn't my idea or Willie's. We might have thought about it, but we wouldn't have proposed it. I blame it on Darla. We were sitting at the Gun 'n Reel, taking a break from the gang at the Party House, nursing beers and watching the usual crowd of tourists and fishermen mingling with a few of the locals. Willie, Darla, Melanie, and I were observing the efforts of two overweight middle-aged men trying to put the make on Mickie. She was getting shit-faced but wasn't having any of it. She was down at the other end of the bar, and the two guys, out-of-towners over-dressed in slacks and knit golf shirts, were huddled on each side of her, buying drinks and giving her the sweet talk. Darla, somewhat over the sobriety threshold herself, was speculating on whether Mickie would make a move with them.

"She could probably do both of them in the parking lot in less than ten minutes. Probably get twenty to thirty each from them and be back on her stool in fifteen." Darla took another swig and turned away.

"You think so? That easy?" Melanie looked at her and then at us.

Willie shrugged and said "Think it would be that easy,

Pete?"

"Not sure, never tried anything like that myself." We were thinking though. Easy money was always worth considering.

Melanie often seemed a bit naïve, although Willie and I both knew there was nothing innocent about her in bed. I think it was her schoolteacher persona, the fact that she spent most of the day around elementary school kids. She had a clean, washed look about her, even when she was chugging Lone Stars with the gang. She also had some pretty impressive breasts, the kind that fill out even the baggiest sweaters. My dad used to describe her kind of figure as "built like a brick shithouse." Indeed it was so, and it was also one of the reasons Willie and I liked to bop around town and drink with her in the other bars. The guys there would always look at her, then at Willie and me, trying to figure out which one she was with and how to get to her. Sometimes we took turns dancing with her, grabbing her around the waist and being as friendly as any boyfriend or lover would. The guys that didn't know us would start getting real itchy, turning on their stools to watch us, meaning they were watching her as she responded to our moves. We didn't get passionate or mushy, just real suggestive. Melanie could do that well. She had great big blue eyes lined with dark mascara, giving them the power of magnets. They pulled you toward her from across a smoke-filled bar and they held you, as if your eyes were prisoners and she had the only key you needed or wanted.

Willie grinned at Melanie and said, "Sure, why not? If you find the right dude with a bankroll, in town for some fishing and gettin' away from his wife—he'd be more than happy to share some of that with a sweet thing like you." He turned to Darla. "Sound about right to you?"

She looked back toward him, considering. "I wouldn't know, I always just give it away." I couldn't tell if she was saying it with pride or resentment, or if putting it on the line for money had never occurred to her. But she was right on. She had given it away a good number of times, even though she was married and the mother of two. I had never been the recipient, and I was pretty sure Willie hadn't been either, because her husband was one of our best friends and a business partner. Doesn't pay to sample the honey too close to home.

I had never patronized a prostitute, that is, a certified money-snatching professional, but I read a lot and had seen the usual movies, so my expertise, needless to say, was in demand. I looked at Melanie as I talked to Willie. "We should be able to pull this off. If you and I acted as her bodyguards, we could let her pick her mark and make sure she doesn't get into trouble."

Our girl and potential moneymaker looked doubtful but interested. "How would that work?"

"We could start at one of the bars, like here," answered Willie. "On a weekend, this place fills up with guys on the make with way too much money. The beer and booze are cheap, and there's no place else to spend the rest of it."

Melanie sat back on her stool. "You might be right, but that brings up a question. If that's all true, why isn't the place crawling with prostitutes, including high-priced ones?" Like I said, she could be naïve, but she wasn't stupid.

Willie took a sip of beer and replied, "They're here, but not in the taverns or cheap motels. You'll find them in the condos along the beaches. The real high rollers have connections and get appointments. That's the hundred to thousand-dollar stuff."

Darla looked at him in disbelief. "How in the hell would

you know about that?"

"I heard Sara's dad, Ray, talking about it with his retired business pals. Where to get pussy, with all of the frills."

"Frills?" I asked, signaling the waitress for another longneck.

"Yeah, good food and fancy drinks, satin sheets, massages, the works. It's for the real businessmen that come down from Austin and San Antonio. They fly in or sail in —you won't see them getting their hands dirty in a place like this."

Melanie spread her fingers out and turned them over. "My hands aren't dirty," she said in mock wide-eyed innocence.

"It's your eyes that are dirty, girl, your eyes." Darla was looking at her and giving her that knowing grin.

"The other thing that keeps the real pros away is all of the summer beach girls and locals, like you. Hard for pros to compete with available amateurs, even though they may not be that accessible to older guys like these."

"Ooh, Willie, you do know your stuff, don't you?" I smiled and took a sip from the fresh bottle that had just been set in front of me.

Willie smiled back. "Yeah, Pete, it isn't all in the books."

Mickie had turned her back on the two guys and was making a point of ignoring them. She tipped her glass toward us and Melanie gave a subtle finger wave back. Willie and I gave Mickie an encouraging smile, and she returned it.

Melanie turned first to Willie, on her left, then to me, on her right. "Then what? Just how are you two going to protect me?"

I jumped on it first. "It's not like we will be real pimps, like with the downtown girls. You'll do the approach, and we'll just be there to make sure no one gets hurt."

Darla couldn't let that one slide. "Who, Mel or her customer?"

Willie provided the plan of attack. "Select someone, well-dressed and drinking a cocktail. Let us know which one. We'll move away and give you room. Make contact with those seductive eyes of yours and he'll approach. Let him know you're available but for a price."

"How much should I ask for?"

Willie and I looked at each other.

"Not less than fifty, and that's for a quickie," said Darla, as if she had been giving it some serious thought.

"Wow, you think he'd pay that much?" More wide eyes.

It was my turn to be gallant. "Hell yes, Melanie, I'd pay you twice that much if I had the money."

She turned to me, put her hand on my arm, and said in her silkiest voice, "You'll never be able to afford me, so it's a good thing I let you sleep with me for nothing." I nodded in agreement, thankful for the little pleasures in a life well lived.

Willie had been thinking also and he elaborated. "Don't let him take you to a motel room. Since it's a quickie, do it in his car on the beach. I suggest you have him drive to a mile this side of the pier and park near the dunes where it's dark. Pete and I will follow you, discreetly of course, and park within sight of you. There are always a few lovers out there and we won't be obvious."

"Collect the money first, Mel. Don't do anything until he puts the folding stuff in your hand." Darla looked at Melanie like a drama coach, giving critical stage directions. Amazingly, for someone who had never taken a dollar, she seemed to know what to do.

"Yeah, good advice," I said. "That's the way the pros do it. Money first, then action." Willie looked at me with a grin on his face. He knew I had never been to a pro but said nothing.

"What kind of action? What should I do?" Melanie was starting to look nervous as she realized this wasn't a romp in the hay with her friends. "Suppose he wants to do something really weird, like tie me up or beat me?"

"Save that kind of thing for Peter and me. We'll be your weird guys, right, Pete?" Willie looked at me, but I needed to answer Mel.

"Get the price agreed on *before* you get in the car. You can do that in the parking lot before you leave. Keep talking to him and encouraging him on your way to the beach. When you get there, start undressing, maybe even let him undo a button or two. If he's got a big car with a nice back seat, do your thing there. If he's an older guy and overweight, he probably won't be up for a backseat session, so offer to give him a blowjob in the front seat."

The three of them stared at me, mouths open. "Whoo-wee," said Darla. "I want Pete for my stage manager. Wanna go into business?" Darla wasn't the cutest woman in town, but she could be persuasive.

"I think Randy would need to be in on that," I replied. I suspected her husband was too wholesome to be completely aware of Darla's wilder side.

"We'll be nearby in case you get in trouble. Scream or jump out of the car and we'll be on it," added Willie. "And Pete's right. If you get some older fat guy, we won't have any problems. The last thing most of them want here is trouble."

We let Melanie think about it for a few minutes while we watched Mickie leave the bar, alone. The two guys moved closer together, and we could tell they were disappointed by the outcome. One of the guys looked like he was in his fifties and he laughed like he was well over the sobriety limit. In other words, just about right for a drive on a dark beach.

Melanie made her decision. "Do you think I look the

part? I mean, suppose they turn me down?" That hadn't occurred to any of us. I would never turn Mel down and neither would Willie. We weren't sure about Darla—she had occasionally swung both ways—but she leaned over Willie and whispered something to Mel. It must have been encouraging, because she nodded and smiled.

Willie gave her one last piece of advice. "Don't go anywhere with both of them. Only one."

Darla added, "I'll keep my eye on the other one."

Melanie walked into the women's room, and Darla led Willie and me to an empty table. We picked a corner spot where we could survey the proceedings. Mel returned from the restroom, eyes a bit darker and a fresh coat of lipstick evident. Most of the time, the Island girls didn't wear much lipstick, usually only protective gloss for the beach. But there she was, sitting at the bar by herself, legs exposed in her blue jean shorts, tight blouse displaying those magnificent boobs, and made up for a date. It didn't take long. The older one sauntered over and plunked himself down next to her, leaned over, and said something. She smiled and he laughed. She laughed, and he bought her a drink. It was a cocktail, something she rarely drank, but she smiled sweetly and sipped at it as he downed another Jack and soda. Darla kept her eyes on the guy's buddy, but he stayed by himself, apart from his friend's negotiations.

Willie went out to sit in his car so he could spot Melanie and her friend when they started for the beach. I would follow them out and join him. After ten minutes of banter, the man paid the bar and they headed for the door, arm-in-arm. The guy turned and gave his buddy a wave and the guy gave him a thumbs-up and returned to his drink. I noted that Mel's drink was still three-quarters full. I joined Willie as she and her mark drove out of the lot.

"Did he pay her?" I asked, parking my butt in the suicide seat.

"Couldn't tell. They talked for a minute before she got in the car, but it was on the other side. I hope so."

We pulled out and headed for the beach, following their taillights at a discreet distance. Willie lit up a smoke and turned on the radio. The taillights turned right on the sand, as scheduled, and we stayed about fifty yards back. It was only about ten thirty and a few other cars were coming and going along the surf line. A half-moon provided just enough light to see the dark shapes of automobiles parked against the dunes, windshields facing out toward the Gulf.

"Hope this is a quickie," said Willie, "I'd just as soon get this over with."

"You know, real pimps often collect the money for their girls. Not always, but some of them do. And, they keep some of it, sometimes most of it." I looked at him, emphasizing the fact that any share of this for our trouble hadn't been discussed. It seemed that we weren't actually involved in the moneymaking business.

"Hmm, I forgot about that," he said. "This is really for Mel, isn't it? She's fulfilling some kind of wish fantasy and this will probably be a one-time thing." He looked at me, as if hoping for an affirmative response. We had known her for more than a year, ever since she had arrived in town as a new hire for the school district. We liked her, in all of the best meanings of the word. She was a friend, an occasional lover, and a lot of fun. It hadn't occurred to us until that moment the adventure was anything more than a whim, a dare resulting from a casual observation at the bar.

I looked ahead and yelled, "Where are they? Where in the hell did they go?" No taillights were visible in the near distance.

"Shit, oh shit," mumbled Willie, grasping the steering wheel.

We looked frantically behind us, hoping to see a car pulling into the fore dunes, but it was only darkness. The pier was still about a mile ahead of us and they had to be nearby, but where? We stopped and looked around us.

"Pull up to the dunes, maybe we'll see something from that angle," I suggested. Willie put the car in gear and turned right, leaving the wet sand and crossing the dry sand. Just where the dunes started, he turned the car around so we faced the water. He looked toward the left, and I looked right.

"I can make something out, looks like a car, about thirty yards away," he said.

"Think it's them?"

"Don't know. The only way I would is if I snuck up on them and read their plates with a flashlight." We had noted the car's number when they left the parking lot.

"I don't think that's gonna be compatible with the sex-for-sale business, my friend. Her friend was giddy but not drunk. That's probably them. Roll down your window and listen for anything that sounds like trouble."

We killed the radio and listened to the waves sliding up the beach. There was no wind and breakers were absent, as was often the condition on this part of the Gulf. We sat there, Willie smoking while I sat and tried to imagine what might be happening in the car with Melanie. We had screwed up big time.

"Suppose that isn't her?" I said. "Suppose this guy knew he was being followed and has taken her someplace and she is…"

"Shut up, Peter, just shut up. Unless you have a better plan, we just wait it out here. Keep looking for lights. She should be finished in less than twenty minutes and it's already been ten. Give her some more time."

"And if we see nothing, what then?" I asked, not sure I wanted the answer.

"Then we start driving back the way we came. I'm pretty sure they're not ahead of us, so we must have passed them while we were talking."

I thought a minute. "Willie, we passed the second beach cutoff road. It's on the way back. Suppose he turned there? They could be anywhere."

He thought a minute. "Yeah, I guess so. We'll run up the beach a bit and if we don't see anything, we'll take the cutoff."

The cutoff road connected to the main highway running the length of the island. *If the son-of-a-bitch turned left onto the highway, we will never find them.* I was beginning to feel sick at my stomach.

Ten minutes passed, then another five. Willie had gone through three cigarettes. As he put the last one out, he started the engine and turned on the lights.

"We go," he said and pulled forward, turned left, and started along the high dry sand. We would be close enough to identify car makes without needing to read license plates—we were looking for a four-door Lincoln. We passed two cars, neither like our target, before arriving at the cutoff road.

"They can't be this far back," I said, "even if they turned around and parked closer to town. Let's take the cutoff."

More in desperation for want of something better, he agreed. We turned onto the gravel connector and drove the mile to the paved highway. Seeing nothing to the left, we decided to return to town and recruit some help in the search. We drove the four miles back in somber silence, pulling into the Party House lot just as Melanie was stepping onto the front porch. We honked and she waved as we stopped and got out.

Willie and I were instantly at her side, asking her if she was all right and what had happened.

"He wouldn't pay me in the parking lot," she sniffled. "The S.O.B. was friendly and told me he would give it to me when we were at the beach, before we did anything."

She nodded toward the Gun 'n Reel. His Lincoln was parked where it had been before. Willie started toward the adjacent bar, but I pulled him back and Mel told him to forget it. He and I escorted her into the Party House, grabbed three beers, and sat on the back porch away from the others.

"We lost your car," admitted Willie, "it was my fault."

"Mine too," I added, "we both fucked up. What happened when you got there?"

She took a swig, visibly recovering and giving us a smile. She put her beer between her knees and her hands out, resting one on each of our arms.

"My fault too. You warned me not to go unless he paid me in the lot, and I didn't insist. He seemed so nice. We were driving toward the pier and he suddenly cut the lights off and turned into the dunes. When we stopped, I asked him for the fifty dollars, and he told me that I was a crazy whore and he would never pay that much for some bar pick-up." She spoke faster than usual but seemed composed. "I tried to stay friendly and reminded him we had agreed on it, and he said he would buy me a drink and something to eat when we got back to town. I told him two of my friends, the guys I was sitting with, were nearby and they would make sure I got paid and was okay. He stared at me for a couple of minutes and told me he suspected he was being followed."

"Then what?" asked Willie.

"He started the car and we came back to town. He dropped me off here and told me to stay out of his face."

"Let's go get the bastard," said Willie standing up. Willie was only five-seven and not particularly well built or tough. I had never seen him in a fight or even overly exercised about anything, but he had consumed enough beer to provide sufficient courage for a confrontation. He started for the Gun 'n Reel with Mel and me trailing, feebly protesting. As we rounded the front of the Party House, we could immediately see the Lincoln was gone. Darla was on her way to the Party House and looked up at us as she mounted the front steps.

"They just took off," she said, "and your friend wasn't looking any too happy. He came in, waved to his buddy, and they made tracks for the door. What happened?"

We filled her in as we went back to our place on the back porch. "I think our pimping enterprise is off to a rough start," I observed. Willie seemed to be happy the showdown had been preempted, and Melanie just wanted to forget the whole thing.

"I think I'll stick with freebies for friends," she said, cuddling up to Willie. Her eyes were still dark, and the magnets worked as well as ever.

Darla and I clicked longnecks and chalked up another get-rich scheme gone astray in the land of disappointed dreams. Later that night, Willie and I walked Darla and Melanie to their respective places. We had mellowed, and the near-disaster was already something to laugh about.

"Do you think we'll ever see him again?" asked Darla.

"I don't think so," said Mel, "after I told them what my body guards would do to him if he didn't pay." She looked at Willie, then at me. "What would you have done, boys, to protect my honor and… well, you know…?"

Willie took a puff on his cigarette, and I lowered my head as we neared Darla's house.

"Damn, well… you know… whatever we had to, I guess," said Willie. "Right, Pete?"

"Whatever we had to Willie, what you just said."

After we dropped off the ladies, Willie and I headed back to the Party House for some serious after-hours drinking and thinking—thinking about what might have happened and drinking because it didn't. My thoughts, however, kept returning to how an innocent graduate student had slid so easily from the world of crab behavior to encouraging my friends to prostitute themselves.

CHAPTER FOURTEEN

Lawnmower Ted

SPRING 1975 TO SPRING 1976

They didn't know if that was his real name. That's what they called him, if they called him anything at all. He was old and scraggly, a man of few words and few beers. The latter because he couldn't afford more, the former because he was able to express his whole philosophy of life, which he did often, in a loud cracking voice directed to the bar more than to the people in it:

"Fuck 'em all."

That was it. Very little else came from LT except an occasional grunt or "shit" or something completely unintelligible. LT's daily schedule was also simple: borrow a lawnmower from Jimmy, the young but three-generation island resident, push it down the street, and find someone who needed a lawn mowed. Most lawns in town weren't worth mowing. A few sparse weeds growing out of the sand and shell that comprised the local "soil" was the best most homeowners could hope for. Renters could have cared less, and most of the town was renting. Still, Ted was able to find an occasional patron willing to give him a dollar or two to cut some of the weeds. They knew what he needed it for, and no one wanted to begrudge a seventy-year something his suds.

He would work for an hour or two, depending on the sun and how long he had looked for a lawn, and return the mower. Jimmy left his garage unlocked, and the mower was always there by early afternoon. By two, Ted was in the Party House, sitting next to the jukebox, sipping on a draft. Drafts were twenty-five cents, a good deal even then. The mugs were chilled, and LT could make a beer last almost an hour before ordering another one. The first two or three were usually consumed in total silence. Ted would focus on the mug he held firmly with both hands, watching the bubbles rise slowly to the surface. When they stopped, he was ready for another. Sometimes he stared at the Corona sign over the bar, lost in his own universe of weedy lots and a past he never revealed to anyone.

The others sometimes speculated, usually on a slow afternoon, just what it was Ted contemplated. Maybe a new lawn mower of his own or a place where they had real lawns? Probably not. Mitch thought about how many more beers he could do a day if they were twenty cents instead of a quarter. Sometimes, one of the gang bought him a draft or the bartender poured him an extra. He added color to the bar and kept some of the more easily offended tourists away.

How did he get the name Lawnmower Ted? Willie thought it was Bart that first called him that, but within a week everyone knew him without knowing him. He showed up in early May, before the students hit the beaches and the fishermen hired the deep-sea charters. Jimmy must have known him first because he started mowing yards soon after arrival. His first "fuck 'em all" graced the Party House on his first night at the bar, and the expression became his handle as much as his nickname. One day, Sherry, during her daytime shift behind the bar, kept a tally of how many times he expressed himself before he stumbled out of the bar: twenty-seven utterances between one in the afternoon and eight that evening. He didn't stumble because he was drunk. Ted always stumbled, coming into the bar, pushing the mower, or walking about town.

Ted stayed at a room in the old Tarpon Inn. He paid for it and an occasional meal with his social security check and a bit of broom pushing for the hotel. But mowing lawns was for beer, Ted's hard-earned justification for living the life of luxury.

Mostly Ted drank his beer and left everyone alone. There was an occasional exception. One afternoon, about five, a group of students dropped in. This in itself wasn't unusual. The Party House was near the docks and in proximity to two restaurants and several other watering holes. Two guys and three girls, all of them with early college freshness and few other clues to life, stepped in and up to the bar. Ted, as was his habit, pointedly ignored them, secure in his corner by the juke. One of the girls, a tanned brunette with short hair and a revealing tank top, stood behind Ted and next to the jukebox. She pulled out a couple of quarters and turned to select some songs. She punched two or three but couldn't decide on the next. She turned back to Ted and said, in an overly cheerful voice that only the perky can muster at that time of day, "What'cha wanna hear, sweetie?"

Ted didn't respond, despite the fact that she was almost breathing down the back of his sunburned neck.

"Maybe something old-timey?" she said, winking at one of her male companions.

Several of the gang farther along the bar, sitting at tables or playing pool, watched in anticipation. Entire hours could pass inside the bar without some excitement or drama. Surely this brazen intrusion into the Lawnmower Man's personal space would do it. Sherry, putting mugs in the chiller, decided intervention might be the best course, but whether it was to rescue Ted or the girl wasn't clear.

"I thank y'all might best jus leave him be," she drawled. "What can I get ya?"

One of the guys indicated they wanted a round of longnecks and Sherry was just about to start checking ID when Ted stood up. He wasn't tall but the perky one was still several inches shorter. She backed up a step, not sure what Ted was going to do. He looked at her, looked at the jukebox, then out at the bar without focusing.

"Fuck 'em all," he bellowed, and walked out.

After a moment of stunned silence, the brunette turned to her friends, eyes close to watering, a slight but noticeable tremor in her voice.

"Did he mean us?" she asked, first to no one specific, but then to Sherry.

Sherry could have said no, that this was Ted's only way of communicating his deep and carefully considered thoughts to the world. Instead, she said, "Sho did, honey. Thas eggzactly what he meant. I've never heard him so upset."

The brunette went running for the door and the rest of her group followed. None of the bar regulars ever saw them again. Sherry could be that way. She didn't own any part of the business, and she got paid the same and drank the same, whether customers were there or not. She just didn't care much for college kids and perky brunettes. Sherry wasn't that old—in her mid-thirties with a hard, darkened skin from a lot of beach time. She had a decent figure and she usually wore a bright lime bikini and a pair of flip-flops when working the bar. But she was nobody's fool and didn't take crap from anyone, especially from anyone whose age she needed to check.

The second notable time Ted was demonstrative was

when someone loaded a new record on the box he particularly liked. It was "Why Don't We Get Drunk and Screw" by Jimmy Buffett. Buffett was a favorite on our music lists—his songs about laid-back island life and drinking resonated with most of the regular customers. This particular song wouldn't play at some of the family restaurants or tourist-oriented taverns, but it was just right for the Party House. The first time it played while Ted was occupying his stool, the effect was immediate and transformational. Ted looked up, turned around, stared at the jukebox, and said, "Well, I'll be damned."

Henry was still selecting songs and Ted stood behind him as he punched the buttons. Henry looked up and asked him if he liked the song. Ted nodded, so Henry punched it again. From that time on, whenever Ted was in the house, someone would play Buffett's raucous piece. Ted would usually sing along or bang his mug in time. Once, after several hours of sipping, he actually stumbled through his interpretation of a solo two-step.

Unlike most business establishment jukeboxes, the Party House owned this one and the records in it. Party House regulars were solely responsible for the contents, and they contributed to the collection, changing the repertoire according to their whims. The screw song was never taken off, even after Ted disappeared.

The only other things that seemed to trigger a predictable reaction from Ted were the dogs that frequented the bar. There were several regulars and a few occasional short-time strays that could be found, either on the porch or inside, usually under a table. The bar kept several water dishes in various corners, in exchange for the dogs helping keep the floor clear of dropped pizza, chips, and whatever. Ted liked them and often stooped to run his gnarly fingers through their coats or give them a pat on the butt or head, whichever was closest. He once poured part of his beer into an empty water dish on an especially hot day. This had to be a big sacrifice for a man who nursed his suds as carefully as Ted did.

"How old do you think Ted is," asked Willie one night. Several of the gang were sitting around with a bottle of bourbon and some setups. The question was also similar to the introduction of another song on the box, one that Ted occasionally requested.

"Gotta be at least seventy-five, maybe more," offered K.C. "Hard to tell. He's spent a lot of time in the sun. Probably did manual most of his life."

"Scrawny people live a long time. His arms don't have muscles, they're made of wires," offered Sherry. She was off-duty, drinking steadily, and sitting between Mitch and Willie. They thought about that a while. None of them had reached forty, and they talked about how someone comes to a town from nowhere, settles in at Ted's age, and becomes a fixture with minimal needs and wants. Most of them had arrived in their twenties; a few had been born and grown up on the island. But old newcomers like Ted were a rarity.

"What's his story?" Mitch asked, not expecting an answer. "Why, 'fuck 'em all?' What do you think triggered his bitterness?"

"What? You're some kind of psychiatrist? What the fuck do you care?" snorted Willie, downing another shot of Old Crow. He was almost as shit-faced as Sherry. With her old man shrimping the Gulf for three weeks, it was easy to guess how this night might end.

Sherry put her arm on Willie's shoulder, gave him her best closing time horny grin, and said, "Let's go play Ted's favorite song."

■   ■   ■

A year later, almost to the day he arrived, Lawn-mower Ted stopped showing up at the Party House. He had rarely missed more than two days in a row, and it had been a week since anyone had seen him. Jimmy comes in and sits down. Asked about the man, Jimmy just shakes his head.

"Hasn't borrowed the lawnmower in a week. Don't know nothing."

Sherry calls the Tarpon Inn and asks her friend at the desk if she has seen Ted. "About five days ago," she is told. "He wasn't looking too good, but I've been off for several days. I'll ask around."

That was all anyone knew for another week. On a slow Thursday evening, Mac, one of the better town cops, stops in. "Need a cold one?" asks Janet, one of the part-time barmaids. She is making pizza for Willie, Arnie and Pete, the only customers in the place except for Randy's rag-tag Airedale. He was asleep and wasn't much of a conversationalist anyway.

"I need to pass on the brew, but I've got some news about Ted. Thought you oughta know." They could tell from Mac's face that the news wasn't good. Mac was usually happy-go-lucky and as close to being a Party House regular as the law would allow.

"The coroner in Snapper Pass called us this morning and asked if we could identify a body they pulled out of the Intracoastal. He was an old guy and didn't have ID, but they thought he might have fallen off the ferry. It looks like he had been in the water for a couple of days. An autopsy is pending. I went over and identified Ted. We checked at the bank and found his social security account. The checks come in for Charles Littlestone. A search for relatives is underway, but there might not be any. Can you guys or anyone else you know add to that?"

They sit in silence—there is nothing to add. They tell Mac to check with Jimmy and he leaves. Janet serves the pizza and pours them all a beer. They eat and drink slowly, still silent, thinking about what they had just heard.

Lawnmower Ted was a stranger they had accepted into their community as one of their own. But he wasn't really. They never knew him, and he didn't know them. What impact did his presence make and what ripple resulted from his passing? It was hard to understand the emptiness that it left. The Party House was sometimes quiet and lonely, often crowded and noisy, but it was never empty. Emptiness is more than just too much open space. It is more about a feeling of hopelessness, of the dreaded inevitability of mortality. It is a somber reflection on the survivors. Willie, waxing philosophical, takes a sip and quietly says to the others, "We will age, we will die, and our party will end."

Did Lawnmower Ted choose to leave the party or was the choice made for him? They would never know.

A quarter hits the slot and Janet pushes a button. Ted's favorite song fills the bar. Willie and Arnie look at each other for only a moment before shouting simultaneously, "Fuck 'em all."

CHAPTER FIFTEEN

It's Not Gambling If You Do It Right

SUMMER 1975

During my first lunch with Mitch two years earlier, he asked me if I played poker. I indicated an interest, and I later joined the Port Tarpon Social Drinking and Card Ensemble. The social drinking part was indistinguishable from all of the other drinking in PT, but the poker games were wide open for anything anyone could dream up, if the person was sober enough to explain the rules. Some of the games were definitely not to be found in Hoyle, and most of them would be banned from any respectable casino. The nice thing was that Charlie's, and the other places around town where we played, were not respectable. The gang consisted of the usual crowd, but not all members were present at any one game. Nick, Willie, Mitch, K.C., Arnie, Henry, and I made up the core, the regular gamers that quickly disregarded other tasks or obligations to gather and play. As Mitch had indicated, the stakes were low, mostly change, and no one lost much to the pot, even after a long night of drinking. It was the gossip, the banter, the wry political rhetoric of Willie, and the good-natured commentary of the group that made the evenings noteworthy. One rule was carefully adhered to—no women. We talked and joked about them, told our tales, real or fantasized, but their presence at the table was neither wanted nor permitted. But even that firm guideline was violated once.

We rotated the host location between various houses and Charlie's motel. My place was too small and on the Institute grounds, so I didn't host, but most of the others took their turns. Nick managed Charlie's, and about half of the games were held there, usually in the same room where Sara and the gals would have their bachelorette party.

We didn't have poker chips, so everyone was encouraged to bring lots of change. A big night of losses or winnings rarely amounted to more than ten dollars. We all brought what we wanted to drink, although the host often provided setups and soft drinks. Our games varied from straight five-card draw, five and seven-card stud, to a variety of high-low games. The crazy games included no peek, a number of designated wild card forms, and liar's poker, where everyone saw your cards but you. Other players occasionally joined in: Bart, Randy, Jimmy, and Fast Eddie, our designated minister from St. Melancholy Island. Leonard and Skip, two of the local musicians, occasionally came by and sometimes we played with ten people and two decks. Interestingly, Texas hold 'em, now the classic worldwide poker game, was unknown to us at the time.

Our single exception to the no-female rule came one night when I brought Eide, a seventeen-year old visiting Port Tarpon from Kansas. Her mother lived on the island, but Eide had left home with a guy when she was fifteen and had only been back a few times since. She would stay for a week or two, then disappear for several months. She was slim, blonde, and had an infectious smile. She looked and acted older than her age, and she had an ID to get her into any place she desired. She got into our game by volunteering to serve us drinks when we played at Charlie's. I didn't actually bring her, but I told her where we were playing and said she was on her own with regard to the motel staff.

Some of the women at the motel also played barmaid and brought us fresh setups or ice during the night. Unlike the motel staff, Eide decided to dress the part for serving. After arriving at the motel, she changed into a special costume as we set up the table and prepared to play. It was also customary to puff away on cigars while we played. We preferred wine-soaked Crooks Brothers—cheap, smelly, and just the right touch for our rough and tumble gambling images.

We had a phone in the room to call for service, and Eide came with drinks and ice about eight o'clock. We had been playing for less than a half hour and expected to see one of the regular staff, usually dressed in cut-off jeans and a summer blouse. Eide was attired in a black French maid negligee, transparent. She was wearing silk red panties and no bra. She entered the room and quietly distributed the drinks while all of us, including myself, sat transfixed and openly gawked.

I had only known her for a couple of weeks. We were not intimate friends, but I had shown her around the Institute and my field sites, and we had spent some time at the beach. But for this display, I was completely unprepared.

"She with you, Pete?" asked Nick, chomping on his cigar and grinning.

Eide smiled at me and said, "Hi, Peter. Is this okay?" She held the thin skirt out from her sides and twirled slowly in a circle so we could get the full treatment.

"I'd say that is more than okay," exclaimed Arnie with untethered enthusiasm, "a hell of a lot more than okay."

"What's your name?" asked K.C. The game had halted, and everyone's cards were face down on the table. Eide had their full attention.

"Eide." She gave him her best seductive smile. "It's always been my dream to play in a real poker game, with real men, not with some kids for bottle caps."

There were seven of us at the table, and we weren't expecting any additions. Nick was the host, and we shifted our focus to him. If an exception was to be made, it would be up to him, pending the group's approval.

Nick was still chomping and puffing. "I've never let Toni play, even though she asked a couple of times. What about you Willie?"

Willie thought a moment and ran his hand through his stringy hair. "No, I never told Toni she couldn't play, but Sara asked once, and I told her it was the men's night out and besides we wanted to be able to talk about the women."

Eide stood quietly, one hip thrust to the side in a pro-vocative pose, not lost on any of the men. I kept looking at her, not recognizing the quiet teenager I had spent a few innocent moments with.

Fast Eddie was the one who proposed a compromise. "Because she took all of this trouble to dress up and serve the Club, I suggest we let her sit in on a few hands. This would fulfill her wish and provide us with a few more minutes of leering pleasure. That okay with you, Pete?"

Before I could answer, Mitch said, "It works for him."

With that settled, Nick instructed her to come back at eight thirty with fresh drinks and ice and she could sit in for a round of deals. It was dealer's choice, so that meant she could play for eight hands. Willie told her we would explain the rules and betting as we went.

"I assume you brought some money, honey," said K.C.

Eide lost her composure and blushed. "Oops, I forgot I needed money to play."

"I'm afraid we don't play for bottle caps," remarked K.C.

I immediately came to her rescue and told them I'd cover her antes and bets. No collusion between you two, Arnie warned. Whatever she owes you, you settle later, as you see fit. I agreed, Eide left with a smile at me, and we continued our game.

At eight thirty sharp, Eide returned with the drinks, passed them around, and sat at the eighth chair. I was immediately to her left and it was my turn to deal. I gave her a couple of dollars change, hoping it would last through the round of play. We all threw a dime in the pot, our usual ante. Thinking I would make it easy for her, I announced five-card stud. Willie, helpful as always, started to explain the house rules, but she gave him a flirtatious smile and told him she knew that one. So she did. Her jack up was the highest showing, and she bet twenty cents. Five callers, including myself, and the next card came around. K.C. drew an ace and he took over, betting a quarter and telling Eide he had a pair of them.

"Do you now, laddie?" Willie grinned, took a sip and called. He had a queen up. I considered dropping but decided to stay. Now there were four of us. Eide's smile never faltered, and she played like she had been racking chips for years. It suddenly occurred to me that maybe she had.

The fourth card came out. It was Willie, K.C., Eide and I. Now K.C. had a pair of sevens and an ace showing. Eide hadn't improved her single jack. Willie had a ten to go with his queen, and I had a five up to match my five in the hole. Betting around was raised twice as we tried to run at least one more player out of the pot. There was almost five dollars in the center, a healthy amount for our casual game. Eide had a cola with ice, and Mitch asked her if she would like it flavored with a bit of rum. He held the bottle out to her, but she shook her head and told him she had already added some, producing a new look of awe and wonder from Willie and Arnie. The fifth card came out.

K.C. hit an ace—he had two pair showing. Eide doubled her jack. He made no attempt to hide his delight as he threw fifty cents, our maximum bet, into the center. "Run fools, run" he chortled.

Willie did just that, but Eide called. I folded. K.C. looked at her, not quite believing what she had done.

"If you can beat what I have showing, you should raise. If you can't, save your money, darlin.'"

She gave him her sweetest smile. "This is only my first hand and I don't want to take all your money just yet." She turned over her jack in the hole for the set. It was actually a smart bet to call, because K.C. might have had a boat, but he didn't. He watched glumly as Eide raked the coins and two bills. The rest of us were laughing and drinking and also getting our eyefuls of Eide's considerable charms. When you have the cards, however, you don't need the distractions.

K.C. wasn't glum about losing. None of us cared that much, and we all took our turns being the goat, either for a hand or the entire night. But K.C. had lost to an under-age girl, the first time one had ever played. He would be immortalized in the annals of the PTSD&CE for being the first, but he wouldn't be the last. Out of the eight hands Eide played, she only folded once and she won four times, regardless of what crazy game we played. "Beginner's luck," she said, each time she raked a pot. After the fourth hand, she refilled her rum and coke, adding a generous amount of Bacardi. She now had about ten dollars of our money in front of her.

The eighth and last hand passed to Eide to deal. She shuffled the cards like a casino dealer, never leaving the table surface, her nimble fingers in complete control. We sat there in silence, mesmerized by her presence and stunned by her success. She called baseball, a seven-card stud variant with threes and nines wild. A four up gave you a bonus card in the hole. Fortune shifted quickly in a game like this, and it usually took a boat, flush, or something better to win. Four of a kind was not a rare hand in baseball. I cut and she dealt them out, each card landing precisely in front of each position.

"Pete, where did you get her?" Willie's mouth was open as he picked up his cards. This last demonstration of dealing aptitude left no doubt in any of our minds that we had been suckered.

"Remember pool table Angie at Ahab's?" I said. "I feel like Cowboy must have felt."

We finished Eide's last hand, a wild betting affair with everyone staying in, trying to beat her and also hoping the final card would bring glory and salvation. It didn't. After the last bets and calls, Eide turned over four tens for her fourth and final win. "Railroad tracks," she proudly announced and stood up. "Thanks guys, this has been a lot of fun. And thank you, Peter, for inviting me." She gave me a big kiss on the forehead and picked up her twenty-some dollars and walked toward the door.

"Will you still be working as a server?" I asked.

"Oh, sure, you don't think I got all dressed up just to play a few hands of poker, do you? Pete, I hope you'll take me home when the game is finished. Just call and I'll be back with whatever you need, guys."

"How about some of your luck and all of our money?" said Arnie.

"A working girl has to keep something for herself, don'cha think?" With that and a quick wiggle of her butt, she was out the door.

It was time to take a piss, refresh our drinks, light up cigars and cigarillos, and talk about the storm, Hurricane Eide, who had just washed ashore and destroyed our manly sanctuary.

"Did you see the way she dealt?" asked K.C. "And the games? She knew them and then some."

"Thank you, Peter, this has been a lot of fun," intoned Willie in a high snotty voice. Then, in a gruffer voice, "You'd better be losing the rest of the night."

It was Mitch's turn next. "Taking her home, Pete? Your place or hers?" They all looked at me, knowing I didn't have a home and I had previously informed them she didn't have any privacy at her place.

"Probably just drop her off at her place," I answered. But then I thought about her lacy negligee. "Maybe after we take a short ride along the beach."

Fast Eddie was usually the quiet one, the least likely to add fuel to the fire. "You know I could marry both of you here, before you leave for the beach. Make it legit." That brought another round of laughter and obscene speculation as we settled down at the table to continue our game, albeit now considerably weaker in financial resources.

Eide was good to her word and made a few more appearances, each seductive and enticing. The game broke at midnight and Eide returned in her regular summer clothes as we cleaned up the room, stacked the bottles, emptied waste baskets, and did our usual post-game replay of who won and lost what. To Willie's (and I suppose everyone else's) satisfaction, I was the big loser, almost fifteen dollars.

"Well deserved laddie," said Willie, his hand on my shoulder. "But maybe you'll end up the big winner tonight after all." He glanced at Eide, but she was talking to Fast Eddie and Mitch.

Eide and I walked out and just before we disappeared through the door, she slipped her arm through mine as we strolled hip to hip down the wooden walkway. We didn't take the beach drive—she and I were both tired, but I still felt like I had come out ahead on the night. There are stakes and there are stakes. Some involve money, and others involve the recognition and envy you earn by the small victories. I felt like it was me, not Eide, that had cleaned the gang's wallets that evening.

Eide left town a week later, and I never saw her again. Other than the kiss at the poker table and a brief kiss when I dropped her off that night, she and I consummated *nada*. It was also the last time the Port Tarpon Social Drinking and Card Ensemble allowed a female to join them at the table. As Arnie put it so succinctly later, "Once hustled, poor you, but twice hustled, you'd be a sorry bastard."

■ ■ ■

THERE WERE OTHER POKER GAMES AND AN OCCASIONAL crap game that graced Port Tarpon from time to time. We never participated because most of them involved a different crowd in the community. Higher stakes games were held in the condos and sometimes a table would set up at one of the other bars, motels, or someone's house. One night in September, word came around that a really big show was scheduled, a high-stakes game with a ten thousand-dollar minimum buy in. Most of the people, even the successful businessmen and property owners on the island, didn't have anywhere near that kind of money. The rumor said that the hosts were a pair of out-of-towners, Arabian owners of several motels, condos, and other businesses along the Texas coast. Other players were flying in from Fort Worth,

San Antonio, and other points to participate.

Much of the news was conveyed to us by Daisy, a looks-to-kill blonde who occasionally joined us at the Party House and during beach parties. She was a part-time fashion model, and we had heard she also appeared in a few soft-core porno flicks. She had been invited, along with a select few others, to help serve drinks and food and provide a pleasant background for the high rollers. Daisy was telling us about the opportunity to pick up some fat tips, especially if she showed a bit of thigh or whatever else was requested.

Patrick was a forty-odd year shrimper who patronized the bar from time to time. He owned his own boat, had a working crew of five, and knew the best fishing grounds in the Gulf. As a result, his once-a-month paydays were fat, and he and his crew enjoyed the good life, be it ever so brief before the next shrimp trip. Everyone liked Pat. He was affable, generous, single, and hard working. He earned his money and spent it on himself and his friends. He was also close friends with the bottle but didn't do drugs.

He did have one other vice, however. He liked to gamble. Cards, dice, horses, dogs—you name it and he'd bet on it. He once bet someone at the bar that the next person to walk in after the clock hit five would be a woman. He made the bet at four thirty and put a hundred dollar bill on the counter. It took five others, placing twenty each, to cover his bet. Now one might suspect that this was a setup, that Patrick had arranged for a female friend of his to hit the door at five sharp. Not so. The first person to enter the Party House after five, 5:03 to be accurate, was Henry. The crowd at the bar, all staring at the door, burst into wild applause as Henry crossed the threshold, bewildered by the sudden celebration. As the c-note was changed and the twenties distributed, Patrick ordered another beer, as if he had merely lost a game of pool or flipped someone for the next jukebox pick.

When Daisy related what she knew about the forthcoming game, Patrick became excited and took her hand. "Daisy, I want to get into that game. Can you help me?"

She looked at him and shook her head. "Patrick, it takes ten big ones just to sit at the table. These guys play in a different universe. You don't want any part of that." We had gathered around to hear the dialog and we were in agreement with Daisy. Patrick had never played in our game—loose change didn't interest him.

"I have the ten grand and more," he stated. "When and where?"

She hesitated but told him it would be the coming Saturday night, at Big Ray's, the business club of a local deep-sea fisherman. Big Ray was retired but generally acknowledged to be one of the wealthier residents in town. Ray, not to be confused with Sara's dad, was also one of the larger game hosts, but no one was aware of any previous game that approached the stakes of the Saturday get together.

"How many players?" Patrick asked.

Daisy wasn't sure. The party would invite about fifty, but this included women, not all of them wives of the male guests, serving staff, and a number of onlookers. If Patrick could provide some proof of his ability to meet the minimum, she would ask Ray about inviting him. Patrick thanked her, and we continued our low-key entertainment in the bar.

Daisy provided Patrick with the answer he wanted. He was in. Show up on Saturday at six, she told him. Dinner and drinks would be provided. Bring your bankroll, wear something nice, and be prepared to play cards with some pros. Patrick was scheduled to go out Saturday morning for his usual three-week run, but he called his crew and told them to postpone the trip until the following Monday. "Even with the luck of the Irish, I may need an extra day to recover," he told them. We wished him luck, but more than one of us feared that our friend was going to be well in over his head and ten thousand dollars poorer before the evening was finished.

We didn't hear anything that evening, which wasn't surprising. A game like that could go for hours, even days in some cases. But Patrick didn't show up on Sunday or Monday. His crew was still in town and one of them came into the bar Monday evening. Bill sat down and ordered a beer.

"How did it go, the big game?" asked Arnie, serving Bill a frosty mug of Lone Star.

Bill's face told the story. "He lost. He lost big."

"The whole ten thousand, huh?"

"Nope. He lost the ten thousand, about ten thousand more, and then…" Bill choked up, about to cry. Arnie waited, saying nothing, feeling the tragedy arrive like drift-wood from a boat lost at sea. "He lost the damned boat. The crazy fucker lost our boat. We ain't goin' nowhere, not shrimpin'—not fishin'—not squat. We're done." He took a long sip and hung his head down.

Arnie stood up straight. "The boat? How did he do that?"

There was a moment of silence as Bill drained the glass and held up a finger for another. As Arnie refilled his glass, Bill started to reach into his pocket, but Arnie said, "No, this one and the first one are on me. "What happened, Bill?"

"I wasn't there, none of us were. But Pat told us yesterday that the boat was gone, new owners, he said. We'd have to get on with someone else, because the boat would be moved to Galveston, and they already had a crew. Pat had already lost most of his cash, and he was in a big pot and he had a full house, aces over. He figured he couldn't lose, so he called a bet and raised by putting his boat deed on the table. Why he even had it with him, I can't figure. They looked at it, checked with Ray on its condition, and approved the bet. The winning hand was four deuces, and Pat had to sign the boat over. He said they bought him a drink before he left. Pat told me he thought seriously about putting his forty-five to his head that night and leaving it all, but he wanted to tell us and thank us for our times. At least we all got paid before Pat threw it on the table."

Mitch and Willie walked into the bar, and Arnie summarized Bill's sad tale. They bought Bill another beer and another one after that. They had hoped Patrick and some of the rest of the crew would appear, but they never did. Daisy provided her version of the game on Wednesday to a larger crowd.

"I didn't see the whole game because they kept us busy bringing drinks and serving food, most of it away from the table. But I knew Pat was losing. The chips in front of him disappeared within an hour. I know he bought back in but those didn't last much longer." She looked at each of us, aware that this was not a story any of us wanted to hear, but we felt compelled to know what happened, especially since Bill hadn't been a witness. "When the big hand played, the one where Pat lost everything, the room got silent and a large crowd gathered around the table. The showdown was between Pat and an old-timer from Houston. Some said he was a professional poker player and was a regular on the high-stakes circuits around the country. I saw Pat pull a paper out of his jacket and throw it on the table. The man he was betting against gave it to Ray and Ray nodded yes. When the cards turned over, Pat was beat. He rose from the table, thanked them, got a drink from the bar, and walked out the door. He saw me while he was at the bar and he nodded but didn't say anything. He just left. He had a deer-in-the headlights stare, and he walked… kinda like a zombie." She held her head down and a tear ran down her left cheek. "I haven't seen him since."

"Do you think it was a legit game or was Patrick set up?" asked Willie.

"I wouldn't know," she said. "They played until five in the morning, but I left at two, I'm so sorry. I was the one that got him into the game. I never thought he would lose everything."

"It's not you," said Mitch. "Patrick isn't a kid, and this wasn't his first rodeo. He may not have been thinking about his shipmates when he bet the boat, but he should have known who he was playing with. It's not a problem if you know what you're doing. He didn't and they did."

There was a murmur as we dispersed. Coins fell into the jukebox, music filled the bar, glasses clattered, a return to normal at the Party House. But for most of us, it wasn't normal at all. We had lost a friend and he had lost his crew and income, all because of a game. Our game was just that, a chance to relax and have a good time. We heard sometime later that Patrick had returned to Illinois and was working in a farm supply store with his father.

Arnie put it best. "It ain't gambling, if you do it right."

Patrick didn't do it right.

CHAPTER SIXTEEN

Affairs of the Heart and Other Places

WINTER 1975

might have been terminally naïve at times, but intimacy wasn't an unknown in my life. I wasn't a virgin, and I was living in the midst of 1970s sexual freedom on steroids. Port Tarpon combined Peyton Place, San Francisco, Gomorrah, and Paris into one small teeming town of sweaty bodies and intoxicated libidos—without the glamor and bright lights. It was heady, fast, and unpredictable. Couples changed partners in the dance of romance and lust. Barroom eyes transformed into bedroom eyes. Other body parts played their roles. There were marriages and loyal partners, straight families and others who neither participated in nor acknowledged the orgy raging around them. Carl and Cindi, for example, remained aloof, untouched by the tremors of sexual energy that were always close at hand. Others I knew were tempted and only infrequently ventured off the marital path, but they weren't perfect. Some I wasn't sure about. Chun, for example, was a mature healthy male, but his dedication to research seemed to preclude any time for efforts to seek a partner or simply relieve himself of the manly burden.

Among the bar set, opportunism was a given. If you had a willing and able partner, you went for it. Hetero or homo, gay, lesbian, or straight up, drunk or sober, there was a time and place to connect for those with the inclination. The summer featured new faces and bodies, young and old, shy and bold. It was a buffet to be consumed and consummated. The winter, full of dark and dreary days, was a time to consolidate and circulate among the familiar, the friends who remained to maintain the island culture. The culture was not recognized by the Endowment for the Arts or represented in the Guggenheim, but it was a distinct form of communication, a language and recognition among the people that comprised the island residents. The Party House regulars were a subculture within the larger island community. They were independent but interdependent as well. The good and bad fortunes of individuals affected those around them. No one was an island on the island.

The winter of 1975 was a lonely one at first. Friends there were, and the Party House remained an oasis in the growing darkness, but I didn't have a mate. The tourists and visitors had gone. A few dates with summer students at MSI had not materialized into anything, and my contacts in Austin had vanished or found new stages on which to play. Melanie, my occasional love buddy, had started seeing one of the long-time island residents. He was also a fisherman with his own boat, and he seemed to provide some of the stability that Melanie needed.

The thought of winter without a lover was enough to drive a man to drink, but I was already doing that and rather heavily at times. Poker games brought some relief, and my graduate advisor encouraged me to write up and publish portions of my ongoing dissertation before it was completed. But I wanted someone with whom to share a warm bed. There again, I was not in the best of circumstances. My bed was a thin, narrow mattress on a bunk bed with squeaky springs. My roommate, although as inoffensive as a roommate could ever be, was not among the assets that would encourage a female overnight guest. A few day-time quickies were all I had been able to manage over the past two years at the jetty cabin, and these were nervous encounters, not conducive to relaxation, much less comfort. Dark nights on the beach worked occasionally, but this wasn't a comfortable option during the winter. Obviously, I needed to find someone with her own place. That or rent a room in one of the few motels open during the off-season. Lack of money was a deterrent for that.

It was a friend of Sara's that provided the first ray of light, the beacon to the Promised Land. Willie, Sara, and I were sitting outside their trailer. Sara had a glass of white wine, and Willie and I each had a tumbler of sipping bourbon. The day was very mild for winter, I was caught up for the moment on my dissertation, and in the mood to relax.

Willie, as usual, had a cigarette in one hand and his glass in the other. He looked at Sara and winked. "Dont'cha think it's about time we fixed Petey up with Rachel?"

Sara took a sip, looked at me, then back at Willie. "What makes you think Pete would like her? She's not for everyone you know. She has some peculiar interests."

"Hell, Pete likes peculiar interests. He is one of the most peculiar chaps I know."

"Hey folks, I'm right here. Is there something I should know or are you talking about a different Pete?"

"Oh, a different Pete," replied Willie. "The Pete I'm talking about spends too much time in the sun chasing little crawly things around and way too much time measuring and watching them. Although he seems to be terminally horny, I am not sure he knows what a woman looks like or what to do with one if he had one."

Sara smiled. "I'm pretty sure Pete knows what to do. I know of at least one of the local ladies who thinks he does just fine."

"Who would that be?" I asked.

"Who would that be?" asked Willie, still not looking my way.

Sara looked at me and smiled. "Should I tell him, Pete? I thought he knew, especially since he was panting over the same lady."

I was puzzled. I didn't remember Willie and myself in pursuit of anyone at the same time, unless… Ah. It had to be Melanie, our school teacher and would-be prostitute. She and I connected one night at the bar and she took me home, we took a shower, and then I spent the night with her. The next morning, we went to breakfast together, but the strange thing was, we never had intercourse. A bit of fooling around and rubbing naked bodies, but no actual sex. That same pattern was repeated a few more times during the year. I looked at Sara and then at Willie.

"We never had intercourse…" I began, but Sara interrupted.

"Peter, I never said you did, did I? Mel simply said you were fine, a real gentleman. Charming, I believe her words were."

Willie was laughing by now and finally acknowledged I was on the porch. "Sounds like Pete all right. Yeah, he and Rachel might get along after all."

I didn't know her, but Sara had a lot of friends, both on island and off. Sara poured herself another glass of wine, and I refilled my glass. "So who is she and what does she do?" I asked.

Once again, Willie directed his comments to Sara. "See, most guys would ask what she looks like, is she wild or does she like to party, how tall is she, how big are her boobs, but no, Pete wants to know what she does. Maybe he wants to see her curriculum vitae and make sure she took the right courses."

I started to protest but Sara again interrupted. "Tell him to screw himself, Pete. You don't need any advice from Willie the Wonder. Most of the time he's so loaded he doesn't know what he's fucking."

This must have hit home or had an element of truth, because all of a sudden Willie said he had to piss and walked into the trailer. Sara smiled and shrugged, then asked me if I wanted to see a picture of Rachel.

"Sure," I said. "Where does she live?"

"In Corpus. She's an artist, a painter. Does some very nice work and her things are hanging in galleries, including one in San Antone." She retrieved a picture from inside the trailer, showing a tall brunette standing on one of the local piers. She was wearing shorts and a tank top—she was very attractive.

"So what's peculiar about her?" By this time, Willie had rejoined us and poured another glass of bourbon for himself and touched up mine. I gave the picture back to Sara, indicating my interest in meeting Rachel.

"I'll give her a call tomorrow and invite her over for a swim and dinner. When are you available?"

Willie couldn't resist. "Available? This is the most available lad on the island, anytime, anywhere. Right, Pete?" Sara gave her husband the finger, but she was smiling. It took a lot to get her riled and she was used to Willie's bullshit.

"Anytime works for me," I said, confirming Willie's taunt. Getting serious, I asked Sara if there was anything I should know, avoid, or anything we might have in common that I could lead into.

"She's not a fast mover to the bedroom, but she's not prudish either, so go slow and easy. Just be you, Pete, and don't let my old man tell you different."

Rachel arrived at the Institute at one o'clock on a Sunday afternoon. The weather was still holding, and she had asked to see MSI, so Sara and Willie brought her to my place of work. I met them by the front door of the main building, and we spent the next hour touring the labs and the jetty, the sheds, and the rest of the Institute grounds. Willie also showed her his geology lab and she asked both of us a lot of well-informed questions. She was quiet and mature but had a spark of energy that seemed ready to ignite at any time. I drove us to the beach, and we picked a quiet place so the four of us could talk and drink.

Under her jeans and blouse was a striking one-piece knit bathing suit, revealingly seductive, especially after it got wet. We had a cooler of wine (Rachel didn't care for beer) and some food. Sara and Willie were in an extremely good mood, as if they were newly minted lovers instead of a live together couple of two years standing. Rachel asked me more about what I was studying and what I intended to do after I received the degree.

I had to confess that I didn't know. I wanted to pursue additional research, perhaps on a different animal and in a different environment, but I hadn't made up my mind. I was also uncertain about whether I wanted to leave Port Tarpon at all. I had friends, I was comfortable, and there was the possibility of working at MSI after I received my doctorate. When I asked her about her work, she invited me to come to Corpus and see for myself. She had a studio, had a few students she taught part-time, and she traveled around the Gulf Coast a fair amount of the time. She was twenty-eight, two years older than I. She had been married when she was younger, but that had only lasted about a year. She had a Master's in Fine Arts, and she was trying to get on at the local university in Corpus as a full-time teacher.

"Painting doesn't pay all the bills," she said. "I find ways to supplement my income, but it's not stable and I need some consistency in order to focus on my art."

Willie and Sara had wandered down the beach to give us some privacy. When they returned, I think Willie was disappointed that Rachel and I weren't locked in a passionate embrace or better. But Sara looked at Rachel and I could see them exchange a subtle, but apparently positive look. We dressed and ate at Blackie's, the Cajun restaurant. Because I had washed dishes in the gourmet eatery earlier in the year, my guest and I received a discount on our meals. We both ordered crab-stuffed flounder, a treat that melted in your mouth. I rarely ate there because the prices were high even with the discount, but I had decided to splurge for the occasion. Sara and Willie also received a discount because Sara did some publicity work for the owner via the weekly newsletter she edited and published. I also wrote a humorous column on poker and a series of fantasy short stories for the hand-printed newspaper. As I had indicated to Rachel, life in Port Tarpon was good and I was torn between staying and leaving.

Rachel drove back to Corpus later that evening, and I agreed to visit her the following Saturday at her place, meaning her studio near the waterfront. After she left, Sara punched me in the arm.

"Smooth, Pete, you're so smooth, like a milkshake." She ran her tongue over her lips for emphasis as Willie looked on in amusement.

"We'll see, we'll see," I said. The next weekend might tell, or it might not.

Rachel's studio was impressive. It was a large renovated warehouse with solid wood floors and more than adequate natural light. She had several easels set up, some for her own ongoing projects and others for students. Two of them were in the studio, working under her supervision. I had parked and walked in as she was finishing some instructions to the two high school girls. Seeing me in the doorway, she removed her paint-daubed smock and came to me, giving me a friendly peck on the cheek as she took my hand.

She showed me around the open space, and I looked at a wall where she had taped some of her work and some by her students. "Can you tell which is mine and which is theirs?" she asked.

Not a problem. Rachel's paintings, mostly acrylic but with a few watercolors tossed in, were bright and bold, very decisive. They stood out among the tentative and more subdued works by her students. I liked them, and I told her so. She had a wide diversity of topics, from churches, piers, ships, and street scenes, to a few animals and some portraits. One of the portraits was of a nude man, seen from the back. "My ex," she indicated, "the only thing he was ever good for." She said it with a smile.

We sat and talked for about an hour and her students said goodbye.

"Instead of going out somewhere, suppose I fix us dinner at my place." It was a most welcome suggestion, since I had spent most of my remaining funds for the month on the Cajun dinner. I followed her car to an apartment complex and parked beside her. It was a modern place, complete with pool and tropical shrubbery. "Mostly young singles," she said, as we climbed the stairs to her second-floor apartment. "Mostly younger than me," she added.

Her apartment had two bedrooms and an easel occupied a corner of one of them. I glanced in the other bedroom—a king-sized bed dominated it. She had a small bar near the kitchen, and she asked me if I would make us drinks. She had the fixings: gin, vodka, bourbon, and rum.

"I thought you only drank wine." She was in the kitchen, taking something out of the fridge and getting a pan onto the stove.

"No, I drink a lot of things, just not beer. Willie thinks I'm weird."

I decided on rum and tonic. *Willie thinks you are peculiar, I thought. We'll see if you're weird. I hope so.* "Got any limes or lemons?"

"Catch," she called, tossing me a fresh lemon. I caught it and was looking at it when she held up a large knife and said, "Catch." She laughed when she saw the look on my face. She handed me the knife and asked me if fried catfish and hushpuppies would suffice.

"Oh yes, that will do very nicely indeed." *Yes, good weird.*

She had never had a rum and tonic, something I discovered was true for a lot of people. She found them tasty, however, because we had each consumed three middle-sized glasses by the time dinner was finished. I helped her with the dishes and then it was time to consider the rest of the evening.

It was eight o'clock and possibilities included a nearby dance club, a movie on her VCR, or just talk and visit. As we were deciding, I poured us another drink and the dance club was quickly eliminated. Neither of us felt like leaving the apartment, so she picked out a cassette tape from a large shelf over the sofa. The television came to life and the Pink Panther flashed on. *A Shot in the Dark* was one of my favorites, and I hadn't seen it in several years. *How did she know?*

We settled down on the couch, sitting upright but reasonably close. We drank and commented on the film as Peter Sellers bumbled and Elke Sommer deceived. I probably should have never poured us a fifth. We were already feeling the buzz and then some. By the time we woke up, the screen was blank, and we were sprawled horizontally on the couch. It was almost midnight and we arose, laughing and apologizing, she for being a thoughtless hostess and I for being a boring guest.

Rachel looked at the clock on the kitchen wall and looked at me. Taking both of my hands in hers, she told me she didn't want to see me drive all the way back to Port Tarpon late at night, especially after all I had to drink. It didn't take much persuasion to agree to stay the night. I looked at the couch—it was large and well padded, much more comfortable than my jetty cabin bunk bed. Rachel looked on with amusement and then informed me that her bed was even larger and more comfortable.

"I didn't bring pajamas," I said, "or a toothbrush."

"I have an extra, unused toothbrush. You're welcome to it. As for pajamas, I can loan you some of mine, if that's a requirement." Again, the amused but relaxed smile. She must have thought I was the weird one. "Sara warned me you might seem strange at first, but she told me to go slow and easy with you, Pete."

Damn, fell right into that!

She put on a light-colored cotton shirt and kept her panties on. I stripped to my shorts, brushed my teeth, and climbed into bed, waiting for her to finish her bathroom routine. She paused at the door, hand on the light switch.

"Lights on or off?"

"Makes no difference, you choose," I answered.

The lights went out and she climbed into bed. Despite the excitement of a new encounter, we were both very tired and moderately drunk. She curled up next to me and was asleep in less than five minutes. I must have followed soon after, because the next thing I was aware of was soft morning light from the window and the smell of coffee, really good coffee. I started to put my pants on but thought the hell with it and I walked into the kitchen in my shorts. She still had her panties and shirt on.

I sat down on a high chair at the service bar and she handed me a cup of the fresh brew. "Sugar or cream?"

"Neither," I said, "that would spoil this." I took a small sip, and it tasted as good as it smelled.

"Ah, a manly man. My ex had to dump in a ton of sugar and milk to drink his coffee." She said it without bitterness or mockery, but I was pleased with her compliment. She drank hers straight as well and we sat side-by-side, bare knees touching.

"Ah, sex," I said looking at our kneecaps in close contact. I caught her with the coffee at her lips and she almost choked.

"Well, Pete, here's the deal. After breakfast, I'd like to go for a ride, if you're up for it. I don't want to have sex with you, not yet. First… I guess second… date and all. Don't want you to think bad of me, okay?"

I nodded.

"However, I want to take a shower before I get dressed. You're invited to join me, in the interests of saving hot water, soap, and being able to reach those unreachable places." Her smile was unmistakably inviting, so we did, enjoying a ten-minute session of soap, scrub and rinse, including some of the unreachable places. She was as beautiful naked as she was dressed, and she returned the admiring looks.

She fixed waffles and we had a nice breakfast with juice and more coffee. After a leisurely drive into southern Nueces County, toward Mexico, we returned to her apartment, ate a brief lunch, then we said goodbye.

"I had a great time, Pete, really. Let's do this again sometime soon." She was holding my hand at the door.

"Maybe next time we'll make it all the way through the movie," I said, giving her a quick kiss on the lips.

"I hope not." She smiled and closed the door.

Rachel and I dated several more times during that winter. I went with her to Austin on an invited exhibit of her paintings, and she came over to the island a few times, but my living arrangements didn't allow us any comforts or privacy, so most often we used her apartment. We had sex, comfortably and easily. There was no pressure and we fell into intimacy as if it was meant to be. Neither of us made demands or promises. By January, it was over. There was no breakup, no sad farewells. One weekend we made it our last, as if mutually agreed to but unspoken. I'm still not sure why. We were compatible enough, but it just didn't seem like our futures ran down the same road. I didn't realize it was the last time I would see her until I was almost back in Port Tarpon. The song on the car radio was "Wasted Days and Wasted Nights" by Freddie Fender. Relegated to memory, yes—wasted, no.

■　■　■

SOME AFFAIRS ARE BRIEF, NOT AFFAIRS AT ALL. A ONE-night stand, a brief encounter in the dark. There were a few of those, before and after Rachel. I never had an intimate encounter with a woman I didn't at least care something for. It might not have been love—it usually wasn't—but I never considered my partners to be mere meat, something to use and lose, as many of the guys put it. Some of the women were easy and readily available, others more selective. Some young, some old, some large and some small. A few were married or divorced. Some wanted to be married, many did not. There weren't a lot of different partners during the three years on the island—I had neither the time, the talent, nor the inclination—but I had my fair share of close encounters with a diversity of ladies. The attraction wasn't me. I was always painfully aware of that —it was the place and time. Never again in my life would I find the opportunities to enjoy the fairer sex in all their manifestations and variety. As T. G. Shepherd would sing a few years later, "I loved 'em every one."

Harlene was a slim blonde I met at Captain Ahab's during the late summer. She had just turned nineteen, was recently married, and lived in Snapper Pass. She and her girlfriends, also married, made the trip to the island to leave their domestic lives behind, if only for a night. The excitement of the island parties and the perceived freedom was a magnet to drink, dance, and let loose. Harlene and I danced several times one night, and she indicated she would be up for some midnight rodeo. I took her to the beach, and we made love in the back of my station wagon. Since she didn't have a way to get home, I invited her to stay the night in the jetty cabin. Chun was working late, so I brought her in, hung an extra blanket from the top bed, and we snuggled together on the lower bed. Chun came in at about two. He never turned the light on that late, and so he went to bed without disturbing us. He probably knew I had company because of the blanket, but as always, he was meticulously discreet. Harlene was asleep and by the time we woke in the morning, he was gone.

I bought her breakfast in the Island Cafe and after we finished, she called her husband to come and get her. By the time he arrived, I had left, and she told him she had stayed at the house of a girlfriend. I doubt if he believed her and the next time she came to the island, he and a few of his friends made the rounds looking for her. Again, we snuck away, did our business on the beach, and used the cabin once again to sleep. However, I knew it would only be a matter of time and circumstance before her husband caught us, so I broke it off while I could. Bruce told me she visited Ahab's a few more times, but always with her husband beside her.

A woman I had known from Austin came down to the beach one weekend. She rented a condo and looked me up at the Institute. Pat was friendly, a bit overweight, and very horny. We had shared a near-intimate encounter, defined as almost but not quite all the way, when I was at the main campus two years earlier. After a few drinks at the marina bars, we went to her room, got naked on the bed, ready to consummate the deed at last. She was ready; I was not. Sometimes that just happens. There were no external distractions, no reason not to go forward, but I didn't or couldn't. Sometimes it is hard to know the difference. We laughed, wrestled, caressed, and rolled over each other's bodies, but I never entered her. I'm sure she thought she had drawn a loser in the love department, but we parted friends, never to embrace again.

I also had a number of girlfriends that were just friends: confidants, drinking buddies, and dancing partners. Shelley was my astrologer and one of the local school bus drivers. We sometimes enjoyed a couple of joints or a bottle of whatever together, but we never had sex. She was bright, a lot of fun to talk to and was uninhibited with regard to nudity and sex, but we never went further than flirting and having a good time. However, she nailed my hidden personality and ambitions to a tee. After learning my exact place and time of birth, she cast a detailed analysis and projection of my life to come. When I reviewed her written forecast in later years, I would be continually amazed by what she had said and written.

Moonshine and I shared a single night on the TML back dock, drinking, smoking weed, and kissing. Both of us had already consumed a fair amount of beer. We were sitting in the stern of someone's pleasure boat, laying back in deck chairs with our feet on the transom, listening to the water lap at the piers. It was never more than that, just an interlude for both of us, almost softly romantic in nature. Even though she was a free spirit and Mitch wasn't the jealous or possessive type, I would not have gone further with his Tinker Bell.

Sara, Toni, and several of the other ladies and I exchanged platonic kisses and hugs as the situation provided or seemed appropriate. This was an accepted and common behavior among the members of our group. Most men, aware that their women's eyes were wandering among the crowd, simply said, "Tain't nothin' to me." So it was. Even during the cooler winter nights, clothing was usually minimal, bodies were pressed or in motion on the dance floor, and alcohol held inhibitions at a distance. A good life, one that many males would envy or be anxious to emulate, and the women seemed more than satisfied to promote it. For the umpteenth time, did I want to exchange all this for the demanding career I had been preparing for most of my life?

■　■　■

Romantic trysts and living arrangements were always subject to shifts and reversals. As independent as they were, Willie and Sara decided to wed in the early spring of 1976. They opted to get legally hitched, with a ceremony, marriage certificate, and all of the trimmings. It became the social occasion of the year, not that it had a lot of competition. The entire Party House community and many others in town quickly got involved in the plans. A decision was made to celebrate the wedding at the Port Tarpon Community Center, not the bar. A local pastor, not Fast Eddie, performed the ceremony and a grand reception followed afterward.

The reception was anchored with a play, *A Midsummer Night's Dream*. Willie took the part of Theseus, and Sara played Hippolyta. Various friends had other roles, from Titania and Oberon to Puck and the Wall. The performance focused on the end of the comedy, including the embedded play. It was well received by the audience, including me. Shakespeare would have been thrilled by the homage and its original interpretations, if not the artistic quality of the performance.

The most exciting part of the nuptials, however, took place the evening before the wedding. This meant the customary bachelor and bachelorette get-togethers for prospective groom and bride, respectively. The men started drinking at about four in the afternoon, but there was very little offered in the way of traditional bachelor party trappings: no strip teasers bursting from cakes, no exotic foods or drinks.

Except for a few toasts over beer and mescal, the send-off was a dull and drab affair. By eight o'clock, we had become restless. One of Willie's friends walked into the bar and told him that Darla, Sara's bridesmaid, wanted to

see him over by Tarpon Marina Labs for a minute. Deciding that it must have something to do with the next day's
ceremony, he left the bar, telling us he would be back in a
few minutes.

An hour had come and gone when we received the
hand-written note to tell us Willie had been kidnapped and
was being held for ransom. The amount was not specified.
Bart raised his bottle and commented, "That's our Willie."
Mitch and K.C. wanted to know by whom and where was
he being held. Arnie wanted to know the amount of the
ransom. There were about a dozen of us, still disgustingly
sober and bored. Three of us went to the Tarpon Marina
Labs to see if anyone knew anything. Randy was with us
and the lab was closed, but a bait fisherman on the wharf
next to the lab had witnessed the crime.

"It was a silver lifeboat full of women," he declared. "This
guy with long blond hair and a beard came up to them on
the dock and was talking to them when one of them threw
a sack over his head, and several of them tied his wrists
and tossed him in the boat. They were all laughing, and
they looked like they may have had a few." He scratched
his head and looked at us as if we must have known what
was going on.

Mitch said, "They probably used the *Dewey*. It's missing
from the mooring."

I turned to the old man. "Did they mention where they
were going?"

"Not sure 'bout that, but I did hear one say something
about St. Joe."

"Shit, they must have stranded him on St. Joseph. We
need to get a boat and rescue him." I thanked the man and
Arnie started down the dock toward a bait shop where he
knew the owner. By this time, it was near sunset and we

didn't relish the idea of crossing the channel to St. Joe after dark.

Arnie brought the boat around and we made the run, pulling up to a mooring site on one of the few piers on St. Joseph Island, immediately across the Gulf inlet. We scrambled out of the boat and headed in three directions. Mitch found him sitting in the sand, hands still tied and a gag in his mouth. Otherwise, he was no worse for the wear. We got him back to Port Tarpon, returned the boat, and made it back to the Party House.

Willie was highly agitated and very thirsty by this time. "I could have been there all night, might not have been discovered for days," he said while downing a frosted mug of brew, chased with a shot of José Cuervo.

All of us were aware that the evening events had revived our interest in having a real party, but we needed some additional stimulation. It was K.C. who asked the essential question.

"Where are the women having their party?" He said this with a gleam in his eye, a spark that was quickly contagious.

Willie didn't know, but Randy, trusted Randy, did. He and Darla kept no secrets and she told him that their fling would be going on at Charlie's Motel on the beach. The women had rented a couple of rooms, had catered food, and were showing porn movies. Randy also knew that Linda Lovelace was one of the featured film stars.

"Let that be a warning to ya, Will," exclaimed Bart. "Be careful what ya say to your wife to be."

Willie looked at him and said with a still sober voice, "At least I'll be conscious when I get hitched."

We quickly finished our beers, grabbed a few cases from the cold room, and piled into four cars. In caravan, we headed out of town, down the beach, and pulled up to the motel. There was no doubt about where the party was. The doors were open, and you could hear the music and laughter fifty yards down the beach. We had killed our lights and coasted into the parking area so we could arrive unannounced. Willie remained behind us and out of sight.

Mitch and Randy appeared in one of the doorways and were greeted by howls of laughter and a few threats. "Get out of here, this is for the ladies only."

"We've got something that belongs to you," said Randy, and Willie stepped out of the shadow. More laughter and shouts as the women in the adjoining room joined us. Altogether, there were about forty of us, and the party commenced in earnest.

"We were going back for him in about an hour," said Sara, "that's why we didn't return the boat."

"Just wait until the honeymoon," Willie promised, "I will make some special arrangements."

We partied until the wee hours, thankful the wedding wouldn't start until one o'clock the next day, or whenever we arrived, whichever occurred first. There was a lot to eat, a lot to drink, flicks to watch, music to dance to—it was a grand party and prelude to the next day's formalities. Our final goodnight message came from Sara.

"Don't anyone forget your lines tomorrow."

No one did. The wedding within a wedding within a wedding was delivered to an appreciative audience, and Willie and Sara now had the State's blessing, whatever that means.

CHAPTER SEVENTEEN

Sharks, Jellyfish, and Hurricanes. Oh My!

SUMMERS OF 1975 AND 1976

There are ancient creatures with long teeth that prowl the waters of the Gulf, many of them within the swimming and wading zones of the nearshore sandbars. We didn't realize just how many of these cartilaginous predators visited our shores until the Great Shark Convention of 1975. It was August, right after the Armadildos had claimed the Port Tarpon Community Softball League trophy and my thoughts and labors returned to biology. But another facet of the natural world was showing its face—or I should say fin—on the beach side of the island.

An occasional triangular projection, often that of a dolphin, was visible from the beaches from time to time. Most of these were beyond the third sandbar. Occasionally, someone would spot a fin between the bars, and most of the local fishermen and residents knew these belonged to sharks, usually sandbar sharks and occasionally a bull shark. Most were small, less than four feet in length. Some were caught off the piers or the jetty. More of them were taken from the deepsea charters, and these included threshers, hammerheads, blacktips, and makos, some of them of respectable size.

Early August, however, brought a multitude of fins, some of them large enough for concern. For the first time since I had arrived on the island, shark warnings were posted along the beach, and police patrolled with loud speakers advising swimmers and surfers to stay inside the first sand bar, in water less than three feet deep. Most visitors didn't get wet, but they came to see the parade of fins, and it was the main topic of conversation in town. Naturally, the Marine Science Institute became a hangout for the news media and anyone they could interview was fair game for an opinion, from chief scientist to custodian. Frank and his advisor were quickly identified as fish experts, and they were on center stage.

When CBS arrived with its camera people and reporters, Frank was invited to fly over the beach and comment. He invited me to accompany him, the pilot, and cameraman. We took off from the small local airstrip and flew the length of Padre Island, Mustang Island, and St. Joseph. What we saw amazed all of us. Especially along Mustang, the near-shore waters appeared to be a living carpet of sharks and rays. The incredible thing was the species diversity. As we skimmed the surface, we could clearly make out the shapes of the hammerheads and large rays, but we could also distinguish the heads of the bull sharks, the slimmer makos, the fins of the blacktips, and many more. They were aggregated, congregated, and situated, swimming along the bars. By this time, no one was venturing into the water.

The questions came but we had no answers. Groups of sharks had appeared before, from time to time, but no one was sure if it was a regular cycle or not. Frank knew what had to be done next. Enlisting the help of several people from MSI and a number of the local townspeople, the group started catching sharks by reel and by net. A couple of shallow-draft boats plied the outer bar and signs posted at the piers and jetties advised people to bring sharks to the Institute. There, Frank, Mitch, Randy, several students, and I opened them up and sorted the stomach contents into pans and into jars of preservative. There wasn't much to sort. Most of the stomachs were empty or contained minimal remains, usually of small fish. One of the female students kept joking about how many human fingers or toes we would find, but nothing grisly materialized.

The phenomenon lasted about ten days, and then they were gone, leaving only a token handful of the usual finny characters to grace our waters. The swimmers cautiously returned to the Gulf, and the warning signs were lifted. We breathed a sigh of relief and continued to examine the sharks we had, but we never did come up with a satisfactory explanation for the Great Shark Convention of 1975.

What's slimy, has tentacles, and repulses most people? Well, an octopus might fit that description, but what if the tentacles could sting and some of them might actually be dangerous? Jellyfish, oh my!

The most common species in the nearshore waters were called cabbage heads. They were large, several inches across, a translucent white, and the tentacles were relatively short. Whether in the water or washed up on the beach, they were harmless. Sometimes the currents brought great numbers of them ashore, and the beaches would be littered with hundreds to thousands of the rotting blobs of gelatin. This didn't present an ideal panorama for the out-of-town tourist and the smell could be quite impressive after a few days in the sun. Cleanup crews from the town, hired hastily by the city and state, would drive along the beach in garbage trucks and remove the rotting corpses, especially where the most popular stretches of beach attracted the most visitors.

The real drama, however, unfolded when the Portuguese man o' war made its infrequent appearances. They didn't come every year and when they did, it was rare for them to arrive more than once during the summer. They were beautiful, their bright blue bodies and thick white sails visible on the surface as ocean and wind currents brought them onshore. Unlike true jellyfish (the man o' war belongs to a distinct family), these possess a gas-filled bladder that allows them to float at the surface with the long tentacles (up to more than ninety feet but usually only twenty to thirty feet) hanging vertically in the water. The tentacles contain stinging cells that allow the colonial animal to feed on crustaceans and small fish, which it paralyzes with a potent muscular toxin.

Beautiful but painful, the tentacles can be hazardous even after being detached from an animal that has washed ashore and died days earlier. The very length of the tentacles almost guarantees that they will break off when the floating bladder reaches the sand bars or other shallow obstructions. This was the problem. Most people, all but the naïve and unaware, easily spotted and recognized the floating bladders. They were up to a foot in length and extended several inches above the surface. In the gentle waves that lapped the Mustang Island beaches, they were hard to ignore, although a few people always did. It was the detached tentacles, floating under the surface, that presented the biggest hazard. During an invasion, most people (again "most" excludes the foolhardy, the intoxicated, the… well, you know) stayed out of the water and avoided the floats and tentacles on the beach.

The paralyzing stings left large painful red welts where they made contact. They felt like bee stings, and a tentacle wrapped around a leg, arm, or other part of the body could produce a large area of inflamed tissue. The paralysis that killed small fish was usually not lethal to most people, although young children and some susceptible individuals required emergency medical attention if stung badly.

I was at the beach in early September with several friends, and a number of the colorful floats had washed up the day before. With us was a visitor to the Institute, the daughter of one of the full professors. She was fifteen and full of energy, running up and down the beach in a very small two-piece. We had warned her to avoid the man o' war but she wasn't as good a listener as she was a runner. Returning to our blankets, she stopped a few feet away to examine the blue string of tentacles lying in the sand. She carefully poked at it with her finger and then looked over at us.

"It's dead, just a dead wet string. I think I'll take it home as a beach souvenir." Her smile of delight left no doubt about what she would do next.

Three of us started to rise from the beach blanket together, our arms reaching toward her and voicing our protests.

"No, no, don't pick it up"

"Sharon, don't, it'll sting"

"Stop, don't touch it."

She made a face, grabbed the tentacles, and held it over her head at arm's length. A slight breeze caught it and it swung away from her, toward us.

"See, it's completely… owww" She dropped it and the breeze was just enough to carry the short dry strip to my outreached arm. It wrapped itself around my wrist and forearm, and I immediately felt the heat and pain. I removed it quickly and rubbed sand across the red skin to scrape away as many stinging cells as I could. Sharon was holding her hand, the one that had held the tentacle. She was on her knees and crying.

We picked up our things and went back to MSI. From the kitchen we retrieved vinegar and meat tenderizer. Both were effective in reducing the effects of the toxin. Although the pain would last only a couple of hours, the welts would be there for several days. No one felt sorry for the impulsive daughter, but two of my companions showered me with extended nursing care and condolences.

I would encounter the purple floaters on other future occasions, sometimes in the water and along the beaches of Florida, Bermuda, and along other parts of the Gulf Coast. Despite the pain associated with contact, I always considered them to be one of the most beautiful and fascinating creatures of the sea.

There were other hazards living on the island along the shore, but many of these were of the human variety. Careless drivers, flying hooks at the end of lines, weekend boaters coming in too close to the beach and threatening swimmers, and occasional dog bites and bar fights were part of the challenges. There are times, years later, when I marvel at my good fortune and that of my friends in running the gauntlet and surviving. Keep running laddie, and don't look back, oh my!

Texas weather, in general, can be dramatic and dangerous. Lightning storms, tornadoes, sudden freezes, the blistering hot sun, and the stars of the show: tropical storms and hurricanes. Sweeping in from the Gulf of Mexico, the powerful storms have visited the Texas coast on numerous occasions. Hurricane Celia hit Corpus Christi on August 3, 1970. Gusts peaked at 180 mph and about one-third of all the homes in the city were either destroyed or heavily damaged. About 90 percent of the downtown buildings were damaged or destroyed by the high winds. Fifteen people in Texas died, in addition to fatalities in Florida and Cuba earlier. The tides were over nine feet higher than normal in Port Tarpon, and the people on the island didn't forget nature's not so gentle visit.

Every year during hurricane season (nominally, June 1 through November 30), many of the islanders plot the progress of the named storms as they form in the Atlantic, the Caribbean, or the Gulf. The latter, although often not as strong, come up suddenly and provide less time for preparation. The answer: always be prepared. Have food, water, car fueled up, batteries, medical kit, boards and tape for windows, procedural know-how, and when to evacuate. Some of the island people took it seriously and others thought it was a lark, an excuse for a 'cane party. Some of the residents in the large concrete condos lining the beach were especially prone to a lackadaisical attitude. "No storm gonna knock down these walls," they would say. Ask the people of Biloxi and other Gulf Coast communities about "them walls."

The Party House was only a few feet from the marina, and the entire area, known as The Flats, was only a few feet above sea level. Although protected from direct impact by dunes, a tidal rise of several feet meant most of the streets in Port Tarpon were flooded. The Party house roof was composed of shingles and the deep overhang of the eaves almost guaranteed substantial damage, even during gale force winds. When the red flags flew at the Coast Guard station across the street, the gang prepared accordingly. Since there were few high and dry places, many people made the decision to leave the island. When the summer crowds maxed out, this could be a problem. There were only two ways to drive out. Head down the twenty plus mile road to

Corpus, a route that was also subject to being washed out by approaching high tides, or the ferry boats to Snapper Pass. Leaving by ferry, unless done well before the storm, presented a bottleneck of the first magnitude. The boats were slow, could only carry about a dozen cars, and they would cease operation as the storm neared. Unless one left early, the only solution left was to hunker down and stick it out.

Hurricane Anna, the first one of the 1976 season, arose in the Eastern Caribbean on a mid-June day and quickly gathered strength, striking Cuba as a category three storm. Weakening over land, it emerged as a minimal hurricane with eighty mph sustained winds and drove into the Gulf. The seas were warmer than usual, and the storm grew, bands reaching out hundreds of miles. Port Tarpon, along with rest of the Gulf Coast from Central Mexico to Mobile, was on the alert. The storm was unusual in that early storms rarely had top power—the sea temperature wouldn't peak until August. The storm was also moving faster than twenty mph, and it was not wavering, not indecisive in its course, one that had Mustang Island directly in its sights.

Some of the summer visitors started leaving and others, who had planned to come, didn't. The Texas Department of Transportation closed ferry traffic to the island to all except emergency personnel and residents. Unfortunately, they weren't as quick in placing roadblocks to do the same on the Island Road. With forty-eight hours to go until predicted landfall, preparations intensified.

The Marine Science Institute made sure their emergency generators would function and provide juice for seawater tanks, computers, and essential equipment. The two-story facility had several large classrooms and other spaces that could be used as an emergency shelter, and these were assigned to staff and their families. They were also prepared to house other individuals, if required. I gathered my field equipment, notebooks, and expensive camera equipment and stored them in an interior lab on the second floor. My friends were going to remain, and I decided to stay with them rather than at the Institute. Randy needed my help in battening down Tarpon Marina Lab, and several of us were transporting kitchen items from the Party House to a safer location. K.C. and Arnie knew there was a possibility we might lose the building completely. I parked my car at one of the highest points on the MSI grounds and several of us crowded into Randy and Darla's house to wait it out.

The forecasts didn't change. Anna would arrive on time, June 23, 1976, scoring almost a direct hit on Port Tarpon. The storm had continued to strengthen, and top sustained winds were hovering between 130 and 135 mph, reaching category four on the Saffir-Simpson Wind Scale. The dark clouds passing swiftly overhead were moving from east to west, indications of the larger counter-clockwise circulation that traditionally signaled the bad news for coastal residents.

Most of our friends had not experienced Celia or any other major storm. We were excited, frightened, and worried about what might take place. The storm was only a few hours away, and the winds and rain had increased substantially, but we knew the worst, by far, was yet to come. It would arrive during the early morning hours and with a high tide. The only good news was the eye would likely make landfall a few miles northeast of the island, still close enough to inflict considerable damage, but we would be out of the dreaded northeast quadrant where most of the tornadoes were generated.

We had sandwiches, chips, guacamole (what else would you need?), beer, cokes, and fresh fruit. Willie and Mitch didn't have pot with them, out of respect for Randy and his children, and there was no hard liquor, except for a bottle or two that Randy had on hand. Everyone knew we had to keep our wits about us and be prepared to take action during and after the storm. It was going to be a subdued party, but a gathering of friends provided strength and reassurance. Randy's children sat with us as we discussed possible aftermaths and the tasks we would most likely face in the coming days.

Tina, Randy's eleven-year old, provided one of the few laughs. "Maybe Anna will wash away the school." Stevie, the eight-year old clapped and we joined him. The kids set the tone, and the adults joined in to offer encouragement, although we knew if the school went, most of the houses in town, including the one we were in, would go with it.

The power failed at eleven, and we were left with lanterns and flashlights. The wind was an unrelenting howl, and we had to yell to be heard. Sleeping bags were scattered around the living room, the kids were in an adjacent hallway, and some of the women were already asleep. There were nine adults in the house: Randy, Darla, Willie, Sara, Mitch, Henry, Frank, Debbie, and me. The windows were boarded, all of the potential flying debris, such as garbage cans and loose tools, had been brought inside, and all that was left to do was wait. We had a portable radio that provided coordinates and a map on the floor to mark the eye's progress as it bore onshore. We could hear occasional loud bangs and the sharp report of a tree across the street that snapped. Randy looked out the front door and told us the power lines on the corner were down and a palm tree was lying across the road. He shut the door and we waited.

The intensity built to a climax and then it came—the sudden arrival of the eye wall and silence. No wind, no rain, as if it had been just another gentle summer night in paradise. We knew it would be a very brief lull and our respite would only allow us a quick look outside to assess the damage. A quarter moon from an almost clear sky provided just enough light to see the scattered debris in the yard and on the street. Randy walked far enough out of the house to view the roof: it appeared undamaged. Frank was explaining how we were in the westernmost part of the eye, a small well-wound one, and that we could only expect a few minutes of peace before the back wall hit us, suddenly and with full force. "That's what we get for hunkering with a bunch of science people," Debbie remarked. We settled back in the house, and three minutes later the winds and driving rain came with full fury. It was a few minutes to two. By three, all of us had crawled into our bags, happy to be dry and alive.

The storm passed quickly, and the next morning dawned, still heavily overcast but with winds from the west. Still without power, except for a generator attached to the refrigerator, we ate cold cereal and cold muffins with cold preserves. Frank provided a small tabletop stove and a can of Sterno, enough to heat coffee, if you were patient enough to wait.

■　■　■

WILLIE, RANDY AND I LEFT SHORTLY AFTER BREAKFAST to see what had become of the marina. We walked, since the streets were mostly impassible due to downed wires and trees. It was easy to underestimate the number of trees in town until you saw them lying in the roads. Amazingly, the Party House still stood, as did most of the other buildings around the waterfront. There were some loose shingles and one of the boards over a side window had blown off, but water damage seemed minimal and a day of cleanup would have most of it repaired. Winds were still high, but the storm had already been downgraded to tropical status and the Coast Guard was out with the police and fire personnel searching for anyone in trouble.

The three of us walked over to the laboratory. From the front, it looked good. The boards had held, and the roof seemed none the worse, but when we entered, the light from the rear shouted out the bad news. Part of the back wall was gone. As we approached the gaping hole, we immediately saw the reason. A large yacht, longer than thirty feet, had broken loose from its mooring and taken out our back dock and with it, part of the building. The boat was heavily damaged and listing to starboard. We had left a small generator running to keep one refrigerator and the aerators working, but the boat had struck at the most vulnerable location, severing our sea water line and taking out the generator. Except for a few of the hardiest fish and a couple of crabs, the tanks were filled with floating corpses. A shipment of electric rays that hadn't been sent, several hundred dollars' worth, were among the mortalities. Randy looked at Willie and me and sighed.

"It's done boys, it's all over."

Willie and I shook our heads in silent agreement. The business had always been marginal, with proceeds enough to cover expenses, including a modest amount to pay for our help and to supplement Randy's TP&W income. The damage was extensive, and the physical structure would be covered by insurance for the building owner, or the boat owner, whichever applied. But the back wall and dock repairs, if done at all, might take months.

Life has a rhythm of ups and downs, and progress depends so much on momentum. Some events break that rhythm, snap the momentum. Psychologically, the damage was the worst. The long hours of enthusiastic toil, building the lab, enticing visitors, attracting business, it had all come to this—a big hole and a building full of dead and dying animals. Mitch walked in as we stood in the main room. The fish were beginning to smell, as only rotting fish can. He looked at the back wall and the ruined dock beyond.

"Bad, huh?"

"Yep," said Willie.

Randy looked at him and then at each of us in turn. "Thanks for all your help and support, fellas. I think we had something good going." A pause. "I'm going to need something harder than a beer. I think I'm going to cry."

"We can clean this up later. I know where there's a bottle already calling to come and get me." Willie turned and exited.

Randy asked Mitch and me to help him dump the fish and crabs that were still alive into the marina, and we did. There weren't many of them. We followed Willie to the Party House where K.C., Arnie, and Sherry were already beginning to clean up and reopen the bar.

The storm had weakened slightly, to 120 mph, before making landfall. Power was restored two days later, and within a week the island was open for business and summer crowds had returned. Commercial business had been spared much of the damage, a miracle in itself. The frequent toast at the Party House and at many other spots on the island was "until next time." We knew there would always be a next time.

CHAPTER EIGHTEEN

Sunset and Sayonara

SUMMER 1976 TO SUMMER 1977

Almost all of my fieldwork was finished by the time Hurricane Anna made its unwelcome appearance in 1976. Good thing too, because the storm changed the mud flats and crab habitats in significant ways. The crabs didn't go anywhere —they had been through storms before and would survive many more. But the roads along the back of the island were washed out, and a major part of the area I had been studying was either sitting at the bottom of the Intracoastal or covered over by sand and dirt from adjacent fields.

Curious to observe the site changes a week after the storm, I hiked into the area from the end of the road at the Texas Parks and Wildlife facility. I didn't recognize my familiar landmarks: the small back dunes, ridges, a few small ponds, and various patches of vegetation. Everything was different and there was only a handful of burrows visible compared to the thousands I was used to viewing. I took some pictures and vowed to come back several times to see how long it would take for the population to recover.

I was scheduled to present some of my findings at a late-summer meeting of the American Society of Zoologists in New Orleans. I had given two talks to the same group before: my first national presentation in Houston in 1973 and a second talk in Tucson in 1974. Both talks went well, and I already had two papers published or in press. My advisor was pleased and again indicated that the peer review associated with publication would facilitate my dissertation defense, provisionally scheduled for the coming December. I was also sending out my curriculum vitae to prospective employers and investigators, but I had not received any positive responses, and I was hoping I might have an opportunity in the Big Easy to meet and greet colleagues who might help me take the next step. In the meantime, I focused on analyzing the data, learning some new statistical techniques, and using the computer to draw graphs and plot habitat maps. The computer was also used by several of the students during the late hours to play a very primitive version of Star Trek, with o's and x's representing the Klingons and Federation ships on a two-dimensional grid. Not very high tech, but it was all we had, and it kept our minds from becoming overly obsessed with real data.

Party house misdeeds and relationships continued as ever, but I found myself increasingly engaged in *the* internal debate. If I scored a job or post-doc position, what would I do? Take it or leave it? It might depend on where and what. I wanted to stay near the coast, to continue with direct access to marine environments, although I had always been fascinated with other animals, including primates. A chance to dramatically switch biological endeavors was not out of the question. However, I couldn't see myself teaching at a Midwest or deep inland college, unless it was a prestigious one with opportunities to build a career.

The New Orleans meeting went better than planned. My talk was well attended, and two professors from a New York university invited me to lunch. One of them had been at my Houston presentation, and she also worked on crabs, but studied physiology rather than behavior. The other person was the Assistant Chair of the Biology Department. I didn't make any other productive contacts or develop any promising leads, so when I returned to MSI, I continued sending out letters.

October brought some encouragement, but not in the form of a job offer from outside. One of the microbiology professors at MSI needed laboratory help with a large project that had recently received funding. He already had an organic chemist, but I was experienced in bacteriological techniques and my analytical work for the dissertation had been duly acknowledged by the MSI faculty and staff. I was offered the chance to join the project as a research associate, my first full-time professional job. I didn't take much time to think about it—I gladly accepted the employment parachute. This meant I could finally move out of the jetty cabin—so long, Chun—and get myself an apartment or small house. I could start living, including a better choice of menu, an automobile upgrade, and so many other things I had been putting off. All I had to do was pass the final defense and get my doctorate and the job, now elevated to a postdoctoral research associate, was mine. They hired me on a temporary appointment, pending the degree.

This change of fortune resulted in a strange compromise. I would be working for the Institute and receive decent pay. I would be helping with someone else's research, much like Willie and Mitch were doing with their respective appointments, but I would be paid correspondingly more. However, my research obligations would leave me adequate time to continue patronizing the Party House, play poker, and, in general, carouse as before. Didn't seem like a bad plan.

Redoubling my efforts to finish the dissertation, I spent

long days at the typewriter and manually drafting some of the illustrations from computer printouts. In those days, each dissertation page had to be perfect: no erasures, white-outs, or other signs of errors. A woman on the main campus checked each thesis and dissertation for any evidence of imperfection, and she had the power to reject the entire work if she found any blemish on the good name of the graduate school. The dissertation was slightly over 200 pages, smaller than many. I assembled and boxed copies of the manuscript for my trip to Austin. My committee had already read much of it because of the publications, but I distributed copies to each member for preliminary approval. The committee and I confirmed the early December date for the formal defense. With only a few minor corrections and suggestions, I was able to prepare the final copy, ready to hand in to the graduate school at the completion, hopefully, of the defense.

Once again, darkness descended on the island and Port Tarpon. It had been a frenetic summer, including the hurricane, the after-storm cleanup, closing the Tarpon Marina Lab, and looking for a new place to live. Mitch offered to let me stay with him while I looked.

"*Muchas gracias, hombre.* I 'preciate that, but I don't want to move twice. I'll stay with Chun until I find something, shouldn't take long."

Sara said she would look around for me. She did have a rental, but it was a larger house than I needed or wanted to take care of. She also suggested that one of the island ladies might be willing to entertain a male housemate.

"Oh, which one?" Remembering Cindi's attempts at fixing me up, I was walking on the cautious side. I also thought about my reporter friend in Corpus, but we hadn't been in contact for some time.

"How about Melanie? She's still single and not firmly attached to anyone yet. Besides, if you were living with her, maybe Willie wouldn't want to hang around her as much."

I thought about that for only a second. "No, I prefer Melanie as an occasional drinking and dancing partner. Besides, I know she has her eye, and a few other body parts, on one of the fisher guys." It was true. In fact, Melanie had stopped hanging around the Party House and neither Willie nor I had partaken of her company in months.

Sara shrugged and gave up. So did a couple of the other would-be matchmakers, but I appreciated the effort and it was always intriguing to learn about whom they thought might be right for me or vice versa. What I wanted was a roomy one-bedroom house or cabin, someplace secure to stow my stuff and in which to be comfortable. I also wanted to buy a real bed and have a real bedroom with real bed partners. Making love in the back of a car on the beach was occasionally romantic, but more often not.

Sara found me a cabin, not luxurious by any means, but it was across the street from Randy and Darla's house and the tenant had just moved out. The rent was quite reasonable. It had a shower, but it was only one large room—bedroom, living room, and kitchen combined. A modern open plan house, Sara joked. I didn't care. I took it, gave her a month's deposit with advance, and quickly moved my stuff over from the Institute. Darla invited me over for dinner, and the gang gathered to celebrate my new digs.

"The next poker game will be at Pete's, next week," announced Willie.

"Yeah," I said, "new venue, new winner." It had been a while since I had left the game ahead.

I joined the two other project investigators on periodic voyages into the Gulf and the Atlantic, each trip lasting from a week to ten days. Our task was to collect water samples, from the surface to various depths, searching for microorganisms that degraded natural hydrocarbons. The idea was to find, isolate, identify, then grow cultures of the bacteria for use in dispersing and metabolizing oil slicks. Tar from naturally occurring oil leaks in Mexico washed up from time to time on Texas beaches. If the slicks could be neutralized while still offshore, cleanup would be less expensive and more efficient. Tourists were much more likely to come to clean beaches where they didn't have to scrape their heels. The laboratory work wasn't particularly exciting, but the project itself was interesting, and I still had a university connection.

On December 7, a Tuesday, I drove up to Austin for my defense. This was a private affair, just my six-person committee and me. Often, graduate defenses were held in a large auditorium or meeting room so that other faculty and students could attend and comment. I had already given a seminar at MSI, and Dr. Stevens indicated that it would suffice for the public performance. I wasn't sure what to expect. I knew my committee members well and they had been helpful during the past two years, but it isn't over until it's over. The only woman on my committee wasn't fat, so she wouldn't be singing.

It was a small room, with a long table and seven chairs. A blackboard dominated the wall behind me as I sat down by myself on one side and my committee occupied the six chairs facing me, four across and one at each end. Noting that I was a bit nervous at the room arrangement, my advisor lightened the mood immediately.

"What do you think, should we torture him here or take him out into the woods?"

This got a few laughs and we were on our way. Most of

the questions were not about the research or defending the data. That had been done before and during publication. Instead, we conversed about the hazards and drawbacks of fieldwork, the difficulties in quantifying behavior, and the rough, deprived life I had been subjected to on the barrier island. A couple of the committee members had seen my jetty cabin and were aware of my diet during the time away from Austin. The psychologist summed it up.

"When I visited Pete in the summer of 1975, the poor guy was down to 175 pounds and four beers a day." I remembered her visit and we had shared some of those suds.

"I hear you have a postdoc with the Institute," said one of the ecologists.

"Not a formal post-doc, but I will be a research associate, working on oil slicks and bacteria," I replied.

"That's quite a change from doing social behavior. Are you going to be happy with that?" asked another committee member.

"For now, it will be fine. I wasn't being overwhelmed with job offers, and I am happy to be there and doing something useful, and… they're going to pay me."

Everyone nodded. They knew my predoctoral training stipend didn't provide more than a minimal living and they also had students looking for jobs. Carl would be defending his dissertation in January and he hadn't found a job yet. Federal money for research had decreased significantly during the seventies, and jobs had disappeared accordingly.

So it went, a lot of light banter, a few requisite questions, and then they stood and told me to wait outside while they discussed my defense. This was not something I was expecting. The casual tone over the past hour had led me to believe it was signed and sealed. I stepped outside the room, worried for the first time that I hadn't met their expectations, that I wasn't qualified to join the academic ranks. That would mean goodbye to the MSI job, my new house, and my cozy future.

Only two minutes lapsed, and I was still standing there when the door opened and my advisor waved me into the room. I took my place, facing six somber faces. Two of them couldn't keep it straight and started laughing, quickly joined by the others.

Stevens addressed me, "Peter, oh Peter, I wish we had a camera to capture the look on your face. A trip to the guillotine would have seemed in order."

The ecologist added, "It was too easy, Pete, it just wasn't a challenge for us. The papers published, the dissertation, the years we saw you work, it was a pro forma no brainer. But, we still had to have the meeting and we wanted to provide you with some obligatory perspiration, if not entertainment."

"It was the right thing to do," said the psychologist.

I guess it was. I did sweat, and I didn't disappoint them with my reaction. But then it was celebration time. Dr. Stevens was hosting a dinner party for me at his house that evening. My committee, a number of other faculty, and students were invited, and Carl and Cindi were there to add their congratulations.

"No hard feelings about Diana, Pete?" said Cindi, bringing me a margarita refill. I gave her a quick kiss on the cheek and told her all had been forgiven a long time ago. I wished her and Carl the same fortune on his defense and luck in finding a job.

"He'll do well, just like you did," she said. "I think we are going back to Canada. We have friends in Toronto and there will be something, I'm sure."

Two of the faculty had rug rats crawling around on Steven's living room carpet. We were amused by Stevens'

Sheltie, herding the kids away from walls and furniture and keeping them in the middle of the room. Food was served, drinks flowed freely, and after dinner music provided the opportunity to dance or talk. As the new doctor, I had to spend most of it talking, answering questions from departmental faculty who knew little about my research. Many of them were curious about MSI —most had never been to the branch campus or Port Tarpon. One of the male faculty members, in his middle forties and well past the inebriation limit, asked the most insightful question.

"How were you able to stay focused on watching all those damned crabs when you were surrounded by women wearing skimpy bikinis?" He had one arm on my shoulder, his right hand wrapped around a gin and tonic, and his head was lowered toward mine, as if our conversation was being conducted in private. Even with a loud rock number banging in the next room, everyone could hear his question clearly. Several looked up to hear my response.

"It was easy, Professor Blackwell. I was studying courtship and sexual interactions, and my animals don't take second fiddle to anyone."

"Fiddle, fiddler, huh, yes, yes, I get it. Fiddler crabs." He slapped me on the shoulder, threw his head back in an exaggerated guffaw, and spilled the entire drink down the front of his pants. This brought a corresponding response of amusement from the onlookers, and I quickly disengaged and found a young female student to dance with.

We partied until almost one o'clock, and Dr. Stevens provided me with a room for the night. In the morning, he and his wife fixed a great breakfast, and I took my boxed dissertation to the graduate office. The clerk examined several pages by holding them up to the light and she measured the margins, checked the references, and compared the numbers in the table of contents with those in the text portions. Fifteen minutes later, she smiled, finally, and said "Good job!"

* * *

FREE AT LAST, I DROVE BACK TO THE ISLAND. IT WAS NOW almost five and time for the second round of celebrations. Willie, Mitch, and many of the others showed up at the Party House during the next hour or two. I didn't buy a single drink and could barely keep up with the line of mugs, shots, and pizza slices on my table.

Bart summed it up. "Pete, you crazy son of a bitch. I hope when you're famous and standing in Sweden or wherever and getting that prize, whatever it's called, you won't forget about us."

"I'll be here, right here. But now I'll have more money to buy you better booze instead of cheap beer."

Mitch looked at me and simply said, "Pete, that works for me."

By ten o'clock I was feeling no pain. In fact, I wasn't feeling anything. I did manage to find the men's bathroom two out of three times, and I was able to acknowledge two different offers from the ladies to spend the night with me. I wish I could remember which ladies and what I said to them, but there was this fog and then I woke up the next morning in my bed, in my cabin, alone.

Darla came over to see if I was still alive. She and Randy had brought me home and tucked me in. I hoped it wasn't Randy that did the tucking. It was after ten, and she wanted to know if I wanted breakfast. I looked at her and asked her what she was serving. A really evil look came over her and she leaned close and whispered, "I have some really greasy, almost slimy sausage and I can fry it real crisp."

I pushed past her, found the toilet, and rid myself of last night's repast and other things. As I came out of the bathroom, wiping my mouth on a wet washcloth, she started for the door, paused, and said, "Whatever you want, Pete, I can get it for you." A cheese omelet and biscuits made the day, and I went to work, a bit queasy but otherwise intact.

For the next two months Port Tarpon was the very epitome of the good life. We made our first sea voyage in January off of the Carolina coast. The sampling went as planned and life aboard was busy but joyful. Back at the Institute, the lab work started out well and we were already getting preliminary results. Our corporate sponsor and administrator of the federal grants was Texas Instruments, headquarters located near Dallas. We were invited, along with other grant recipients, to visit the TI campus and give an initial report in February.

In the meantime, I had hosted two poker games at the cabin. Space was limited, but I did have a kitchen table and we borrowed some extra chairs to accommodate the boys. I also managed to take more than my share of the pots on one of those occasions. Best of all, companionship arrived when one of the relative newcomers for the year, a graduate student in botany, decided she wanted to visit my place from time to time.

Carol was short, platinum blonde, and passionate. She had been a grade-school science teacher but had decided to return to school and get a master's degree to teach high school or community college. She was bright, had a sense of humor and—did I tell you?—she was passionate. In her middle twenties, Carol had never been married and was the only child of conservative parents in Waco. She had gone to a Baptist school in a Baptist community, and she was leaving it all behind as fast as she could. Her time at MSI was as much liberation as it was an education, maybe more.

It didn't take long for our discussions to arrive at the possibility of finding a bigger house and cohabiting. I liked that word, much better than shacking up, but she was in favor of it, no matter what we called it. I didn't have a lease, and she was already tired of the room she had at the MSI dormitory. Her room was in the same building, just down the hall, from the first room I had occupied at the Institute.

When I returned from the Atlantic trip, nearing the end of January, we asked Sara to keep an eye out for a suitable house with two bedrooms. Carol wanted a bathtub and a decent-sized kitchen. We also talked about getting a dog. Heaven only knows, the island needed another dog, but we knew there were always some in need of a home and we wouldn't have to search far. February started with a promise of domestic stability, a sense of belonging at last. The month would end somewhat differently.

■　　■　　■

IN THE SECOND WEEK OF FEBRUARY, DR. ROBINSON, THE project director, Dr. Sam Hardaway, the organic chemistry post-doc, and I made our way to TI for the research conference. We toured their extensive environmental laboratories and part of the instrument division. At the time, TI calculators were one of the top brands. We were amused by two things at TI. Although we only saw a glimpse of their computer operations, we were forced to undergo a security clearance that would have done justice to the War Room at the Pentagon. We were issued visitor badges, had to sign in and out each time we left a building, and had to be accompanied by a TI employee when we used the bathroom. All of this took place inside the environmental facilities. The second thing that drew a smile was the office space assigned to the environmental scientists and analysts. It was a huge open room filled with several hundred cubicles. Each cubicle was identical, with identical furniture and computers. As we passed by the workspaces, we noticed that no personal items were present on the desks or cubicle walls, except for one family picture on a corner of the desk. The only color in the entire space was provided by the binders and books on the single bookshelf over each desk. It was a grim reminder of big corporate protocol, and we became evermore appreciative of the freedom we enjoyed at the Institute. No sandals, cutoffs, or T-shirts at TI. Lunches and break times were proscribed, and the time clock regulated everything on a twenty-four-hour basis. It was a technical factory.

The next day was spent listening to reports by various investigators and the modern conference room was well equipped to display slides, overheads, and a few videos. It felt more like the academic conferences we were accustomed to, which wasn't surprising since the majority of participants were from universities. That evening, the three of us were relaxing in our motel room. We would be on our way to MSI in the morning, and we had just finished a big steak dinner at a local restaurant. Stomachs full and mentally satisfied with how our data had been received, we were talking about our next sea trip when the room phone rang. Robinson answered it and handed the receiver to me.

It was from Penny at MSI. Although it was after hours, she knew it was important to reach me and so had waited until we were in our room. She had received a call for me from a university in New York and they wanted to get in touch with me. Penny gave me the number and name of the person to call. Penny told me I should call immediately, despite the time difference. The call was from Doctor Matthews, the crab physiologist with whom I had lunch in New Orleans the summer before.

As Robinson and Sam talked quietly, I dialed her number. It was eleven o'clock in New York, but she thanked me for phoning and wanted to know if I had found a job yet. I told her I was working on an oceanographic microbiology project, and I was in Dallas attending a conference with our sponsor. When I mentioned this, Robinson looked at Sam and the two of them stepped out of the room, so I had some privacy.

"Peter, well, I guess it's Doctor Gilbert now, and congratulations, I'm happy you are employed, but I am calling to offer you a teaching position with us for the coming fall."

I was flabbergasted. After sending out almost one hundred resumes and never getting an interview or follow-up, here was an offer without having applied. "You mean you would like me to apply and come for an interview?" I asked, still not sure I had heard her right.

"No, Peter, we are offering you the position, an assistant professorship in biology, tenure track. You didn't know it, but when Alex and I attended your presentation in New Orleans, we were impressed enough to interview you over lunch. You just didn't know that was what we were doing. We also weren't sure we would have the position funded, so we couldn't say anything about the possibility at the time. But we always had you in mind."

"Wow, I'm glad I'm sitting down. This is sudden."

"Are you interested? Is this what you would like to do?" She paused. Leslie Matthews knew I was a westerner and had never been to New York. We had talked about how different the culture was, especially compared to barrier island Texas. She had no idea what the *real* differences were. "Oh, and we can arrange for you to have a non-paid research appointment at the American Museum of Natural History."

"Leslie, that would be fabulous. I've dreamed about visiting it, but the chance to work there… well, I am truly at a loss for words."

"You don't have to give me an answer tonight, Peter. I know this is a big decision, especially since you already have a job. We would like to have your decision within a week, if that's possible. If you decide to pass on it, we will advertise it. Is that agreeable?"

"Yes, I would need to give my team adequate notice and I have some personal things to consider." Matthews knew I wasn't married but she could probably guess that I had some relationships to work out. I thanked her and we ended the call.

I stepped into the hallway and motioned to Robinson and Sam that I was finished. They returned to the room and I informed them what had happened. Robinson said very little, but Sam, who had been a good friend and office mate for the past three months, displayed the expected reaction. He encouraged me to take the job, since he knew it was the break I had been looking for and it represented some great opportunities. On the other hand, he enjoyed the inter-personal dynamics of our research team—we worked well together. More than that, we had started playing Dungeons and Dragons, the popular fantasy board game. His wife and fifteen-year old son had joined in, and I had recently invited Carol to participate. This usually came with dinner and some serious wine sipping, a cheap and clean evening of entertainment that effectively replaced much of the bar life. Sam didn't push me either way, but we had some wine in our room and the three of us toasted to the offer and to the decision I would need to make soon. Robinson finally spoke and told me I would be welcome to stay with his lab as long as I wanted and that our few months together had been productive and enjoyable. I reminded him that even if I accepted the position, it wouldn't start until September. In the meantime, I could still work for him, probably until July or August. I said it as if I had already decided, but I was far from that.

I chose not to tell Carol right away about the job offer. If I declined, I could discuss it with her later and let her know that she was one of the reasons I decided to remain in Port Tarpon. If I accepted, then we, actually she, would have another big decision. Should she come with me or stay and finish her degree? Would she want to come? Was our relationship that strong? There were a lot of questions I wanted to avoid until I had sorted it out for myself.

■　　■　　■

WE RETURNED TO THE ISLAND THE NEXT DAY, AND I talked to Carl about New York. He was excited for me and didn't think there was any decision at all.

"Go for it, heh, what have you got here, really?" Although Cindi and I had kissed and made up, my Canadian friends still didn't approve of my Party House exploits and they were not overly enthusiastic about Carol. They considered her a wild one, a bad influence on my future professional reputation, whatever that meant, and not much better than the other women on the island. At one point, Cindi had referred to them as the Party House sluts. When I quietly informed her that she was speaking about my friends, she apologized, but I knew her mind hadn't changed.

My next round of consultations was held with Randy, Mitch, and Willie. Sara and Darla were also present, but they didn't say much. The Party House was quiet. Willie was watching the bar, but there were no other occupants. The six of us sat around a table. The ladies were drinking wine, and the rest of us had drafts. The scene was all-too-familiar as I looked at each of my friends, wondering if this would be another late night and too-early morning.

"This might call for something more potent," said Randy, looking at Willie.

"I have a bottle of tequila in my backpack," said Mitch. The backpack was in the corner by the pool table, and he rose to fetch it.

"I'll get the lemons and salt," added Sara and she sauntered into the kitchen with an exaggerated sway of her hips, letting everyone know she was ready to party.

I looked at my friends again, my reliable island buddies, always ready for happy times but willing to console anyone in the not-so-happy ones. Willie gave me a questioning look as glasses and the full tequila bottle arrived at the table.

"Works for me, every time," I said.

Willie poured a healthy slug of the stimulating clear liquid into everyone's glass. "Here's to Pete," he said. "May he make the right decision… and stay with us." Thus departing from any hint of neutrality, most of my friends gave me endless reasons why I would be happier in Port Tarpon and miserable in New York. All of the eastern urban stereotypes were paraded for my careful consideration, but only Sara and Willie had ever been to New York, and that had been a short visit.

Randy had said very little, but he kept watching me. Instead of the salt and lemon (we were out of limes) routine, he nursed the tequila and chased it with beer. Finally, he offered his considered opinion.

"Pete, this might seem like I'm trying to encourage you

to leave, but that is only partly true. I think you should go to New York and take the job. If you don't like it, you can always come back. Right? Won't Robinson hire you back?"

I thought a minute. Another hit of the potent stuff. "I don't know. Maybe. If he fills the position, and he probably will, I might not have anything to come back to." I looked at each one. "Then I'd be just like the rest of you sorry bastards."

"What about us? We'll never be sorry bastards," said Darla, indicating Sara and herself.

"No, I could never be like you and Sara," I answered, "not even sure I want to try, although I've heard anything is possible in the Big Apple."

"Ah, stay with us sorry bastards," said Willie. "You know we love you, in spite of all your obvious faults and handicaps."

"Handicaps?"

"Can't play second base worth a damn," he retorted. Another round of shots.

"I'll still be here this summer, so don't warm up another second baseman just yet."

Darla reached across the table and took my hand. "Shit, Pete, does that mean you're gonna go?" I didn't answer. "What about Carol? We like her. Give her another month or two and she'll be just like the rest of us."

"A sorry bitch," said Sara, sitting back in her chair, now completely relaxed.

The conversation deteriorated as it always did after several drinks. Darla punched a few songs on the jukebox, including "Why Don't We Get Drunk and Screw." The music lifted our spirits, and the mood changed to Party House happy. They knew as I knew, the real decision was ahead but time was ticking and by the end of the weekend I would be calling New York to announce my decision.

■   ■   ■

Saturday morning dawned bright and clear, nice weather for mid-February. I had arrived on the island almost four years earlier, committed to a research plan but without a clue about my personal future. It seemed that some things change a lot and other things change very little. Carol had been out of town for a couple of days, so this was my first chance to tell her what was pending. Although many people at the Institute and most of my island friends now knew about the offer, she had been out of contact and was unaware of recent events.

I picked her up at her dorm and we drove down the beach, several miles away from town. The beach around us was completely deserted except for seagulls and plovers. We spread a blanket, and I opened a beer for each of us.

She picked up a can and took a healthy sip. "We can get naked and screw, if we want. No one here but the birds and they don't care." Carol's whitish-blonde hair slipped over one eye. She looked like she was ready to peel her clothes off, so I took her hand.

"Carol, we need to talk about something." I must have sounded more somber than I had intended, even though it was a serious topic. She froze and her sexy come-hither smile disappeared. "When we were in Dallas, I received a phone call."

"Oh Pete, not bad news, I hope. Your mother, someone else in your family?"

"No, not that. It was a call from New York, Carol. They offered me a teaching job, a chance to be a biology professor and to have a staff appointment at the American Museum of Natural History."

She remained still, very still. Finally, she asked, "What

are you going to do, Peter?" She only used my formal name when she was teasing or when she was upset. I knew she wasn't teasing.

"I don't know yet. I wanted to talk to you first. It's a big decision, one of the biggest that I've ever made."

"When would you leave?"

"If I leave, it would be this fall. I would continue to work, play ball, play poker, you know, play around… " I gave her a big smile, trying to reassure her. I didn't let go of her hand.

"If you leave. If you leave." She said it mostly to herself, a monotone that signaled a sense of resignation before I had made my choice.

"What if you came with me? You could continue your degree in New York, at my university. You're smart, you wouldn't have any trouble getting in. We could get a place there and see a lot of wonderful things, meet new people, we could…"

She jerked her hand out of mine and drew back. "Damn it Pete, damn it! What are you saying? I don't want to leave here. I'm happy at the Institute, and I like the island and all the people I've met. We were starting to fit in. Have you forgotten that we were going to get a house together? We were going to be a couple, you and I. Have you forgotten all that?"

I let her rant, hoping that once she expelled her frustration and resentment we could take a more reasoned tack, sail a quieter sea, and work it out. She reminded me that I had a good job, made enough money to keep us fed and sheltered, and we enjoyed the good times, with Sam and his family, with the Party House gang, and at MSI. Like my earlier bar room friends, she told me that New York wasn't what I wanted or needed. It's crowded, dirty, and full of nasty people, she said. She had lived in New Jersey for two years when she was in grade school. She would never go back, not for anything or anyone. Not for me.

I was stunned. Not because she didn't want to go to New York, but because of the dramatically harsh tone of her voice, the terminal declaration that she wouldn't consider it.

Tears followed, and mascara ran down her cheeks. She made no attempt to wipe them, and her chest heaved as the sobs increased in intensity.

"Don't go Pete, just tell them no. Tell them you're happy here, that you have a job and you have a lover, and you don't need them. Please, oh please." She threw herself in my lap, her arms around my waist and continued crying.

I felt as helpless as I could ever remember, and I had been helpless any number of times. I had almost made my mind up to accept, but this was another reason, a compelling one, to stay. I let her cry it out and when she finally sat up, she took out a Kleenex and wiped her face.

"I must look like shit," she laughed. "I don't have any eye-liner with me."

"I'll settle for some fresh lipstick and a long, hot kiss." I held out my arms, and she hugged me. Our clothes came off and we sunbathed, but somehow the mood to make love didn't return. We lay there holding hands, listening to the waves and screaming calls of soaring gulls. One car drove by, slowly, but went on and no one else disturbed our peace.

In the afternoon, we slowly dressed, returned to town, stopped at a small Mexican restaurant that was open on weekends, and had chicken enchiladas. She didn't say anything further about our proposed house or about New York. We went to my cabin and fell asleep. Tonight was not going to be a Party House night.

Carol and I had breakfast in the Island Cafe on Sunday morning. She had some things to do in the lab Sunday afternoon, and I didn't see her the rest of that day. I spent a restless afternoon and evening, a sober one, debating the pros and cons, what I would lose with each choice. I didn't go to the Party House. I sought no company or other confidants. This was my decision and mine alone.

I called Leslie Matthews at eleven o'clock in the morning on Monday, two in the afternoon her time.

"I would be pleased to accept your offer of employment for the fall," I said.

"Great, Peter, that's great news. I'll pass the word to the department chair. He'll have to communicate with the university provost, and the official letter of appointment will come from his office. Expect it in about one or two weeks. But as far as we are concerned, it's a done deal." Her voice was excited, the enthusiasm palpable and one of the reasons I could cite for deciding to join her. She would be a great colleague.

She gave me some further details about my office and lab space—my own laboratory! She also provided me with details about the research position at the American Museum. She and I would be in the same office and lab complex. We talked about living arrangements, and she told me a number of the faculty lived in and commuted from New Jersey because it was considerably more affordable than downtown Manhattan. The mention of the Garden State reminded me of Carol's exhortations. Leslie would send me some newspapers with ads when the time came, so I could hit the ground running, as she put it. I told her I had some of my own equipment and a lot of books to bring and she suggested I ship them by post, and they would put them in my lab for me.

"Welcome aboard, Doctor Gilbert. We look forward to your arrival."

I thanked her and hung up the phone. I was in a bit of a daze, still wondering if I had done the right thing, made the best decision. How does one ever know at the time? Only a look back in a few years would the truth be known, if then. The next task was to meet with Dr. Robinson and Sam and let them know I would be leaving in early August. They took it well and wished me success, but they said the formal farewell and congratulations wouldn't come until mid-summer. In the meantime, there was a lot of work to do, so "Peter, get the hell into the lab and get to work."

That left two other sets of informants: the many friends in town and Carol. She was in her laboratory in the adjacent wing, but I wanted to tell her after hours, when we could be alone. She knew I was likely to make my final decision that day, but she didn't know when. I wanted her to know first, before anyone at the Party House, so I met her at five o'clock, as she was preparing to leave. We walked back to my cabin, small talking, avoiding the big one. She could probably tell what I had decided; otherwise I would have given her the news already. As we were nearing my small house, Randy came out of his and waved at me from across the street. "Any word yet?" he shouted.

I waved back and told him I'd let him know later. Carol and I entered the house and sat on the bed. "Would you like a beer or a glass of wine?" I said, ready to get her something from the kitchen.

"Okay, Pete, get it over with. What did you do? Are you going or staying?" She wasn't angry, and there were no tears. She appeared calm but resigned, expecting the bad news.

I gave it to her, as gently as I could. I once again explained to her why I needed to go, why the professorship and position at the museum was my dream, actually more than I expected. I told her about the months of sending out a hundred letters, the encouragement from close colleagues but lack of response in the greater world, and the need to take advantage of this one opportunity. I told her I could return to the island, even though I was far less certain about this than I sounded, and that New York wasn't necessarily fixed in stone.

"Once I have established myself, gotten a few grants, published more, earned tenure, then I'll be competitive for other positions. You have to start somewhere."

"Do you? I thought you had already started. Several things," she added.

"Change your mind. Come with me." I knew it was hopeless, this was a token gesture, and that it wouldn't work. I would not be able to do my best if she was miserable. She was right to say no, but that doomed us as a couple.

"I can't Pete. I understand why you want to leave, but I just can't agree with it and you won't be able to agree with what I need. I won't come with you. Let's be friends, continue to enjoy each other for the few months that remain, and then we go our separate ways."

I nodded slowly as she talked, knowing that this was the way it would be. Again, I asked her if she wanted something to drink, either here or at someplace in town. Choices to eat out during the off season were limited, especially on a Monday night, but she said she was tired, didn't feel like it, and wanted to go back to her room at MSI. I told her I would drive her, but she said she needed the fresh air and the walk would do her good. She left after giving me a brief hug, a sisterly embrace that also seemed predictably formal.

I sat for a while. By this time it was almost seven and I was hungry, so I walked to the Party House and ordered two pizzas.

"Both of these for you, Pete?" asked Janet. She noted that I was sitting by myself, and the only two other people in the bar, playing pool, were not part of our regular crowd.

"And a mug of Shiner and keep it filled, please."

"Sure thing, honey. Arnie will be here in a few minutes." She hustled into the kitchen, and I gazed at her backside as she prepared the pizzas for the counter oven.

The men and women, my long-time friends, drifted in over the next hour or two. Not all of them. They rarely gathered en masse during the winter unless there was a special celebration or entertainment. But I informed them I would be leaving in August, and they suggested that I had better party hardy for the next few months.

■　　■　　■

So I did. The six months flew by fast. Two more trips into the ocean, publication of another paper from my dissertation, shipping books to New York, and time to visit Austin, see a few friends for the last time, and travel a bit around Texas while I had the chance. I was at second base again, but our team had a split win-loss season, and we finished fourth in the league. However, my batting and fielding average improved, and I was satisfied I had done my part for the team.

Doctor Stevens was delighted that I had a job. "Didn't even have to write a letter of reference," he said. He had written several in my unsuccessful bids earlier. Carl passed his dissertation defense, and I celebrated with him in Austin. He and Cindi left for Toronto in late May.

Carol and I saw each other around the Institute and stayed friendly but distant. She and I were in the Party House a few times, but we came and left separately. I was serving one night and kept filling her glass without charging for it. When she got up to leave, she handed me a ten and told me to keep the change. She couldn't have drunk more than two dollars' worth. It was the last time we spoke. I also had a few short-term affairs with a few of the island ladies and spring visitors, but nothing of note, nothing to remember anyone by. So it goes.

The gang threw a party for me at the bar in late July. There were some parting gifts "to remember us by" and a lot of drinks, dancing, and a few tears, mine and theirs. We usually celebrated every permanent farewell with a party, and mine was just one in a long sequence of good-byes over the years, but it was my goodbye, my sayonara. The party was in the Party House, where else, but we were closed to the public for the duration, most of a Sunday evening. Willie, Randy, and Mitch bought me a bottle of mescal and after helping me finish it, I was obliged to swallow the worm. Each of the ladies I had known well either danced with me or gave me a big kiss on the lips. Once again, I thought about calling New York and telling 'em to fugget about it.

My colleagues at MSI honored me with a more sedate affair. Sam and his wife had already said their farewells over dinner earlier, but they were there along with Robinson and his wife, some of the administrative staff, Penny (looking as foxy as ever), and many of the students, some of whom I didn't know at all. Free food was always a reason to attract a crowd. Cindi and Carl had already departed for their new position in Canada, but they had also invited me to dinner the week before they left.

Notably absent was Carol. Even after several months of little contact, I missed her and had hoped to see her again before I left. It was not to be. I found out later from one of my friends that she never returned to MSI after the summer and didn't finish her degree. She went north somewhere and disappeared from the radar.

▪   ▪   ▪

THE DAY CAME AT LAST, TUESDAY, AUGUST 16, 1977. I had bought a used Saab to replace the station wagon. My beach car had served me well, but it was about to give up the final ghost. I packed my clothes and personal belongings in the trunk. I had finished shipping my books, and I had sold a small television and a few other things from my cabin during a garage sale. My farewells had been said, perhaps too many times, so when the morning came, I was ready. I took one last slow walk around the Institute, staring out at the Gulf from a rear second floor window. Chun was in Austin, so I didn't have a chance to wish him well and thank him for being my roommate. I walked down the jetty from my small former cabin to the tide trap and peered into the sheds that had once housed my crabs. I acknowledged a few waves or nods but didn't linger. I got into my car, passed the Coast Guard station and drove slowly around the marina, past the restaurants and bars, stopping briefly to look at the rear of the Party House. Bart was sleeping on the back porch, but I didn't wake him. I drove to the end of the Ferry Road and got in line, ready to cross the Intracoastal and head toward the Atlantic Coast and my new beginning.

A rainy morning in February 1973 came to mind, driving onto a ferry, chugging across the Intracoastal toward an island in the sun, a strange place filled with strange people. Now, I was one of them and yet, I wasn't. *Peter, you don't even know how far you've come or where you've been. Do I know, even now, where I am going?*

Return to the Island in the Sun

SPRING 1996

THOMAS WOLFE WAS RIGHT. YOU CAN'T GO HOME AGAIN, not even to a temporary home, a place that served the purpose and provided the things you needed. Wolfe was also right in observing that life was not about the desire to escape life, but to prevent life escaping you. Life had been good, twenty years of an academic career, four of them in New York. Other places beckoned: Alabama, Mississippi, and Oregon, with stops in Bermuda, Costa Rica, and the Galapagos Islands. The biological world is beautifully vast, and I have sampled only a small part of it, but then, how many have seen it all?

The original Marine Science Institute was permanently established with a few wooden buildings in 1946. A fifty-year celebration was announced, and the former faculty, staff, and students were invited to return and help celebrate (and leave a few dollars in donations, as well). It was an opportunity to visit MSI for the first time in almost twenty years and to see Frank, Willie, and a few others again. Willie no longer worked for the Institute, and Frank had a job in Houston managing large research projects, but we talked about the days when we played and beat the Longhorns, about the Great Shark Convention, and the barroom bicycle race. The Institute had also changed considerably. It was much larger, and the facilities had been renovated and expanded. The old tank shed was now a research building, and a new educational wing for the public had been added to the main building complex. What had not changed were the cafeteria and dormitory buildings. Newly painted and trimmed, they stood as before. And at the land end of the jetty was a small two-room cabin, one of the first buildings from the 1940s, still standing, used now as a storage building for nets and other sampling equipment.

Penny was gone. Someone told me she had married one of her out of town men in the early '80s and left the island, but she wasn't sure where. A librarian who had encouraged my research and helped me publish my first crab papers had retired. She was still in town, but I didn't see her.

There was, of course, another reason to visit Port Tarpon. How many of the town people were still there? Willie took me to the Gun n' Reel. That and Mary's Place were there, having survived additional storms and thousands of visitors. Their names had changed, but the insides were mostly as I remembered. Willie and I sat at a table near where we had encouraged Melanie to play prostitute. We ordered draft Lone Stars, and he filled me in on what had happened. The shell of the Party House building, more or less, was there, but it had become a beach club, filled with bright lights and new bodies, mostly students. The music was 90's techno-pop, and no one left from the Party House gang patronized the new owners. There weren't many of them left in town anyway.

Mitch had left for Iowa, and Randy had a job in Galveston. Sara was still there, selling real estate when she felt like it, but she and Willie had split. The *Midsummer Night's Dream* had ended, and he had been drifting from brief affair to another, from one traditional island bar to another. Arnie and K.C. had also moved on a few years after I had left. That was the way Port Tarpon was, a long-term place only for a few. For most, it was a transition, a way station. Melanie still lived and taught in town, now at the high school that had finally been built so the island kids didn't have to commute two hours a day. She had married the fisherman she had been dating when I left. They had three kids who were now in high school and middle school. The only other person that I talked to from the seventies was Mickie. She was still around, still crazy, still liked to flash her boobs once in a while. She sat down with Willie and me for a quick drink. A kiss and a smile, and she was out the door.

I asked Willie about Bruce. I had to remind him who I was talking about, a reflection on how little Bruce mixed with the Party House bunch, how reclusive he had been at Ahab's. Then he remembered.

"Mad Dog, yeah I remember. He left town about a year after you went to New York. Bad thing, Pete. We got word back he put a shotgun to his head not long after leaving."

"Shit. I hate to hear that. I guess he never got back with his wife, huh?"

"Actually, he did. She came to town and a couple of us saw them walking around together. He had cut his hair, shaved the beard, and wasn't carrying a bottle. Some of us thought he was about to join the human race, or at least what passes for it here."

"So what happened?" I asked, finishing my drink.

"I think they left together. No goodbyes or explanations. None of us knew him very well, but Mitch said he thought they were going back to St. Louis. He seemed happy, but I guess it didn't work out. It was Mitch that told me about the suicide."

"Shit. I had hoped for better. He was a nice guy and… well, I guess I'm not completely surprised."

Willie nodded, downed his beer and filled me in on a few other changes. Ahab's had disappeared in a storm, and Charlie's motel had been moved to the Island Road, just outside of town. The Coast Guard station and much of the town—the ballpark, Catholic Church, Island Cafe, and the cabin where I lived across from Randy—were still there.

"Oh, yeah. Baseball. What happened to Bad Bart, our manager and all around drunk?"

Willie smiled as he retrieved a cigarette from his shirt pocket. "You won't believe it, Pete. Bart actually married Connie, for real, in a ceremony. They have two kids, and they're living in Corpus. He works as a mechanic in a high-end car dealership, and Connie is completing a degree in accounting."

"Damn, Willie, that is a shock. He's the last one I thought would ever make the transformation to… what? Normalcy?"

What was normal? After several years on the island and two decades in the "real" world, I was not sure of how to define the word. And what about the island? It felt different. Port Tarpon had aged. Or was it us? I looked at Willie, and he seemed a bit older, a bit slower. Clearly not as cavalier, not as witty and fast on the draw. But he still liked to talk, and he was happy to see me.

"Ever thought of returning, maybe eventually retiring here?"

I looked around at the bar. I had seen most of the town. It was larger, more condominiums and a lot more tourist traps, restaurants, gift shops, miniature golf courses, water slides—all bright plastic, neon, and cheap looking. Not as good on the eyes as the type of cheap we had known, the weathered boards, the shacks and bungalows—they were rapidly giving way to new. I had passed a McDonald's on the way from the ferry. Willie told me What-a-Burger and others were slated to follow.

I answered him. "No, Willie, this isn't it. I'm fairly content in Oregon. Married, have two kids, might not stay there forever, probably won't. But, this, no this will look like every other suburban ghetto in another year or two. This isn't Port Tarpon.

"Sounds like you found your place, Pete. Good luck." He shook my hand as we got up.

"Works for me," I said, and we left the bar.

Although I retained fond memories of the place and its people, I never returned to the island. It was sunset when I drove my rented car into Corpus Christi to catch a flight home.

THE END

LAWRENCE W. POWERS HAS AUTHORED NONFICTION ON medical technology, marine biology, and western history. He wrote a critical examination of *The Winter of Our Discontent* for *Steinbeck Review*. He has contributed articles on natural and cultural history for *Oregon Encyclopedia Online* and has served as an editor for *Laboratory Medicine, The Journal of the Shaw Historical Library and Timberline Review*. Larry wrote the narrative film script for *Fields of Splendor*, a 2005 documentary film by Anders Tomlinson. and served as assistant director for a locally produced film, *Wiseacre* in 2017. His first novel, *The Home*, was published in 2017 under the name L. Wade Powers. Luminare Press published a collection of his short stories, *Falling in Love and Other Misadventures*, in April 2019. This is his second novel and a third is in preparation. A retired professor of natural sciences, Larry lives in Eastern Oregon with his beautiful wife Alla and crazy cat Molly. Visit his website at www.lwadepowers.com